CHULIE THE VAMPDOG

First in the Immortails Series

Suzy Jackson

PROLOGUE:

Becoming

I used to love our kitchen in the morning. The sounds and smells of coffee percolating, the soft light. Our cook, Miranda, darting around, making coffee, eggs and grits. The polished oak floors were dusted with powdered sugar from freshly made beignets, the griddle still popping. Miranda always had Top Forty hits jamming on the radio, the announcer blared the next song: "Take on Me," by A-ha. Not that I understood popular music, or that the year was 1985, dogs don't understand charts and calendars and such. It was merely an energy and a vibe I picked up on. I was very in tune with the emotions of the humans around me. My owner, Lucy, would glide into the room and slip me a piece of bacon without Miranda seeing. Her voice was like soft bells when she told me I was good. Lucy was beautiful with honey-colored hair, peach-kissed cheeks and teenage exuberance. I adored her. I would stare up at Lucy, careful not to let her out of my sight. As she flitted out of the room, I always followed close at her sneakered heels, ever her faithful companion.

I lived for her belly rubs.

That is, while I lived.

A young man entered her bedroom one night. He appeared to be not much older than Lucy and it was clear they knew each other. As always, I was curled up next to her in the bed on my own silk pillow. I had been more tired than usual in those days. Lucy sat up in the moonlight and nodded at him. He stepped forward onto one of her cassette tapes that were strewn about the floor; it buckled under his weight with a loud *crack*. I barked a warning. I could feel a mixture of fear, longing, sadness and something primal in Lucy. They stared at each other. She pulled me close and when he leaned in, I felt a chill. He smelled familiar, like he'd been a guest at the house. But I'd never looked closely at eyes like his, so intense and rimmed in red. I trembled but was silent, burrowing next to my human. As the young man drew closer, she presented me to him, lifting me between her face and his. My memory is cloudy. Did she actually nod her consent? She gave me a hug and her cheeks were damp with tears. Without seeing him move, I felt his teeth sink into my neck. A biting human? Was he human? I had not a moment for a yelp before I went limp.

That was the night I was changed forever—and my Lucy vanished.

Now I am aware of what visited our room that night because I am that creature, too. In the French Quarter, I wander over uneven sidewalks pushed out in sharp angles by the tree roots that snake beneath. I live amongst the gutter punks and vagabonds who inhabit the night. No longer am I the bougie Pekinese-Poodle mix (a Peek-a-Poo, how adorable is that.) I only have memories left of my life nestled in the parlor of a wealthy hot sauce magnate's mansion, regarded as plaything for his teenage daughter.

If you ever have the misfortune of looking closely into my face now, you'll see the large black spheres of my eyes rimmed in red. I pass up half-eaten chicken wings on the sidewalk because I no longer eat dead flesh. The smells of gumbo, beignets and vomit no longer intrigue me.

After thirty years in this new reality, my Lucy would be a middle-aged woman by now. She was my everything, my world. My devotion to Lucy as a mortal dog or in my immortal state is unchanged. She will always be my beautiful Lucy with the honey-colored hair.

I long to hear her call me by my name, Chulie, once again.

CHAPTER ONE:

Vampdog

T onight, I swung by our old house as is my nightly routine. I am compelled to do so, forever hopeful my humans will return. My dog brain always anticipates that moment when Lucy will reappear, whether she's gone thirty minutes or thirty years. Now it's closer to the latter. My vampire brain had become slightly more jaded after decades of disappointment. But still I found myself staring expectantly at our stately old manor on Esplanade again, my tongue flapping, eyes darting back and forth, until eventually I gave up. Hunger called.

I walked back into the Quarter, staying near the edges of the buildings where the streetlamps didn't reach. Someone had dropped a cell phone. I had no need for such things but gave it a sniff. Aloe, mint, vodka and sweat. Further down, a discarded vape pen. These are things humans obsess over. I know this from exploring their thoughts.

I passed a 24/7 bar with a lump of a bouncer seated in the doorway. His eyes looked alert as he scanned the street. He'd be worth a go. I stood before him and made an irresistible whiny noise. He looked down at me with a kind face. Jackpot.

"Hey little friend, you got no place to go?" He leaned toward me to let me sniff the back of his hand, a sure sign of a of a dog lover. I stared into his face, locking eyes and he froze. In I went to search his mind for any trace of my Lucy. A mind meld is a curvy path to the truth because it's one person's interpretation of what they have seen. In this man's mind I saw lots of women in festive outfits celebrating a bachelorette party. One woman in particular gave the bouncer a smile and now he was imagining them laughing together. He then pictured a woman who was saying goodbye to him in what looked like his apartment, but she barely looked up from her phone and implored him to take the garbage out this time. I was feeling his mixture of guilt and fondness. Was it because he was thinking about someone else? His mind flooded with a variety of people trying to get into the bar, pushing down his other feelings. I searched their faces for any resemblance of Lucy. Most of these people were younger than she'd be now. The bouncer was remembering some young dudes with fake IDs he had to turn away. The boys reacted with anger and aggression, I felt his fear. His thoughts jumped back to the pretty girl who had smiled at him, but now he was picturing doing some carnal things with her. I abruptly looked away, breaking the mind meld. Enough of that. The bouncer shook his head, unaware of what just happened.

"Do you want some water," he started to say but I was already on the next block.

I continued over the chaotic geometry of gray slabs with blue and white ceramic tile street names on every corner. The night air was a thick blanket of humidity even at that hour. A cat slithered by and made its way over to a tree. I soon saw his target, a nest of baby birds. The mother bird, a robin, squawked frantically over her helpless babies. Nature can be so very cruel to the small and helpless—even for unnatural creatures like me. But I have learned survival skills and have discovered my vampire powers.

I was on the cat in a flash, a dark streak to the naked human eye because of my preternatural speed, my favorite skill.

I didn't kill the cat, just drained enough blood to feel full and make the cat loopy and harmless. I knew he had to eat, too. All animals do. But maybe just not those baby birds. Go find yourself a nice can of tuna, kitty.

Feeling satiated, I pranced around the corner and landed smack into a huge gathering. A swarm of female humans adorned in sparkly red outfits skated past me. This must be the Running of the Bulls parade, a strange New Orleans ritual I did not grasp, but it happened every summer and people seemed to enjoy being chased by these roller girls. That year it was happening at night.

I was generally okay with crowds because of my size and speed. I could zip out of the way of perilous surges or stampedes. This was especially helpful living amidst the parade culture of New Orleans where parades are plentiful, exuberant and long. They are the person at the party who doesn't know when to go home.

On any given day or night a second line parade can spring up like a blast of confetti, to celebrate a life or a wedding or the feast day of a saint … not to mention the spectacle that is Mardi Gras and Carnival season. Steppers, brass bands, marchers, floats and festoonery are all woven into the fabric of New Orleans.

I got out of the way of the spectacle to wait behind the crowd for the parade to end. I began to daydream. My owner, Lucy, loved parades. She'd even dress me up to match her own costume and carry me in a baby sling to the neighborhood parades. The baby sling held me near enough to her chest that I could hear her heartbeat. *Thump thump thump.* She wore a heart-shaped locket with a picture of me inside. I think there was a picture of a boy, too, but that didn't concern me.

I found myself transported to these sunny day memories, the only way I'd see a sunny day again. There we were in my mind's eye, my Lucy singing to the tune of Al Johnson's "Carnival Time" as we bopped through the crowd looking for a good spot to watch the parade.

"Oh well, it's Carnival Time and Chulie and me havin' fun," she would sing.

Her joy radiated and if a dog could smile, I beamed a wide floppy-tongue grin. She was dressed as a purple, green and gold harlequin and I had a frilly matching collar. Everyone loved everybody on Mardi Gras, and I loved my Lucy. We passed people covered in feathers, sequins, body paint, superheroes and circus stars. People danced, sang and swayed to jazz, rock, folk or their own internal rhythm.

"You see that, Chulie? There's the Zulu king! Let's see if we can get a coconut!" She put an extra hand on my sling as we weaved through the crowd to get a prized coconut, the Krewe of Zulu's signature throw. Her heart thumped faster. At the front of the crowd, a krewe member saw us and said, "Look at that cute doggy. Have a Zulu coconut, miss."

My Lucy was ecstatic, and I felt like a hero. We had won the grand prize, a lovely gold painted and spangled coconut. She let me sniff it all over and it smelled sweet and synthetic. We danced through the streets with the other revelers, my Lucy cooing and singing to me the whole time. "You are the goodest boy of all," she told me. Heaven thy name is Mardi Gras.

When we got home that day, we entered the stately mansion on Esplanade like a sunbeam bursting through the window and there in the front hall stood Lucy's mom, a cold, dark lump of displeasure.

"Have you been consorting with those sinners? You better not have been drinking alcohol."

"No, ma'am," Lucy had said, deflated like yesterday's birthday balloon. On our way to escape to her bedroom, we passed her father's den. He was less of a party pooper, giving us a thumbs up on the coconut, but quickly looked distracted when his phone rang.

In my doggy head, I was rolling in every detail of that day like it was fresh cut grass. All I had left were those memories. I let the images swirl, my eyes closed, almost forgetting where I was, waiting for the current day parade to end and everyone to go home.

CHAPTER TWO:

Vampire Tour

It happened a year before he was born but the story of Lucy's disappearance in 1987 was pivotal in the life of Chad Russo nonetheless. When it happened, the news of this missing girl not only captivated people in New Orleans, but those across the country, including Iowa where Chad had grown up. His parents and older brother watched the news coverage showing the signs people posted throughout the French Quarter, demanding:

"FIND LUCY"

"CHULIE + LUCY FOREVER"

"REUNITE CHULIE & LUCY!"

Always the news story would flash on the girl's parents, the mother stoic as if she were in a trance and the dad a wreck.

Chad only heard the stories second hand, the tale of a missing teenage girl and her vampire dog. The dog still roamed New Orleans. It had grown into a legend.

Now in 2023 the fervor had calmed down. People had given up, frustrated by lack of resolution or explanation. But not Chad Russo, vampire aficionado. He remained obsessed with the story. So much so that most of the few friends he had grew bored with him and fell out of touch. Except for one—his longtime girlfriend, Maggie.

Chad stepped into the shade of a tree to escape the New Orleans sun and took the cover off of his iPhone. He pulled out the newspaper clipping he kept tucked inside. The paper was soft and yellow now. He read the headline for the millionth time: "Girl gone, dog becomes vampire." A picture under the headline showed a glimpse of Lucy in her debutante ball gown running down a dark street with a leash in her hand, glancing over her shoulder. It was taken by a local resident who happened to be walking home from work that night. Something seemed off in the photo to Chad. Lucy didn't seem worried or scared, but rather excited. She was never seen again after that night.

Chad had found this clipping in his older brother's room. Pete would have been forty-seven years old now if he was still around, a full twelve years older than Chad. He'd been gone for decades, but Chad thought about him every day. Part of him was stuck back in a time when his brother was still alive. He folded the article back up and held it in his hand for a moment like a talisman. Sometimes he felt if he didn't help the girl and her vampire dog reunite, he'd be letting his big brother down. Chad put so much importance on this quest he sometimes felt frozen in his ability to act on it. It was as if the mere act of assigning it such importance forced him to face his own limitations. It was his brother's wish. Or at least that's what Chad thought.

Chad put the article back in his phone case and tucked the phone into his pocket. He plastered a wide smile on his face to greet his next tour group.

"Welcome to the Vampire Legends Tour, Fangs for the Memories."

For years now he led groups of tourists on vampire tours through the heart of the French Quarter in New Orleans. It was about the only job he could keep gainfully, the only occupation where his obsession with vampires was an asset and his wandering mind didn't get him into too much trouble.

He played his part even when he wasn't giving tours, always dressed in black head to toe, black eyeliner and black nail polish, too. The story of Chulie and Lucy was naturally woven into his talk track and his obsession only enhanced it. He'd become a vampire subject matter expert as an adult, which suited him and his desire to solve the Lucy & vampdog mystery.

He invited the tour group to stop in front of a stately manor on Esplanade Avenue.

"Here we stand in front of the puppyhood home of Chulie the vampire dog and his beloved owner, Lucy, back when the dog was still mortal." The tour group buzzed excitedly.

"Lucy vanished without a trace over thirty-five years ago," Chad continued, "the ever-elusive Chulie remains part of our vampire community." Chad paused for dramatic effect as he always did. He could recite this speech in his sleep and sometimes did, much to the annoyance of Maggie.

"Why do you know so much about vampires?" one pimple-faced kid in the tour group asked. He reminded Chad of his teenage self. Chad sighed; he got this question a lot. Why indeed. He gave his stock answer to be theatrical.

"I am in the service of the undead."

But in his heart, he knew the true origin of his obsession with vampires and especially the Lucy & Chulie story. It felt like everyone had moved on, except him and an occasional cold case true crime episode.

"Have you ever seen the vampdog, Chulie?" the same kid asked, undeterred by Chad's being in the service of the undead.

"Indeed I have had the good fortune of seeing Chulie the vampdog. Though some might not call it *good* fortune." As always, he had the audience hanging on every word. He was an excellent tour guide.

"You may spot him, too, one evening on a stroll through the Quarter. But heed this warning: Don't get too close and be sure not to stare for more than five seconds into his large, red-rimmed eyes. It has been said that he can burrow into your thoughts and put you into a trance."

Only one place on Earth made sense to Chad and that was New Orleans. He was sucked in, so to speak, by all the stories that were soaked into the walls, courtyards, bumpy brick streets and wrought iron balconies. He adored the way French words were mispronounced like rough hands handling lace. And of course, the casual acceptance of vampires living among us, haunted apartments, Voodoo religion and supernatural beings. You might call it vampire-friendly. There were more vampire residents per capita than any other city in the United States, much to the delight of the tourists.

The tour wrapped up as usual and Chad parted ways with the group. He was checking his Venmo for tips when he got a ding alerting him to a comment on his latest article in *Bloodlust,* a blog he had created for vampire enthusiasts. His last article for *Bloodlust* had gotten over 300,000 likes. New Orleans gave him endless source material for stories about the undead. Here the dead are mostly buried above ground which might have something to do with the prevalence of true vamp stories. Reports of vampire encounters dated back hundreds of years. In modern times, New Orleans had some of the most tolerant ordinances for the co-existence of vampires and humans in the country. In fact, vampires were amongst his most avid followers. Lately, unfortunately, there had been a growing number of attacks on vampires.

Even with the ordinances, it was an uneasy co-existence fraught with divisiveness. Most vampires practiced ethical feeding and sought ways to feed without killing. But a group called The Darkness believed in respecting a vampire's true nature to hunt and feed despite the human casualties. And a deadly counter to that was an ultra-religious group called The Impalers who believed all vampire kind should be eradicated. Chad didn't want to see anyone hurt, human or vampire.

Chad scrolled down to the comments under his blog entry. Only paid subscribers were allowed to comment, which helped minimize the craziness. There was one comment posted from the handle CasketGirl76, an old nun historian at Ursuline Convent who had recently been helping him and Maggie. It read, "They're going to shut down Lucy's missing person's case for good. Tomorrow City Hall 8:00 pm."

Chad stopped in his tracks after reading this. He felt like someone had launched a cannon into his stomach. Of course he knew this was possible, even imminent after all these years. But why now? He felt like he might be on to something new. Oh why hadn't he been working harder on this all these years? He cursed himself and his procrastinating. Indeed, he'd join the other protestors at City Hall tomorrow night with bells on.

CHAPTER THREE:
A Blog for Vampire Enthusiasts

*B*loodlust, *A Blog for Vampire Enthusiasts, July 13, 2023, by Chad Russo*

Heed my warning, fiends and followers, the myths and rumors are true. A vampdog exists in our midst. I myself had another sighting (!!) and I was only two cocktails in at the time. Mind you my alcohol tolerance is quite high.

The streets of the Central Business District (CBD) were quieter than usual, even though it was the occasion of *The Running of the Bulls*. For those unfamiliar with the New Orleans' version of this tradition, it involves roller derby queens, or RollerBulls, in skimpy red sequin outfits and horns, whacking runners with foam bats. As a member of the media, I was one of the VIP invited.

After the revelers had cleared, there were bits of evidence of the raucous spectacle—a dozen or so red boa feathers wafting through the gutters and a few discarded cardboard fans. In the darkening calm after the parade, I slipped through the shadows and passed by an urgent care outpost of the New Orleans Musicians Clinic. Thousands of our treasured musicians and culture bearers have benefited from the health *services offered here, especially during the recent pandemic. I cut right to head toward my streetcar stop, passing by the alley behind the clinic. It was fully dark by then. There, near a medical waste dumpster, I caught sight of the undead canine. I could tell even from a distance that he was in a moment of rapture as he fed on a discarded blood bag. I froze in my tracks but couldn't stifle the slightest gasp. Vampdog sensed me immediately and turned to size me up. I slowly lifted my phone and luckily it was still in camera mode. But in the instant I snapped the photo, he was gone, almost as if he'd vaporized. His movements were too quick for my human eyes. Oh, sweet coven, believe me when I say, this streak you see captured in the photo below is indeed the vampdog in all his immortal glory.*

IMPORTANT NOTE: For those of you still following the mysterious disappearance of Chulie's owner, Lucy, there will be a rally on the steps of City Hall tomorrow night, July 14th, after dark. The authorities are going to officially close the case and leave it unsolved forever. We must not let that happen. We need resources left on the case. We must find Lucy for the sake of her poor vampire dog. Please show your support.

@Chadrusso #bloodlust #vampdog Please like, follow and share.

CHAPTER FOUR:

Case Closed

I made my way to City Hall on my own four paws. I'd heard through the grapevine the "Find Lucy" movement would be gathering here; vampires can be a gossipy lot. The protestors wanted to make sure the authorities didn't stop looking for my Lucy. Many of them were true crime groupies, both humans and vampires. I needed to see what happened next in this investigation. I was frustrated in not being much use in the search so far, being a dog and all.

I cloaked myself in the shrubbery of Duncan Plaza across the street. There was a dog park here so I sniffed the perimeter for good measure before finding my hiding spot. Thankfully, they held this rally at a vampire-friendly hour after sunset. The offices would be closed but the news media trucks were lined up and that's what mattered. The protesters came with signs. Not that I can read, but I assumed they said something like "Find Lucy" or "Don't Forget Lucy." I recognized her photo on some of the signs. Her blonde hair pulled up in a side ponytail that girls used to wear back then. I don't see many girls with that style anymore. I'd also noticed some posters that tried to show what she'd look like now next to her school photo. The doctored photos looked like her older aunts, not my Lucy. I knew she'd be ten times prettier than those phony pictures.

I recognized the geeky guy in black who does the vampire tours. He always turned up at these rallies with some skinny woman with short pink hair. They followed everything to do with my Lucy. When I'd snuck up close to him on occasion, I liked the way he smelled, musky, sweet and a little like grass.

I decided to stay near enough to hear what they were up to. Luckily, I could hear and smell well from a distance. If all of these people wanted to solve the mystery of Lucy, why hadn't she been found yet? I know humans often harm one another but my canine brain couldn't conceive of a way to make someone vanish into thin air like she had. As a dog, my investigative skills left a lot to be desired. As a vampire, I knew more than an ordinary dog, mostly from penetrating human minds. Maybe I'd recruit some assistants. I was desperate to not let Lucy slip from the public eye. I kept thinking she'd just come back. I needed help.

I recognized some people from a group called Krewe du Vampdog. They were a krewe, which is sort of like a Mardi Gras club to put it simply. This group was bonded by their obsession with yours truly, the one and only vampdog. At least the only one I knew. They met regularly, organized blood drives for me and posted photos when they sighted me. They'd even tried to catch me in assorted futile ways. I crouched back into my hiding place.

"If I could have your attention!" a voice boomed over a megaphone. He waited until every last person was quiet. Jordan

LeBlanc, the Chief of Police, was compact but mighty. He commanded attention.

"First, we'd like to thank this group for their dedication to finding Lucy Broussard over the years, those who were around when it happened and many more who have who have joined the cause as the years have gone on. You've kept a small flame of hope alive."

The crowd broke out in cheers and applause.

The Police Chief continued, "But now that flame has burned out. The Broussard family have requested that no more efforts be made to find their long ago lost daughter, Lucy."

The crowd rustled with disapproval.

"I know you are all disappointed and the family insisted we let you know directly. They are grateful for your thoughts and prayers. After the recent passing of their patriarch, Victor Broussard, God rest his soul, the family feels the time has come. He alone had provided funds to keep the investigation open to reduce the burden on taxpayers. Now his surviving family says no more. They are asking for respect and privacy. They want to thank you for your dedication, some of you for many years. But it is time to let it rest. Thank you and good night."

The crowd began shouting.

"Don't give up on Lucy!" "Does this mean she's dead?" "What about Chulie? He needs Lucy!" I had to agree. There was a buzz in the crowd that I was picking up on about a conspiracy behind this. Someone trying to hide something. But who had a secret they wanted to keep? The cops brushing a botched investigation under the rug? I also heard people speculating on the involvement of a sect of vampires called The Darkness. I knew of this group. I spotted Vampire Tour Guy again, shouting with the protestors. I decided then and there I'd try to stick by Vampire Tour Guy. The rumble of the crowd grew and vampires hissed their dissent. The official with the megaphone tried to regain the crowd's attention, news cameras and phones with bright lights swirled everywhere. It was getting too chaotic for my taste. As I looked around for an escape route, I saw two figures behind a tree and a flash of metal. A gunshot cracked through the night. A policeman in a patrol car stationed nearby shouted into a radio. People started screaming and scrambling like fleas on bath night. The commotion was enough cover for me to make an exit unseen. As I bolted through the park, I passed two people slipping through the trees, escaping into the night along with me. A familiar smell wafted through the air as they ran. Was it some kind of cleaner scent? I also smelled gun powder. One of these shadowy figures must have fired the shot. They appeared to be two women.

CHAPTER FIVE:

Tilt

The arcade was in a back room of an Uptown bar called Bar Sanchez where locals and a few cops hung out. This is where Chad had met an old retired cop who was on the Lucy Broussard missing person's case long ago, and where he went to think. Tonight, Chad hoped to run into the cop, but in the meantime, he needed some time to process the rally that ended in chaos. Maggie went home to turn in. This wasn't really her scene. *Another gunshot*, Chad thought. What was this city coming to? But he couldn't help but think it wasn't random.

Pinball was his escape. Another throwback to time spent with his brother, Pete. They used to play *Attack From Mars* and *Addams Family* at a local 7-Eleven for hours until the owner would shoo them out to get some fresh air.

The tables at Bar Sanchez did not disappoint either. Four pinball machines lined the wall. There were a handful of tables and chairs and two young men sat at a table smoking and drinking beer even though patrons weren't technically allowed to smoke inside bars in New Orleans. But no one here really cared.

Attack from Mars maintained all its retro glory. There was even an old Bram Stokers Dracula game that was Chad's personal favorite. With the comforting sound of quarters jangling in his pocket he brought the machine to life and let himself become mesmerized by flashing lights and spinning silver balls.

Pete used to smoke. Even as Chad concentrated on pressing the flippers and keeping the ball in play, he could almost hear Pete cheering him on. It was after one of their pinball sessions at the 7-Eleven that Pete told Chad the story of the missing girl Lucy and her vampdog; Chad was ten making Pete twenty-two. Pete was really into all forms of vampire stories … Anne Rice, Buffy the Vampire Slayer, Dark Shadows, so the story of Lucy and her vampdog captured his imagination. They were sitting on a bench in front of the convenience store on a scorcher July day, drinking blue Slurpees, Pete smoking as he told Chad about how a teenager named Lucy, the daughter of a hot sauce magnate in New Orleans, had vanished the night of her debutante ball, the same night her beloved pet dog was turned into a vampire. Chad was enthralled. Later that night, Pete went out and never came home. A drunk driver had crossed the line and hit him head on killing him instantly.

For years, Chad preferred to think that Pete had been turned into a vampire and had to stay away from their family for their own safety. In fact, that's what he told everyone at school. This added to his weirdo reputation and prompted many conversations with counselors because Pete was in fact dead and buried, not a member of vampire society. Chad had long since come to terms with his brother's death. Now as he stood in Bar Sanchez, he tipped his beer glass and poured out a tiny bit onto the floor in his honor.

"Hey there, Bad Chad." Frank the retired cop interrupted the moment as he entered the game area. "Was that for your brother, Pete?" He knew it was. Frank lined himself up in front of *Attack from Mars* and poured a drop of beer out before slipping it into the cupholder attached to the machine.

Chad returned to his own pinball flow state until the silver orb slid down the hole, then turned to face his buddy.

"Hola, Stanky Frank, how's it hanging?"

Frank still looked like a cop with his crew cut and stiff trousers, but now he wore a stained polo shirt and walked with a limp. He smelled like Bengay. He gave Chad a yellow-toothed grin and a throaty laugh.

"How about that gunshot at the City Hall rally? I know you were probably there."

Chad confirmed it with a, "You know I was."

"I'm thinking it wasn't a coincidence. This case has always been strange," Frank said.

Chad nodded. "What have you heard about the case closing?"

"Once old Victor Broussard kicked the bucket, the family was no longer interested in humoring him with this flim-flam investigation."

Frank hobbled over to the T2 game next to Chad's Dracula game and dropped his quarter in the slot for that satisfying *bing bing bing* and rush of silver balls.

"Ready for another beer?" Chad offered. The vet cop nodded. Chad knew this was the best way to get Frank talking and it was always interesting when Frank started talking. Frank kept his ball live for a good 10 minutes at least and paused for a swig from his tulip glass.

"Why do you say flim-flam investigation?" Chad asked.

"Well, you know most of the family didn't want it to go on. He was the only one."

"But there had to be people pushing for the investigation. There was so much public outcry."

"A lot of people were fascinated by the case. But not enough to actually do anything."

Chad thought about his own lack of action. "I'd be one of those people."

"Don't beat yourself up about it. There were a lot of dead ends. We all did our best to find that poor girl." Frank chewed on that thought a bit. "If I didn't know better, I'd say someone was trying to hide something. Someone didn't want that girl found."

This gave Chad pause. He hadn't really thought of it that way. Why on Earth would anyone not want this young girl to be found? What secrets could she possibly reveal?

"Did anything come up early on in the case about The Darkness vampires?" Chad recalled the people in the crowd at the rally talking about The Darkness vampires. Chad was familiar with them as an extremist coven that believed in a vampire's animal instincts to kill. Of course this made humans fear them more than the average vampire.

"There were so many theories. It was a fact that Victor Broussard had some vampire associates, I believe they were Darkness vampires. His daughter, too. Strange coven to be associated with."

"Interesting," was all Chad said. He still thought there was something there. But he knew it could be a dangerous place to poke around. "Did any theories about The Darkness take you back to the night Lucy disappeared?"

"Yes and no," Frank went on, "nothing concrete ever came of it. Plus, most of us were afraid to go there."

"Afraid of being killed by a vampire? Don't you have special vampire apprehension procedures?" Chad asked.

"Sure do. The Darkness vamps weren't afraid of cops, though. In fact, one rookie cop even got glamored by a vamp when he tried to ask questions. Couldn't sleep a full night for weeks."

Frank shook his head at the memory.

"Here's something we didn't share with the public. I can share it now that they are shutting it down. The son of a big shot Darkness vamp disappeared the same night Lucy did."

Chad was floored. "You've been holding out on me, Frank. That could be pretty key."

"Well what most of us old cops suspect is she's been dead a long time. Maybe even since the night she went missing. We even had a running bet about it. But there's no way to settle the score. No hard proof, anyway. Her father wanted to hold out hope and we were okay going along with that. It was on his dime."

They both went back to playing their games. After some time, Frank said, "Sorry, Chad. I know that's not what you want to hear. But maybe now, you can look at it with fresh eyes. Maybe you can give it the attention the cops never did."

Chad just nodded. He had a lump in his throat he couldn't swallow, even with a beer chaser. It went deep for him.

"Here's an idea," Frank offered. "Why don't you keep tabs on that crazy Krewe who keeps following the vampdog? Or maybe watch where that little undead dog goes?"

"I've done both, but maybe it's time to take it up a notch." Chad lost his third ball and took that as a sign to head back home.

CHAPTER SIX:

Encounter

It was the next night after the drama at City Hall, and I was on my evening stroll looking for din din. The sound of that gunshot freaked me out. I hated loud noises; they made me jumpy. But there was something niggling my brain about the humans I saw running from the park after the shot rang out. Was it the smell I recognized?

I was desperate for Lucy to not be forgotten and couldn't get that thought out of my mind; I stopped to stare through the tall, stately windows of a mansion on Esplanade. It was similar to my mortal family's home and wasn't too far from it. I kept tabs on a girl with honey-colored hair who lived here at this mansion. She was a dead ringer for my Lucy. This blonde angel was probably a few years older than my Lucy was when she disappeared; but if I squinted my eyes, they could be sisters. Or maybe she could be a niece. I had seen her out walking and tried to get a mind meld while she waited at a traffic light to cross a busy street. I had to see if she indeed was related to Lucy. But nothing in her thoughts supported that possibility. I even tried to project an image of Lucy from my mind but she was only confused.

Tonight as I watched her house, no one paid me any mind. I could blend in like another sad little stray with shaggy blackish-brownish hair, unless you looked closely at my red-rimmed eyes. No one recognized me except for Vampire Tour Guy, who was following me again and recording things on his phone. In my mortal life, there weren't such gadgets, but I believed he was some sort of journalist, too. Or maybe he was just another fanboy obsessed with the undead. I was hoping there was more to him than that.

I allowed Vampire Tour Guy to follow me, and I was planning to follow him back. I was curious about him like he was about me. Humans assume I have the same faculties as a mortal dog, sniffing through a colorless world of unintelligible sounds and a vocabulary of five words. They underestimate me, giving me an advantage. While I can't speak, I understand them. Their thoughtless drivel. Their hateful jabs. I was in tune with their emotions, too. The fear, lust, joy, grief and yearning. I felt it all.

I'll never forget seeing all the colors for the first time. A mortal dog's world is limited to shades of brown, gray, yellow and blue. Upon becoming a vampdog, my world burst to life in green, purple, red, a full-spectrum experience. At first it scared me. But like everything, it brought me beyond what alive dogs can do.

I watched the girl with the honey-colored hair through the window. She looked up from her book at a young man who burst into the room. A growl vibrated in my chest. The young man looked as if he was yelling, and the girl shrank back into the couch. He grabbed the book out of her hands and threw it against the wall. After he stormed out of the room, she put her lovely face in her hands and sobbed. I was on the move in an instant. I ran so much faster than I did as a mortal. I was a furry blur as I dashed from one side of the boulevard to the other in a blink. My paws hardly touched the grassy neutral ground between the paved streets. I had seen this brute shove her on occasion, and I wasn't having it anymore. He would rage at her and then head out for a smoke to blow off steam. That was his abusive pattern. Then he'd go back in and apparently apologize or bring her flowers. Bastard. To me, this girl with honey-colored hair was a prisoner in this castle, and the physical similarities to my mistress endeared her to me.

On cue, I saw the brute head out the side door. He had a small waist, flatiron chest and swollen biceps stretching his polo-shirt sleeves. He was wearing preppy cargo shorts and loafers without socks. By outward appearances, he was just another rich boy. I pranced over until I was close enough to see his bloodshot eyes and drunken sway. I did my cutest head tilt, usually irresistible even to the biggest of assholes.

But all I got from this guy was a kick.

"Get outta here mutt, no handouts from me."

Charming.

He flicked his cigarette butt toward me and then bent to pick up a nickel. Sure, you rich bastard, you could use another coin.

It was the opening I needed.

In an instant, my mouth was around his wrist like a vice. I transformed into something primal and uncontrollable. I became more monster than dog and lost all sense of my breeding. A thousand beasts from a thousand jungles possessed me. I sucked with all my might and before he could shout or shake me off, he was weak from blood loss. He collapsed in a heap. I took an extra-long draw from his radial artery for good measure. He wouldn't be raging at that lovely girl again anytime soon. My snout was a bloody mess. I heard a brass band start up a block away. I'd pretend it was a celebration for my conquest.

Sure, I could be an angry little dog. Part of me had grown cold and bitter as the years without Lucy went by. I was probably extra angry with the news of Lucy's case closing. You might say I took my anger out on people who had it coming. But now I'd move on from stalking this particular girl and on to someone else. That was my pattern as I pined for my Lucy.

The Vampire Tour Guide was now on the same side of the street as me. He must have witnessed the whole bloody affair and was now taking pictures of the passed-out lug. I needed to figure out how I could connect with him, but that might be awkward at this moment in time after witnessing a feeding. Though most modern vampires stopped feeding in time for the blood host to survive it, the idea of the action still scared and unnerved most humans. Yet, something told me this Vampire Tour Guy might be different. He seemed to have a deeper understanding of vampires and I didn't sense fear. I wanted to believe his devotion to Lucy's case was genuine, and I was willing to find out.

CHAPTER SEVEN:

Witness

*B*loodlust, *A Blog for Vampire Enthusiasts, July 20, 2023, by Chad Russo*

Moon's out fangs out my friends. The sky over the Mississippi is blacker than Lucifer's soul. With Mercury in retrograde this month and an ill wind stirring, the mayhem is reaching a high. For instance, at a protest I attended last week in regards to the closing of the Lucy Broussard missing person's case with other like-minded humans and vampires, a bullet rang out in the crowd, sending us running for cover. Luckily no one was hurt. We had gathered to protest the closing of the Lucy Broussard Missing Person's case. They never caught the shooter, so if you know anything that would help the police, please contact them. This blog writer is still a bit shaken. The case may be cold, but something unexplained is causing a new chill. In other news, multiple vampire sightings and encounters were reported to me from Baton Rouge to Slidell, but none quite as incredible as the one I saw with my own two eyes. More on that in a moment. Mary Pat from Mid City was hit upon in the Carousel Bar on Royal Street by a pale hipster who didn't order a drink for himself but insisted on buying one for her. He said he was a local musician and invited her to come see him play with his band. Normally, Mary Pat was immune to flirts like this, being that she was a pro who worked a pole on Bourbon, stage name Glitter, adept at juggling a steady stream of suiters. But she felt herself being charmed nonetheless. What had thrown Mary Pat off her game? Was it the circular motion of the famous rotating bar? Or this charming stranger's piercing blue gaze? Luckily, her friend intervened and insisted she leave with her at once. Outside the bar, the friend told Mary Pat she had been consorting with a known vampire. Mary Pat looked back and the gentleman was now staring at them through the window. When he caught her eye, he ventured a smile revealing a glimpse of fangs. A near miss, Mary Pat. If it weren't for your friend we may be telling a very different story. Unless of course that's your thing, and there's nothing wrong with that.

Over in Kenner, police were called to an old warehouse that had fallen into disrepair and was thought to be abandoned. A neighbor reported strange noises in the wee hours of the morning. Upon investigation, it was discovered that five full-sized coffins and one baby-sized coffin had been unloaded into the warehouse. This particular group of cops had a vendetta against the vampire species born out of their own fear, most of which was valid for them, but lacked any nuance or empathy. The division between anti-vamps and co-existers remains in our town. Erring on the side of caution, the cops called the bomb squad to come open up the coffins in the full light of day with murderous intent. As the sun stabbed down, they pried the first lid open with no regard for what might happen to the vampire inside. Then another and another until all six were open including the little one.

What do you suppose they found? Nothing more than a thousand kilos of weed with a street value of $500,000. So more of a drug bust than a Dracula smoke out. But it further demonstrates how certain members of law enforcement are less than sympathetic to our vampire residents … as well as a criminal element willing to appropriate vampire culture as a cover. Meanwhile, attacks on vampires are still on the rise. But the highlight of my updates, dear coven, was when I witnessed the infamous vamp pooch chowing down on an abusive boyfriend. I'm telling you, this guy had it coming. I watched this creep bully a young lady and then exit their home in a huff. I could hardly believe my eyes when vampdog latched onto his wrist and got savage on him. It was spectacular and frightening. The brute was left in a heap like a pile of garbage, barely breathing. Vampdog of course was gone in an instant, but I took some snaps of the guy before he regained consciousness. (Below). I called the paramedics but didn't stick around to get tangled in the drama. My blood sugar was low, and I needed to get something to eat. But as I departed, I noticed I wasn't the only witness. It appears as though some of my followers are literally following me IRL now. Stop that! Seriously. If I'm not mistaken, I believe it was a woman by her curvy outline. Human or vampire remains to be seen.

@Chadrusso #bloodlust #vampdog Please like, follow and share.

CHAPTER EIGHT:

Free Dinner

C had looked at Maggie's face across the table in the twinkly café lights in the courtyard of Café Amelie. Her face was also lit with love as she smiled at him and this was indeed the perfect romantic setting. But Chad was not thinking romantic thoughts. He knew Maggie longed for more romance and a more official commitment. Chad wanted it too, he couldn't imagine life without her. But right now the vampdog was heavy on his mind, especially after witnessing him feeding on a human. He hoped his obsession wouldn't eventually push Maggie away like it had so many friends. She was way more than a friend. But despite the enchanting setting they were in, he spoke what was truly on his mind, breaking the spell of Café Amelie.

"What do you think of The Darkness connection in Lucy's disappearance?" Chad spoke loudly over the music of a jazz trio. That turned a few heads of nearby diners. He lowered his voice. "I mean, there's Victor Broussard's business dealings, and the police started to look into it but then gave up. Makes me wonder."

Maggie drew her hand back from where it was on top of his and took a thoughtful moment before answering, "Frankly, I'm still stuck on the gunshot at the rally. I still feel shaky about that. I know you mentioned it on your blog. Could someone like The Darkness coven be trying to scare us off? Your old cop buddy said it was a dead end, though, right?"

"Actually, he said they were discouraged from following that lead, and by discouraged I mean there was some vampire influence. And I still feel uneasy about that gunshot, too."

"Well, why would The Darkness want to stop the investigation unless they had something to do with Lucy's disappearance?"

"Exactly. Or something to hide," Chad replied.

They were both silent for a moment, mulling this over.

"Speaking of your blog and the vampdog feeding session, I read this article about a chemist who has created a synthetic form of blood vampires can feed on. Can you imagine what that might do for human/vampire relations if they got their food from a lab instead of people?"

"Indeed," Chad replied intrigued by the thought. "I know many vampires who take supplements, but never anything that totally replaces human blood."

A waiter swept their empty fried green tomato appetizer plates away and two other waiters simultaneously set down entrées. The service was impeccable here. From the minute Jordan the waiter introduced himself as their server for the evening they felt attended to. He was a likeable guy and they shared an easy banter. Shrimp and grits for Maggie and crab cakes for Chad. They were silent for a moment while they dug in. The jazz trio was taking a break so they were able to speak in hushed tones over the gentler house music.

"If The Darkness doesn't want people digging into Lucy's disappearance, we could be treading in dangerous waters," Maggie said. Chad nodded and sat back for a moment, looking around at the other patrons. There were an assortment of couples, groups of friends and parents with a baby and a toddler strategically positioned at a back corner table so as not to ruin the café's mood. There were also vampires with goblets of red liquid in front of them. A few of them looked familiar. It made Chad wonder who among them could be Darkness vampires.

Maggie had a wistful look as she scoped the room too. Chad noticed and thought of something to brighten her mood.

"Hey Mags, I got an invitation to the Krewe du Vampdog's Blood Hound's ball. It's coming up. What do you say we get all fancy and make it a night? It's sure to be weird and wild. Plus maybe we'll learn something to help the case."

Maggie's blue eyes sparkled as she smiled. "Um, yes." She brightened as she started talking about what she might wear.

That's when Chad noticed Sister Eloise standing just outside of the courtyard gate. He raised his hand to give her a wave but she ducked out of sight. Maggie looked in the direction of his gaze.

"That's odd, I think she saw you," Maggie said.

"Maybe she was embarrassed about peeping on us."

They both giggled.

"She's a funny one," said Maggie.

"I wouldn't mind another visit with her. From what she's told me her life is like its own New Orleans legend. She was definitely around when Lucy disappeared."

"Let's do it."

Chad loved how Maggie was always game to indulge his curiosity. Although, she was curious, too. The weirder the story, the better in her mind it seemed. After they declined an offer for dessert menus, Jordan their waiter elegantly slid the check folio onto the table.

"Looks like dinner tonight was on an anonymous friend," the waiter explained.

Maggie and Chad were perplexed.

"What? Who?" they both stammered.

"Anonymous. Big tipper, though," Jordan replied. "Left you a note," he informed them before gliding away.

"Do you think it was Sister Eloise?" Maggie asked and Chad shrugged.

"I don't see her as having money to throw around." Chad opened the check folio. Inside was a photograph and a note written on a cocktail napkin. The faded photo had rounded corners and a date stamp of May 10, 1987, the day before Lucy was reported missing. Chad's mouth dropped open as he held up the note and photo for Maggie to see. The note said, "The truth must come out." The photo was Lucy's discarded debutante ball gown, covered in blood.

CHAPTER NINE:

Doggy bag

I made sure they didn't see me watching them. I followed Vampire Tour Guy home again. I looked through the window as he was doing something on his laptop and the girl with the pink hair was coaxing him to get up and go somewhere. He obliged and didn't seem to mind much. As far as human relations go in my outsider's perspective, they seemed sweeter than most. He put on a fresh shirt and she primped in front of a mirror. They smiled at each other as they strolled outside their apartment and she bounced along beside him. She called him Chad. Even from a distance, I could smell her perfume and serotonin. He got a sappy look in his eyes when he watched her. I have to admit, it made me feel good too, but also sad and lonely at the same time.

Tailing them was easy because they were mostly absorbed in each other. When they arrived at Café Amelie she told the host that they had a reservation in her name, Maggie. Maggie. That suited her. I disappeared into the shrubs at the edge of the courtyard, just a dark spot in the shadows. I was able to sit very still, unlike mortal dogs who pant and shake.

I watched as they ate and chatted. I even had a feeling that I might be a topic in their conversation. That was a very good sign. I so badly needed to connect with someone else who felt compelled to find my Lucy. I needed a familiar in the classic vampire sense. I was content to watch people. I looked at all of them. But I was only really interested in Chad and Maggie. I watched the vampires, too. One may have even seen me. Some I recognized. One vampire especially. He was a leader in The Darkness coven and stirred up some very old memories for me.

I knew my own vampire origin story was tangled with The Darkness. The night I was turned into a vampire comes to me in dreamy snippets sometimes. My last mortal memory in Lucy's bedroom is followed by waking up in an unfamiliar room in a lot of pain with the young vampire watching over me. I remember him telling me Lucy would come soon. That thought sustained me through the painful transition.

On this night, a different vampire sat with a large goblet of red liquid in front of him. As he took a long slow slip, his eyes slid to the side and I realized he was looking at Chad and Maggie. What could he want with them? Was it their search for Lucy? I suddenly felt afraid for them. Watching him drink the red liquid from his goblet reminded me of my hunger. Once again I was famished. I turned to go, vowing to stalk these two another day, and almost ran smack into Sister Eloise. I slipped back into the bushes before she saw me. She was spying through the fence. I hid because I wasn't in the mood to be interrupted before dinner. She had helped me in the past, but she had this weird thing about trying to save me. I knew her when she was in her twenties and now she was in her sixties. She had started a movement to convert vampires from their natural ways and help them to find salvation through religion. It got to be a bit much. I saw her suddenly scurry off. Ha! Maybe someone caught the old snoop.

I made my way toward the CBD (Central Business District) and one of my favorite spots. Behind Mother's restaurant, the cook left scraps out near the back door after they closed. Not that I had any desire for leftover human food at all, but it attracted a bunch of other strays, both dogs and cats. I liked to watch them. I liked to mix in with them as they tussled over the food.

Tonight, sure enough, I could smell the roast beef debris, the scrapings from the bottom of the stew pot. I stood back to see and hear the dogs gather, tentative at first, then unable to resist. I cornered a rat by the dumpster and had my fill. With an abundance of rats in New Orleans, I'd never starve. The dogs settled into their feast, tugged at bones and chomped on thick chunks of gristle. I arranged myself on the ground nearby like I was one of them. They paid me no mind. I loved feeling like I was part of their pack even for a moment, even though I could never be.

Having their fill, a few of the strays dozed off. I felt so comfortable, I did, too, or at least something close to sleep. My dream took me back to that place where I was kept after being transformed to one of the undead, waiting for my Lucy to come find me. I remembered loud banging on the door and yelling. There was an unearthly howl, either human or animal or both. I was so confused and terrified that I ran through the open door and into the night. I got far away.

Then, there was a scream. Definitely a scream from a human female. Was it my Lucy screaming? I shook myself from my dream state and realized the screaming was now coming from the back door of Mother's. The wife of the chef didn't take as kindly to all the strays getting too comfortable there. She waved a broom and screeched at us all to git. The strays scattered into the night and I ran with them, by far the fastest of the bunch.

CHAPTER TEN:

Scheme

Maggie and Chad huddled in their kitchen, Chad hunched over his laptop, tapping out another blog article. He was thinking of how he could stir up public interest again in the Lucy Broussard's missing person case. When he thought of the story, Pete's voice whispered in his ears, the same hushed reverence he used when he told him the story for the first time. He needed to find a new lead, to give people something to be hopeful about.

"What sounds good for dinner?" Maggie asked.

"Uh-huh," was all Chad said. She sighed and Chad got up to give her a quick kiss on the cheek, then sat back at his laptop. She knew he was wrapped up in another article.

Maggie fussed about the kitchen, retreating like she did whenever Chad escaped into his vampire obsessions, his own little disappearing act. Charlie the mutt was curled up under the table content to be home. He was the neighbor's dog who they babysat (or dogsat?) until she returned from a theatre excursion in New York. They both loved having Charlie around, but Maggie especially.

Chad was bopping along at a steady clip on the laptop keys, never at a loss for inspiration when it came to the vampire dog and the mysterious disappearance of his owner. The vampire stories in New Orleans were relentless, but when it came to this mystery, Chad felt like he was living inside of it. Maggie interrupted again.

"Do you suppose that vampire dog was there at the rally last week?" Maggie asked.

"I do indeed," Chad said.

"You know that band the vampdog hangs out with near Frenchman Street?"

He stopped writing. "What about them?"

"I was thinking that might be an avenue to engage with the dog," Maggie suggested. She did her best to involve herself with his work, Chad knew.

"I'm listening." Chad turned from the laptop for a moment to listen and also to grab his glucose meter. Chad had been a Type 2 diabetic since he was in high school. He pricked his finger and dabbed it on the test strip. The meter read 125, not too bad. Need to watch the sweet cocktails, though, he thought. Maggie watched him do this for the umpteenth time.

"So what about this band?" Chad said.

"You know my blonde wig? That one from when I was in *Annie Get Your Gun*?"

Chad blinked at her.

"What if I were to use my acting skills and plant myself where the band and the vampdog would have to engage with me? With those blonde curls I could get vampdog to follow me, maybe get him closer to us. You know how he is. You've told me how he's drawn to women with the same color hair as his Lucy."

"I do but I'm not sure, Mags. Vamps can be unpredictable. Too risky."

Maggie had the blonde wig clutched in her lap and she stretched it over her bright pink bob now for dramatic effect. "Think of what we can learn for the case," she insisted.

God, she was beautiful, Chad thought. He had been in love with Maggie since the day he met her in second grade. She had wanted to be a movie star even back then. He was grateful she still hung around. He didn't want to disappoint her. He relented.

"Let's try it," he said. She threw her arms around him. She loved a good scheme, especially one in which she could play a lead role. "I could go for some live music."

"Chad, speaking of music, did you get those Helen Gillet tickets at Snug Harbor? I just saw a post that the show's sold out."

Chad paused now and shook his head. She sighed loudly.

"You know Chad …."

He looked up at her. Her face softened when their eyes met.

"Never mind." She kissed him on the head.

They had known each other since they were kids, two geeky misfits in Iowa. But they weren't kids anymore. Chad had his hesitancy about commitment. He knew at some point his self-obsessions would interfere with his life with Maggie, and impossible choices would have to be made. He could never let the vampires, Lucy and the vampdog go. So, he found avoiding long-term commitments of any kind was easier. He was well aware that Maggie put up with it because she knew the difficulties in his past, his brother dying in a car crash, his mother running off. She was the closest human being on the planet to him, but still he kept a shield around his heart. Maggie was his only true friend. Well lover, too. Vampires weren't his only passion.

As kids they used to pretend they were characters in their favorite TV shows. Right after high school Maggie went to L.A. aiming for her star on the Walk of Fame. Chad was her sounding board during the ups and downs. When she got a part in a feature film, she sent him a text full of star emojis, only to find out a month later the project had been shelved before they had even started shooting. It was then that she gave up on La La Land and joined him in New Orleans. She still employed herself as an actress in town, in plays and TV show walk-ons. A lot was produced in New Orleans.

Maggie darted around their apartment now, clearly pleased with herself and charged up about her scheme.

"So crazy it just might work," Chad called to her. "You're right about that dog's fixation on women with a certain shade of blonde hair. I've observed him staring at them in windows, following them down the street, he can't take his eyes off them. He follows, he stares, but never ever harms them. In fact, did I tell you about that girl with the abusive boyfriend who was Chulie's snack?"

"Ha! Had it coming. I read it in your blog of course, silly," Maggie shouted from the next room. She danced back into the kitchen, striking poses like Madonna. Chad grabbed her hands and started swirling her around.

"You should wear that blonde wig when we go to that Krewe ball next week," Chad said. "You'll look like a movie star." Maggie's eyes got misty when he said that so he changed the subject. "There will likely be vampires on the guest list."

Maggie's eyes narrowed and her grin widened. Chad recognized the mischievous gleam in her eyes from when they were kids.

"I am so down with that.".

Chad hugged Maggie and then happily got back down to work while Maggie dove into her closet to experiment with outfits.

Maggie still had the blonde wig on when the doorbell rang. Chad motioned his hand to Maggie to answer as he was absorbed in his work.

"Hey, Sister Eloise," Maggie said brightly as she greeted her at the door. "Chaddy, look who's here." *How strange,* Chad thought, they had just caught her spying on them at the restaurant. Chad typed the closing line to his blog entry and shut his laptop so he could join Sister Eloise and Maggie in the living room. Added bonus to Sister Eloise's arrival was that she knew so much of the vampdog's origin story.

"I hope you don't mind me dropping in, I was passing by and I thought I'd see how things were going with your little investigation," Eloise explained.

Once they settled in, Chad busted out his burning questions, "What more can you tell us about how The Darkness was involved in Lucy's disappearance?"

"Well, you know Lucy's boyfriend was a Darkness vampire and that boy's dad was the head of The Darkness at the time." This was indeed a revelation.

"Did he disappear the same night as Lucy?" Chad asked, thinking about what his cop buddy, Frank, had told him.

"What on Earth made you think of that?" Sister Eloise said taken aback.

"Something someone told me. Never mind."

Chad soaked up every word Sister Eloise said. This had to be the same vampire Frank said disappeared. Sister Eloise went on to tell them the history of The Darkness as an extreme coven that formed in the 1800s and believed coexisting with humans was unnatural. She quickly added, "No vampire is really a lost cause in the Lord's eyes."

"Where is Lucy's vampire beau now?" Maggie asked.

Sister Eloise got a faraway look and teared up. "I'm sure I wouldn't know," was all she said. Then she made her apologies for needing to take her leave. She left so quickly it made them wonder if they had touched a sore spot.

CHAPTER ELEVEN:

Nest

Frenchman Street & Esplanade was the corner where our band played. Correction, it was *our* corner. The Plasma Casters were individually Strings, Beanie, and Glory. I was stationed by the bucket to use my puppy cuteness for sympathy tips. Busking turf was part of the unwritten code of the Quarter so that everyone had a space to perform and collect tips from tourists and passersby. That's why this was our corner. Everybody knew that. It was a line nobody crossed unless they were looking for trouble.

For the most part, the locals were respectful, even though our entire band was comprised of vampires. New Orleans embraced the supernatural. There were ghosts, zombies, witches and vampires in countless stories that captured the imaginations of visitors from around the world who flocked here to rub elbows with immortals.

As we walked to our gig we passed under a hanging wooden sign that read: "Apartments for rent, haunted and not haunted." Locals had a reverence for the dead as well as the undead. Funerals were celebrated with parades and brass band music. Voodoo and witchcraft were respected practices. Vampires were accepted as fellow members of the community, at least in polite company. We suffered a fair amount of discrimination as outliers. As a canine vampire I was the furthest out of outliers and the only one of my kind as far as I knew.

I scampered close to Glory's heels. I'd mostly spent a decade surviving alone in the shadows of the courtyards, shotgun houses, and cemeteries. I had no relationships with other vampires. Then, I met Glory. She observed me feeding on a rat and was delighted to discover a dog vampire. She showed no fear of me and took me in her lap, feeling compelled to tell me her vampire origin story like we were already kindred spirits. She'd had a rough go of things and being a vampire was an improvement in her viewpoint. She introduced me to Beanie and Strings and after a bit of arguing, they agreed to accept me as their nestmate.

Glory warmed up her voice as we walked, her vibrato as sultry as melted chocolate.

"Sounding good, Glory," Beanie, our drummer, said smiling to reveal a severe overbite which made his fangs look like surfboards. When Beanie hit his solo, his sticks moved too fast for the human eye to see.

"Step it up, Beanie," said Strings. Beanie did as told, hoisted his drum case and stepped double time. He idolized Strings who was the leader of the pack and had the looks that made mortal and immortal females swoon. He was a player in more ways than just the lead guitar and vocals in the band; often he picked up women in bars, charming them with gas flame blue eyes.

When we got to our corner to set up as usual, just as the streetlamps turned a jaundice glow, we saw a tarot card reader with her dog in our spot. Strings set down his guitar case with a *thud* and we stopped.

We always followed Strings' lead.

The fortune teller looked up from her tarot cards as we approached and had the gall to wave and say, "cute dog."

How dare she. I could almost taste her salty skin. The others knew how I'd feel about this "cute" remark and Glory stepped in front of me just as I was coiling back. The fur on my back prickled and my ears moved back a notch. Glory's black combat boots and flowy skirt blocked my view of the interloper, but not before I noticed a wisp of honey-colored hair slipping out from her head scarf.

Beanie spoke first. "This is our corner." He looked over at Strings for approval.

Strings nodded and took a step toward the girl. "Beanie, where are your manners. Clearly, she is a newcomer or she would have known. I'm Strings, nice to meet you."

I peeked around Glory's skirt and saw the girl's smile drop and her baby doll eyes click open a notch wider.

"I'm sorry. This is my first night out. I'm new here," she said and stood up to talk to us.

"I'm Strings. Where are you from?"

"Iowa. I came to visit an old friend."

"Must not have given you pointers about what to look out for," Beanie said, staring at her throat. "She? He? They? from here or one of those hipsters gentrifying the life out of this place?"

New Girl backed up a step. "He's not a—he's from Iowa, too—not a hipster. He writes a blog about vampires called Bloodlust. I'm not all into that stuff."

"Bloodlust. I know all about that," Strings said.

Why was her backstory feeling familiar? I thought. Something didn't feel right, but I was intrigued.

She gestured to her dog and said, "This is Charlie. He's friendly." The pathetic hound lifted his head expectantly when he heard his name, tail swishing behind him. She gave him a pat. My insides clenched at the thought of once being such an innocent, hapless creature. But that was long ago. We stared back at her silently, long enough to make her uncomfortable.

"Look, I can clear out of here and give you your little spot back," she stammered as she packed her cards and talismans into a canvas bag. Strings took another step closer. He chose his words carefully.

"We understand you may not know the rules yet, but we can show you the Buskers Map if you'd like to come back to our place."

He was charming her. I guess the band wouldn't be starting until later tonight. Beanie and Glory stashed all the instruments behind the bar at Dragon's Den, a nearby pub where a fellow vamp tends bar.

New Girl fell into Strings' charms and happily followed us to our place. Charlie dog sniffed everywhere, taking a keen interest in me and my backside, but I would have none of it. The woman slipped off her scarf, freeing her honey-colored hair to bounce around her shoulders. Oh, my heart.

Strings and Beanie were the perfect escorts, flanking New Girl on either side and pointing out interesting landmarks. Marie Laveau's House of Voodoo, Muriel's Séance Room, St. Louis Cathedral with a statue casting a giant shadow of Jesus with outstretched arms on its back exterior wall. Glory acted like New Girl was her BFF, though I saw her licking her lips a few times. She spotted things in store windows that "would look *great* on you. You should really come back for that purple fascinator," or "You could really pull off that sequin skirt." New Girl was taken in by their seduction; she didn't stand a chance.

Despite wanting to get a taste of her earlier, I suddenly felt like I wanted to protect her and her dog, too. Maybe it was the hair. Okay, it was definitely the hair. But I knew I'd have to confront Strings if I were to save her, which was nothing to trifle with. As much as I craved her flesh, I didn't want her to suffer. She bore a vague resemblance to Lucy. She had the same honey-colored curls, the same peach complexion and even the pitch of her voice was similar. If she were to say, "who's a good boy?" I'd be undone.

We arrived at Fifi Mahony's Wig Shop in the French Quarter and darted down into the cellar, where once wine had been kept safe barely above sea level. It was impossible to keep the water out. Even now, I watched a dozen rats wriggling together through a crack to reach an underground nest. That was exactly what we were doing, too. This is where we hid from daylight, in a damp, cement, windowless hideaway with all of us piled together. It suited my pack mentality.

New Girl's phone bleated some stupid ringtone and she grabbed a hold of Charlie's collar and started backing away from us in a flurry of apologies and excuses as to why she couldn't join us. I sensed that she was spooked. Did she wise up? Was that her escape call? Beanie and Glory each grabbed one of her arms and hissed. But Strings raised a hand and they released her. Strings bowed his head, and New Girl and her dog ran like hell.

I needed a break from the vampires in my coven for the moment. Sometimes their antics were a bit much for me. I heard them cackling as I ran after the young woman. I couldn't be sure they wouldn't come after her. It was a game to them. But like most modern vampires, they didn't kill when they fed. I'd find them later playing jazz on our corner, scoping for another victim. They were talented musicians and always drew a crowd. I could rejoin them at my post by the tip bucket when I liked. For now, I'd take my leave. They were used to me disappearing on my own.

I caught up with New Girl and her dog in an instant given my preternatural speed. But I maintained my distance. I was still mulling over the right approach. She reached the door to a courtyard that flung open for her. There appeared Chad, the Vampire Tour Guide, pulling her inside to safety.

"Maggie." He hugged her.

Of course. It was Maggie. Iowa. Vampire blogger boyfriend. I don't know why I didn't recognize her sooner, but I'd only seen her from a distance. Her hair was different. Wasn't it pink before? I sniffed around, this was the apartment where I watched them before they went out to dinner. Was this their lame attempt to connect with me? Game on. Now I'd take a more direct approach.

CHAPTER TWELVE:
Close Call

Maggie poured herself a glass of red wine. Her hands were still shaking a little. She was telling Chad every detail of her adventure with the vampire musicians. Before this incident, they were fans of the band's music on Spotify. As long as he'd been writing about vampires in this town he had kept a certain distance. *This was progress*, Chad thought. They knew the location of vampdog's nest. Maggie had both of her hands wrapped around the wine glass as if it could generate warmth. Chad watched her dainty fingers with their short nails painted a sparkly purple and gave her space to tell her story while he tested his glucose level with a finger prick.

"What if I had stayed in their lair? He was charming me. What if I had given in? I was glad to have Charlie with me, I'll be sad when he goes back to his own house tomorrow."

"I wonder what it is about you that you were able to resist being charmed?"

Chad couldn't bear the thought of anything happening to Maggie. He had this strange feeling that the vampdog didn't want her harmed either. That little undead doggy wanted to connect. Chad was convinced he held the key to Lucy's disappearance, even if he didn't realize it.

"The vampdog followed you all the way back here you know, Mags."

"That's like no dog I've ever seen and like every dog at the same time. When he looks at your face it's like he knows exactly what you are feeling. So weird."

"Yep, crazy little critter. I have a feeling our paths will cross again without us even having to plot and scheme."

Maggie gave Charlie some water and kibble and then curled up on the couch to finish her wine. Chad joined her. He raised his own glass of sparkling water.

"Here's to the vampdog and all his wondrous secrets."

Maggie raised her glass to touch his.

"You know it's bad luck to toast with water," she told him.

"Are you with me in this investigation?"

Maggie nodded and clinked her glass to his.

Chad smiled at her and said, "Then we're going to need to take the bad with the good."

CHAPTER THIRTEEN:

Observed

I found the perfect spot to stay and watch them. I spun around a few times before settling in under a tree where I blended in with the ground in a little doggy circle. The lights were on in the blogger's second story flat illuminating the kitchen. I saw the Tour Guide Blogger and his imposter girlfriend, Maggie, conspiring. She no longer captivated me after she ripped off her beautiful blonde hair. What could they be getting up to? I watched him prick his finger, squeeze out a drop of blood, and touch it to a device. Mm, yummy, don't tempt me. I'd have to feed before getting back to the nest, I was already feeling a little shaky. From what I could gather from their expressions, the blogger and the imposter seemed pleased with their ruse. Good for them. They knew I'd follow her. Maybe they even knew the reason—the curse of longing for Lucy and her honey-colored hair. It is an obsession equally as strong as my need to feed on blood. I see a young woman who has golden ringlets and it stirs something at my core.

Finding the real Lucy has been impossible for me. The entire family vacated our old home on Esplanade not long after I'd been turned and she disappeared. Needless to say, they left me no forwarding address. I wasn't even sure if she was still alive. I pictured her a middle-aged woman with a family of her own, maybe even new pets. I tortured myself with such thoughts.

Since seeing them at the Court House rally, I was considering how Chad and Maggie could be helpful to me. Enough of this cat and mouse game! Or rather, vampdog and human game. I needed to connect with these two. I would need to get into their minds. I had to use that power sparingly, though. A mind meld took a lot of my energy but was worth it for the information I received. Maybe it could be the partnership I needed to finally find Lucy, dare I even think it. I felt so limited by my canine body.

I wanted to get closer. I crept down the grassy embankment to the sidewalk. No sooner had I stepped into the streetlight when I felt long, cold fingers grab me around the waist. Strings. I kicked my legs and my paws flailed but to no real effect.

"There you are little one. Time to go back to the nest," Strings said.

How long had I been out here? I must have missed the entire gig that night after I followed Maggie here.

Strings and the others really were fond of me. At the least, I amused them. I think maybe I reminded them all of their lost human lives. Strings tucked me into his knapsack and slung me on his back so I could peek out behind us. Despite the way vampires now lived peacefully with humans, there were a number of characters we had to look out for. Vampire hunters. Dog catchers. Overly zealous fans. Vampires who hurt other vampires. True deaths among vampires were on the rise.

So many times I wished I had long human legs and arms with fists on the end to teach the bad guys a lesson. If I could exact small doses of justice for the downtrodden, maybe I wouldn't be such a despicable demon. Maybe I could prove I was a good boy still, worthy of love. But here I am, trapped in this small dog body for eternity. I watched our back as Strings carried me back to our nest, whistling as he strolled.

"I've got a treat for you," Strings crooned to me. "We found another tourist. A chubby blonde girl whose skin smells like strawberries. We found her on the way back from the gig, passed out on the sidewalk outside Tropical Isle on Bourbon Street, green plastic novelty cup still in her hand." He chuckled.

Tropical Isle was known for ridiculously strong drinks that took tourists by surprise, such as the Hand Grenade in a foot-long green plastic cup with plastic hand grenade garnish and the Tropical Itch in a tall yellow cup with a back scratcher for a stirrer. The cocktail recipes were a well-guarded trade secret, or so the bartenders on Bourbon Street said. This girl was easy pickings for Strings and the gang. There were always easy pickings on Bourbon Street, a vampire's paradise.

"We left plenty for you. Silly pup, chasing after a blonde girl again when we already have one here for you."

We slipped through the rear entrance of the wig shop and into the cellar and Strings released me from his bag. I scurried into our living room, or should I say unliving room? Beanie and Glory were sitting on the floor, Beanie playing the guitar, Glory a violin. They were serenading a limp, motionless audience of one girl sprawled across the floor. I could see bite marks on her neck, wrists and legs. I could feel her pulse throbbing in my ears. She had bleached white hair, nothing like my Lucy.

"Hey Chulie, score any tail?" Glory said and Beanie snorted a laugh at her joke.

I stared at them like I do. Beanie scratched my head with his scraggly fingernails and encouraged me to eat.

"Go on, we saved you some."

The hunger in me took over like a beast unleashed and I clamped onto the girl's wrist. Sweet liquid spurted into my mouth. The others howled at my actions, but Strings called for us to finish up.

"That's enough. We need to leave enough in her that she chalks it up to a bad hangover when she comes to. Though the bite marks may be a giveaway."

"I could go for seconds," Beanie moaned.

"Go get yourself a supplement," Strings ordered. We never crossed the line into actually draining until death. That just wasn't done these days. At least not very often. It's mainly why humans tolerated our kind living openly amongst them.

As I ate, I didn't feel anything for this girl. Her blood still had alcohol in it, making me a little dizzy. It did occur to me this could have been Maggie and that made me feel uneasy. But I was back with my nest and satisfied. Puppy's got to eat, after all. Soon after, I curled up in my square-shaped little casket, which used to be a trunk. I fell asleep with blood on my teeth and dreamt of my Lucy again.

CHAPTER FOURTEEN:

Soiree

*B*loodlust, a Blog for Vampire Enthusiasts – August 5, 2023 By Chad Russo

Greetings fiends and followers. In this week's edition of Bloodlust, I will divulge my sordid experiences at the Krewe du Vampdog Blood Hounds Ball, as well as provide an update on my encounters with the undead canine with whom the Krewe is obsessed.

For the uninitiated, let me describe the essence of a New Orleans "krewe." A krewe in New Orleans typically stages a parade or an event associated with Mardi Gras. They range from smallish neighborhood groups to mega krewes with membership in the hundreds. Some krewes of note: Endymion, Bacchus, Krewe de Vieux, Zulu, Krewe of Red Beans, and Muses. There are nearly a hundred others, the oldest dating back to 1856. Some krewes identify themselves as Social Aid & Pleasure Clubs, serving to unify and support communities. The Krewe du Vampdog unites the stalkers of a diminutive vampire pooch that wanders the Quarter at night. Also of note, the Krewe du Vampdog takes the "Pleasure" part of Social Aid & Pleasure Club to a twisted level of kink this blog writer has never seen.

So picture me, entering the stately manor where the Blood Hounds Ball was being hosted, personal invitation in hand. I was regaled in the requisite tux and had my beautiful blonde girlfriend by my side. I was in my element. Given the infatuation with vampires I share with you, dear readers, New Orleans is the only place for me, and only in New Orleans could there be a party like this.

The foyer was swarming with people in period costumes, S&M outfits, furry costumes, and elaborate masks. It was a carnival for my eyes. A woman in a full Victorian corset and gown had her face and décolletage as generously powdered as a beignet. She pulled the face of a pink panda to ample breasts that bulged from atop her corset like Pillsbury biscuits from a just-cracked tin. A large tuxedo-clad man sporting a long beaky plague-era mask snatched two glasses of champagne from a waiter's tray and brought them to a gaggle of women wearing ornately feathered masks. They were loudly discussing the blonde tourist found staggering through the Quarter at dawn this week covered in bite marks.

The wait staff in crisp white uniforms swirled silver trays filled with delicate glassware and tiny savory and sweet delights while guests grabbed at them, sipping and stuffing their faces with canapé. Another tray had shot glasses of blood for the vampire guests. I was jostled about and my cufflink snagged a feather of a spectacular pink flamingo costume. My date was enchanted by the spectacle and wandered off, chatting with a man in a top hat. On closer look. I noticed he had a snake draped over his shoulders. I wandered alone through a corridor called, the Hall of Captains, which was lined with portraits of former Krewe du Vampdog Captains and other notable New Orleanians. One portrait looked to be from the turn of the Century, as in the early 1900s, way before The Krewe du Vampdog began in the 1990s. The historical portrait depicted a father and his grown son. Next to it was a portrait of the same father and son but this one looked like it was from the 1980s based on their attire and hairstyles. They looked to be exactly the same age as they did in the 1900s. Vampires. I wondered how they related to the Krewe du Vampdog.

It took about five minutes before a trio of fans of my blog were on me like flies on fly paper. (No offense, love you all dearly my readers.) They were dressed like sexy vampire animals and they sucked me into their conversation, pun most definitely intended.

"It's no conspiracy theory, Chad. The pandemic started with vampire bats and was spread to feral cats and dogs," one sultry cat woman purred. A rabbit with large fangs chimed in, "Of course you twit, Chad knows all that, right Chad?" It was clear that they cared less about what I had to say and more about gaining validation for their nonsense. I nodded and escaped to a bar in the corner. Bloody Mary's, of course.

A guest dressed like a sexy demon dog took my free hand and pulled me down the hall to the krewe's infamous party rooms. We passed by one open doorway that revealed a room filled with real dogs. The door was marked the "Tribute Room." Did people actually want to create their own vampdogs? That's a little twisted, people. I understand the intrigue of a vampire dog and I share that fascination. But to arrange the creation of such a creature seems a cruel thing to do to a mortal dog. It also seems to interfere with dark forces that make this blog writer uncomfortable. But here we have a roomful of dogs meant to tempt the vampire dog into biting and turning them. Sure enough, the woman guiding me down the hall confirmed it.

"Yeah, everyone wants their own vampdog. But making one is a lot harder than it sounds. At least making one that doesn't destroy itself that is," she told me.

I wondered how she knew this. Please leave a comment if you know. To my knowledge, the vampire dog has never turned another creature, let alone another dog. But maybe a companion is in his future? I don't pretend to know his every motivation.

My Doggy Diva guide kept tugging me toward the ballroom at the end of the hall and my drink sloshed over my hand. She stopped to lick it off while staring at me with her smoldering eyes. Once at the ballroom door, she whispered a pass phrase through a tiny window. As the double doors opened, an assortment of half-naked, half-costumed humans and a few vampires were tangled in a variety of sex acts. Dear readers, I am no prude. But I saw things that I think defied physics. The night was a blur of debauchery from that point on, but believe it or not, the most remarkable event happened on the way home. My companion and I extracted ourselves from the decadence while it was still at a fever pitch without saying a single goodbye. My ears were still ringing from the thumping techno music in the ballroom, muffling the sounds around me – the wind, an owl, our footsteps. That's when he appeared in our path just a half block ahead. I am convinced he was allowing me to see him, beckoning me. While we have been tracking vampdog for some time, now he has been following us right back. The stalked becomes the stalker.

Touché. There he stood in front of us, as still as death. Even from several feet away, I felt our eyes meet and in that moment a flood of images entered my mind. I knew I was staring into the eyes of a knowing, sentient being. I saw blood, rats, a trumpet, a parade, laughing tourists, rogue chickens, dark courtyards, wavy brick sidewalks passing below me at dizzying speeds. It was so disorienting I thought I'd surely pass out. I held my head in my hands but I couldn't make the visions stop. The last image was the clearest. It was a female in a window with soft lamplight illuminating her honey-colored hair. She had an energy surrounding her like the pull of quicksand, an inescapable force. The only way I can describe what was happening to me was a mind meld between me and vampdog. He was gleaning thoughts and images from my mind as surely as he was projecting his to me. It was a full sensory experience, I heard chants at a protest, people screaming the names Lucy and Chulie, I heard a gunshot and strangely I smelled Murphy's Oil soap. The rally. I have never felt anything like it. It was as if our minds were not contained in our heads but were as powerful as a flood breaking a levee, as deep as the universe and more enormous than a city. They swirled together like a kaleidoscope's fragments. My date was rightfully freaked out and wondered if I needed medical attention. But no. At this moment, something I have suspected about the vampdog had become crystal clear. He can extract thoughts from a human's mind, giving him an awareness and cognitive ability miles above an ordinary dog. While having this epiphany, I received his message loud and clear. He was asking for my help.

Take with you, dear readers, this last revelation. In the nano second before the vampdog vanished, I heard a female scream, "Chulie run!" and I saw a cloaked figure holding a wooden stake and hammer but I could not see his face.

Mercy me, I was mind melded by the vampdog.

Please like, follow and share. @Chadrusso #bloodlust #vampdog Look for my TikTok videos coming soon!

CHAPTER FIFTEEN:

Tributes

It was quiet and dark in a stretch of Woldenberg Park along the Mississippi River. My claws clicked rhythmically like brushes on a snare drum as I scurried along the promenade they call The Moon Walk. Giant, shadowy barges filled the formidable river to my right, moving so slowly one could hardly tell they were moving at all. The park to my left was an expansive green space, likely buzzing with activity during the day, but how would I know. Now it was populated only by the nocturnal: racoons, possums, and me. I needed to be away from humans for a bit to clear my head.

Doing a mind meld with Blogger Guy was overwhelming. So many bizarre images imprinted on my mind like when Lucy would flip through the TV channels so quickly it was impossible to focus on one thing. I know the Blogger Tour Guide is Chad, and I confirmed he bears me no harm. While I'd preferred if his blog didn't bring so much attention to me, I wondered if we could use it to keep Lucy's story alive. So many possibilities if we could work together.

I drew closer to the water near a drain where I knew rats liked to go, their wet, grey bodies wriggling deliciously. I had one in a flash. I needed the sustenance. I felt the frantic creature's heart thumping, enhancing my hunger.

During our mind meld, I had discovered that Chad the blogger and I had something in common. He is a diabetic, constantly monitoring his blood sugar for "lows" and "highs." When I don't consume enough blood, I feel shaky and weak, the same as he does when he experiences a sugar low. Now seeing him prick his finger made sense. After I sucked the life out of the rat, I felt more like myself. Renewed. I reflected how it was all an endless cycle of death and renewal, an infinite resurrection story.

I had achieved my objective of letting Chad know I needed his help. I thought, or at least I'd hoped he understood, my need for him to help in the search for my Lucy. I was fairly certain he did. Maybe he wasn't as dumb as he looked.

But there were many distracting images that I extracted from his mind, including an array of kooks in all manner of costumes and strange behavior at the Krewe du Vampdog party this evening. There was one image that disturbed me most. I saw a dozen mortal dogs of various breeds being held in a cramped Victorian-style parlor. "Tribute dogs" was how Chad saw them and I felt his distress. The Krewe was annoyingly obsessed with me. Sometimes they hosted blood drives and left bags of their own blood out on the street for me. They loved posting photos of their sightings of me and so far, I've seen it in their minds. But offering live dogs as tribute seemed over the edge even for them.

As I reached a plaza where the Moon Walk branched off, I turned left, heading deeper into the Quarter and back toward the scene of the Krewe du Vampdog ball. It was near the same stretch of Esplanade where my Lucy and I lived several decades ago before I became a night creature and object of unwanted fascination. I didn't feel fascinating, even after all this time. I felt funky and not in a good way. I am the smell of death and blood, I am the chill of an ill wind, I am a rolling black sky before a storm. I felt unlovable, even while I still pined for my Lucy. Even though I longed to be a good boy.

I passed statuesque homes ringed in ornate wrought iron balconies, bespectacled with tall windows like eyes opened in shock, with elaborate detailing as subtle as a drag queen's make up. Each had that charming, Southern flair that spoke of debutante balls and secrets. Canopies of moss hung from oak trees older than vampires, lining the boulevard. I was nostalgic for my walks here with Lucy on the other end of a pink, bejeweled leash as I pranced along the sidewalk, sniffing "messages" left by other dogs as if it were our own social network.

I am not sure why, but I felt a surge of empathy for the tribute dogs that were trapped in that parlor. They still had a chance at loving homes, warm kitchens, long walks and belly rubs. I had never turned another creature, human or animal, into a vampire and I can think of nothing more selfish and cruel. Although, I'd be lying if I said the idea of a vampire dog companion wasn't appealing. It was downright intriguing.

But this bunch of hapless canines? Ridiculous. I knew I needed to head back to the party to do something.

I went back to where I had the mind meld with Chad and then got closer to the Krewe du Vampdog's Blood Hounds Ball.

I stood close by on the parkway in the shadow of one of the magnificent Oak trees. Though Chad and Maggie had left the party earlier, in the wee hours of the morning it was in full swing. The windows were lit up and revealed an assortment of oddities. Humans were decked out in finery, others in furry animal costumes. Some were passing fruit back and forth without using their hands, only the crooks of their necks. Trays of frothy drinks swished back and forth. Many guests laughed in a chemical induced hysteria.

Floor-to-ceiling windows on the first floor revealed the Tribute Dog Room. This was the room I saw in Chad's mind's eye, the one that had left him uneasy. I observed the dogs, some curled up on the floor, some tugging at the same toy, others barking at phantoms. Pathetic, but endearing. One was clawing at the door, likely wanting to get out to join his master or mistress. I hear you, brother. Dogs have a singular devotion.

Oh, to be unaware again.

If this was going to work, everything would need to snap into place. In a flash, I was up on the porch outside the window. It was open about 10 inches from the ground with a piece of fabric loosely covering the opening so the air-conditioning and dogs wouldn't escape, but a clever vampire canine such as myself could slip in. There was a trail of what smelled like chicken blood leading to the window. Maybe I'd take a lick?

Wait a minute, was this bait ... for me? People, we don't enjoy the blood of dead things. The dogs noticed me and whined and yelped. A labradoodle bowed to me in that namesake yoga position downward facing dog. I knew this because I watched Glory and Beanie doing her yoga videos.

I entered the room and stared into each one of their eyes until I had them spellbound. It only took a few moments to enthrall them all, but even that was too long. Footsteps approached. I made a noise somewhere between a bark and a yelp at a pitch so high only the dogs heard me. They knew at once to follow me. I dove through the open window and there on the porch was a mountain of a man dressed like a soldier. He lunged toward me. When his meaty arm reached for me, I noticed the mark. It was the bat with the sword. That particular symbol was imprinted on my brain, along with all the other images from the night I was turned. It was on the hand of one of the dinner guests and the vampire boy who snuck into Lucy's room and changed me forever.

I shook my whole body to free myself of the memories. The need to get the dogs out of there super-charged me.

In an instant, a dozen or so dogs dove out the window after me. It was enough to throw this hulk of a man for a loop. I ran into the front yard and zig zagged back and forth. The pack of dogs followed me like a pack would instinctively do. We moved as a unit, making ourselves impossible to catch. A few other goons joined the chase and they all tried to grab at the dogs in our wild herd. But not one got caught. We eluded them and managed to cross Esplanade away from the party house. We were a dog stampede, racing through a residential neighborhood, leaving the crowd of flabbergasted party guests and bouncers far behind.

I knew where I wanted to take them. Winding through a few dark streets we came upon a public park with a huge fenced-off dog park. We stopped here. The dogs sniffed, climbed, explored, and enjoyed their freedom. I watched. I knew it wouldn't be long until they were found and each dog I hoped would be returned to its owner. I'd be long gone by then.

I savored the glorious moment of canine exuberance. I hoped this small act of rebellion would make a statement. No one should exploit those of us condemned to immortality.

CHAPTER SIXTEEN:

Sister Eloise

After some recovery time from the krewe ball, Maggie and Chad were anxious to get back to their investigation. Later the next day they'd arranged to pay Sister Eloise a visit. Chad ventured out to grab coffee for himself and Maggie and was nearly plowed over by group of drunken tourists. *Starting a tad early* Chad thought. It reminded him of another rowdy bunch he'd encountered on one of his vampire tours earlier that year. That was the day he'd met Sister Eloise for the first time.

It was the start of Carnival season earlier that year, just after the St. Joan of Arc parade. The number of tourists in town was on an uptick as it was every year leading up to Mardi Gras and then the spring festivals. And so Chad's tours were booming, too. That one particular group he recalled was extra festive, having done their share of day drinking before the tour. They thought their added commentary would help embellish his talk track, which was always not fun.

"The Ursuline convent in front of us is recognized as the oldest surviving building in New Orleans, even in the whole Mississippi Valley," Chad told his group.

"Do the nuns still live here and is it true New Orleans nuns are allowed to do the nasty on Mardi Gras?" The group of drunk friends thought this was comedy at its finest and they erupted in laughter. Chad wasn't amused.

"No, in fact that's not true but feel free to indulge your fantasies," Chad said, earning him some laughs. "Almost all of the nuns live in a different location now and the building you see here is mostly a museum."

"What does an old convent have to do with vampires?" another tourist blurted out.

"I'm so glad you asked," Chad replied. "The Ursuline nuns came over from France in the earliest days of the colonization in the 1700s to help establish the church and educate the children, at least for the wealthy citizens. But the colonists wanted the marrying type of women, too, so they sent a group of women known as the Casket Girls who are rumored to have brought the first vampires to New Orleans in 1719."

"1728," came a voice from the back of the group. Well that was a weird heckle. The voice called out again, "They came to Biloxi in 1719 and then to New Orleans in 1728." That's when he saw her, standing at the back of the tour group in her long gray habit—Sister Eloise.

"I stand corrected." Chad smiled.

That was the first time Chad met Sister Eloise. Since those many months ago, they kept up with each other. She attended his tours and Chad attended hers. She gave daily tours at the convent and tourists hung on every detail of the Casket Girls and the mysterious third floor of the convent that was sealed shut. Chad

had been observing Sister Eloise's tour guide techniques; she was a master storyteller. She had told Chad about her lineage in New Orleans going all the way back to the early settlers from France and a long line of prostitutes and jazz musicians. She was always religious, fascinated by the stories of saints as a girl. She had become a nun to break the cycle of prostitution and vice in her ancestry. Even her mother worked the streets, her father was a "customer" who disappeared when Eloise was a baby. Late one night, her mother was struck and killed by a car near her post when Eloise was only eighteen. The Church was literally her saving grace.

Chad was feeling inspired by the connection he had made with Chulie during their mind meld and couldn't wait to tell Sister Eloise about it. She may have even read about it in his blog. He blushed thinking about Sister Eloise reading the sordid details of the Krewe du Vampdog party in his last post. Oh well, she'd probably heard it all by now. She left in a rush after her last visit and he wanted to make sure things were okay between them.

Chad and Maggie stopped at nearby bakery Croissant D'Or just after the breakfast rush to grab some pastries to share. Sister Eloise was the only nun in residence at the convent and she lived in a simple room upstairs from the chapel so she could still oversee the tours and curate the exhibits.

"Hello, my dears!"

Sister Eloise greeted them with her typical spunk and Maggie and Chad followed her upstairs, amazed by her agility, even in her long gray habit. Chad felt relieved that she was in a good mood after their last awkward goodbye.

The apartment had a mix of religious and New Orleans artifacts, reflective of the cultural mix in the town. Chad detected the smells of candles and Murphy's Oil Soap, probably used to clean the wooden pews downstairs.

They sat in her parlor and Maggie set out the pastries they'd brought.

"You know, that bakery uses recipes that some of my ancestors brought over from France," Sister Eloise started.

"I know your ancestors were amongst the first settlers here," Chad nudged mostly for Maggie's benefit, so she could hear Sister Eloise tell her story firsthand.

"Oh yes. And before you ask, yes the Casket Girls, too, I am a direct descendant."

Maggie and Chad exchanged looks of marvel. They couldn't believe their good fortune to be in the presence of someone whose life was so intertwined with the history of New Orleans. It was a far cry from the folks they knew in Iowa.

"The Church leaders at the time wanted to ensure there were plentiful good Catholic families. But oh, if they could see what's become of this town now." Eloise shook her head.

"Is it true they brought vampires to New Orleans?" Maggie asked. Eloise seemed slightly annoyed at her enthusiasm.

"I don't think that was entirely up to the Casket Girls. But no one is beyond redemption." Sister Eloise spoke with a passion that made her eyes light. Chad wasn't quite sure what she meant by that but decided not to press.

"Speaking of vampires, can you tell us more about the night that vampdog was created and his owner disappeared?"

Sister Eloise paused to stir her tea. She stared into her cup.

"Oh that. Best to let go and let God." Now Chad was slightly annoyed. He did not agree. He was about to protest when Sister Eloise's next statement gave him pause.

"You know I once kept Chulie the vampdog here with me, to protect him," Sister Eloise offered in a casual way. Chad dropped his croissant and Maggie set her coffee cup back in its saucer. Maggie and Chad were both fake sipping Eloise's horrible coffee anyway, and Chad knew they'd laugh about it later.

"What? Really?" Chad said. "A lot of people believe he holds the answers of what happened to Lucy."

"If he knows anything, I'm not sure how he'd tell anyone. He pines for her all the time. Poor pitiful demon. He lived with me not long after he was turned into one of the undead. I felt sorry for the little creature. The nature of a dog and the devil combined. But still vulnerable."

The devil is taking it a bit far, Chad thought. But he was never one hundred percent sure what Sister Eloise thought of vampires. She read his blog so he assumed she was at least interested in them.

"He slept in my ancestor Colette's trunk, the one she came over with on the ship. Imagine, just a trunk for all your things." Chad noticed that she hadn't used the word "casket" or even the French "casquette."

"Do you still keep in touch with Chulie?" Maggie asked.

Eloise opened her mouth to say something but choked a little on her coffee.

Sister Eloise gathered herself to answer Maggie's question, wiping her mouth with a napkin. "I wouldn't say I keep in touch with him now. That was decades ago. But I do see him from time to time. He's not as vulnerable anymore."

Maggie and Chad exchanged a look.

"Sister Eloise, I need to tell you about an encounter I had with Chulie recently." Chad took a breath to slow himself. "I think he connected me to his mind."

Sister Eloise stared hard at him, expressionless. Something flickered in her eyes.

"Connected to your mind?" she said, rising and shaking out her habit. "Even if he did, what could he possibly show you? Chulie is a poor sad creature, unnatural, and no doubt very confused to find himself in this position. Don't you think?"

"But he seems more than that," Chad pressed.

A timer buzzed from the kitchen.

"Oh my, I need to take the cookies out of the oven. Big bake sale tomorrow. Will you excuse me for a few minutes?"

"Oh yes, Sister. Of course," Maggie said.

Sister Eloise flitted out of the room. Chad and Maggie whispered about how odd Sister Eloise could be and how terrible her coffee was. They wandered about while they waited for her to come back, looking at all of Sister Eloise's mementos: Mardi Gras trinkets and glass beads, statuettes of Saints Joan of Arc, Francis of Assisi, Bernadette, crosses, prayer cards, gris gris bags, candles and kitschy vampire souvenirs, such as tiny caskets with pop-out vampires, a glass case with a wooden stake, small vials of fake blood. It was like a museum of voodoo Catholicism. Even her wallpaper had an intricate pattern of people walking through a cemetery.

"Now then." Sister Eloise came back into the room with more coffee. Chad and Maggie waved a hand to decline a second cup. Sister Eloise set the pot on the table and sat in her chair. Chad side-glanced at Maggie, who nodded. This was the break in the conversation they had been waiting for. "Sister, Eloise, Maggie and I want to apologize for the last visit. When we asked if The Darkness coven was connected to Lucy's disappearance, it seemed to upset you. We were just genuinely curious," Chad implored.

Sister Eloise hopped up and moved some items that they had touched back into their original place on their shelf with a clank. She then straightened her habit before replying. Chad held his breath, hoping he hadn't offended her.

"Well that girl may have gotten herself in trouble by hanging with the wrong crowd. Her mother is a decent God-fearing woman. Not sure how she bred such a wild child." Sister Eloise's expression hardened.

"Teenagers," was all Maggie could say.

"I have it on good authority that Victor Broussard, Lucy's father, had business dealings with The Darkness vampires. They say his wife, Fiona, didn't want anything to do with them. But their daughter, Lucy, may have been exposed to them," Sister Eloise explained.

"Did you know her mother, Fiona?"

"No," Sister Eloise answered quickly. "Why would I know her? We may have crossed paths at a prayer vigil for Lucy, but I wouldn't say I knew her, no."

Sister Eloise gathered herself and softened once more to her sweet spunky self, "Would you look at the time, I think it's about time you were leaving."

Chad and Maggie could take a not-so-subtle hint. They thanked her for her hospitality and left quickly. They had a lot to talk about on the way home. They were a half block away when Chad turned to Maggie and said, "She's hiding something."

CHAPTER SEVENTEEN:

Second Line

I was out on my nightly hunt when I wandered into a second line parade, the uniquely New Orleans style of celebrating someone who has passed. The elaborate nature of the parade told me it must have been a big shot who had croaked. A tuba honked a foot away from me, making me jump to attention. The buzz in the crowd suggested the deceased was someone in the hot sauce industry. There were women dressed as shiny hot sauce bottles made of sequins. Even without the ability to read, the labels looked familiar. It was my Lucy's family's hot sauce. This all made sense with the announcement that Victor Broussard had passed and her case was closed. I wondered and watched, pleading in my cold heart with the universe that somehow Lucy might be here to mourn her father. I watched intently.

Like grander parades such as the St. Joan of Arc Epiphany parade, this parade told a story in chapters, or stages of marchers. This was a bit unusual for a second line, further emphasizing the stature of the honored dead. The first chapter was the pepper plants being harvested in the fields. This was represented by dozens of flag girls and drummers, dressed in bright red, with flags of green like the fields. I heard a kid near me reading the lead banner aloud, "The Harvest."

The kid announced each banner as it passed by. This was helpful since I hadn't yet mastered the ability to read. The second chapter was led by a banner that said "The Making" with rows of horses dressed in shiny silver vestments to evoke the machinery at a factory. This was followed by "The Magic" which was a throng of people on stilts with giant wings and a brass band playing a funky, modern version of "Do You Believe in Magic."

The "chapter" that followed was rather curious. It was called "The Secret Ingredient" and it featured synchronized dancers dressed in bright red satin. This was stirring something in me I couldn't describe, but my senses were on high alert. Someplace locked away, I knew this story.

A giant float was next, with banners on the side reading "The Empire," looking like a city made of Broussard Hot Sauce bottles.

The final chapter was comprised of the mourners. It was led by a horse-drawn carriage with a coffin inside. The carriage displayed a placard reading, "The Glory." The family members and other mourners walked behind it dressed in black, carrying signs with giant pictures of the deceased. I felt a current of emotions as I recognized some of Lucy's family members, her brothers, cousins, all older now. The signs showed their patriarch, Victor Broussard, with thirty years added to my recollection of him. Of course, his death was what prompted them to stop the investigation into Lucy's disappearance. My desire to find Lucy soared in this encounter with her family. I darted about staring laser beams into the crowd to try to find her in the chaos. Then it happened. There ahead, honey-colored curls and a sweet voice chiming, "Who's a good boy? You are!"

I felt electrified with a hope renewed. I bolted toward the sound of that voice and the glimpse of blonde hair. My guard was down and I was nearly stepped upon by a marching band. The sound came from the entrance to a courtyard a few steps out of the fray. With my unnatural hearing I was able to single out the voices above the noise and hone in on it. I could smell a floral shampoo and something else. Peanut butter? I raced over.

Alas, I came upon the source of sweet voice—not my Lucy— but instead a young mother with pretty blonde curls, a boy of about five human years and a French bulldog. The woman was holding up a peanut butter treat to make the pooch dance on his hind legs and the boy was squealing with delight.

"That's a good boy, Pierre!" she encouraged.

Not my Lucy, I thought again. Another in a decades-long series of disappointments. Another sweet lady with honey-colored hair. But maybe this could be the next best thing? I could work with this. I could care less about peanut butter treats any more, but I could dance circles around this clown dog.

I got their attention with a bright, "yip." The boy looked at me and pointed. With their attention on me I pulled out all the stops. I used my speed to spin in a circle so fast I was a blur of fur. I posed, then did a few flips high up in the air above their heads. The mom gasped but the boy shrieked with laughter. I was going to go from "good boy" to "great boy," I thought. I landed gracefully on my feet, giving my tail a good wag to send friendly vibes and then did a twisty little jazz square on my hind legs. I stopped and waited for her praise. The mom smiled at me, and I felt clouds parting in my chest.

Then her smile fell as she looked past me.

What I hadn't realized was that my antics had drawn a crowd of onlookers. The group was the true "second liners" who danced and marched behind the family of mourners to convey the celebration portion of the ritual parade. The mom's face set firmly and she ushered her little boy and dog deeper into the courtyard and inside the building to safety. Something was wrong. Very wrong. I smelled something metallic along with incense. The touristy types in front clapped and cheered my performance, calling for more. Gathering behind them was a wall of red and black cloaks, a formidable gathering of priests wearing medieval armor over their cassocks. I was familiar with this particularly militant religious order because of their hatred for vampire kind, including the canine variety. I was so wrapped up in trying to win the affections of someone who resembled my Lucy, that I wasn't paying attention to my surroundings. Big mistake. They were fixed on me with the intensity of a tracker beam. I was in deep shit without a poop bag.

The circle of priests squeezed in and forced out the innocent onlookers. One hulking man of the cloth brandished a dog catcher's stick. Another had a silver chainmail blanket, a vicious thing that could render a vampire immobile while their skin welted up under the silver links.

An innocent bystander recognized me as the vampdog and saw the group closing in on me. He shouted, "Run vampdog, run" and ducked away from the scary priests. Others in the crowd started yelling, "Go vampdog, go!" and "Leave him alone!" The advantage of being a legend in my own time.

Who knew this hateful group would be at this celebration of life for Mr. Broussard? That didn't seem appropriate. I wondered what the connection to the Broussards could be but didn't have time to linger on it if I were to survive this encounter.

The shouting crowd created a distraction. My speed and size helped, too. I needed to get far away from the freaky fathers, but they were closing in tighter. I was out of options. As I tried to somehow make myself smaller, tail between my legs, Nola's finest intervened.

The bleep of a siren ripped through the night. It was the crowd control detail, warning everyone that it was time to disperse. They had a bright spotlight that made both humans and vampires cringe. Their megaphone barked orders to the crowd. Some in the circle of priests started to break apart, some were trying to make a quick grab for me and got tangled up with each other.

I had a tiny window to escape and I took it. I was like lightning as I bolted past the dark cloaked wall of priests. I darted into a nearby promenade and zipped behind statues and trees in hopes they'd lose sight of me. I didn't stop until I reached a small cemetery on the edge of town where I'd hole up for the night rather than lead them back to my nest. I waited for hours to make sure the coast was clear. Then, before dawn, I snacked on a small rodent and burrowed down into a hole I had dug deep in the ground near a crypt to shield myself from daylight. I dreamed about humans in hot sauce costumes, honey-colored curls, and scary priests.

CHAPTER EIGHTEEN:

Research

C had had always been intrigued by vampdog. But now he felt a deepening fondness for this blood-sucking dog. He gave Chulie mad props for his stunt with the Tribute Dogs. Chad wished he'd had the courage to intervene. This was a pooch with a conscience. And in some weird way, his interactions with Chulie made him feel like Pete was close by.

"There's more to this story," he could hear Pete say, "dark forces that have something to hide." *Right you are,* brother, Chad thought. But which dark forces? At first he wasn't sure if he should be afraid of the vampdog, but he didn't get a sense of darkness from him, only desperation.

Since Chad had been writing about the vampdog for a few years, tourists had been flocking to the Quarter with the hopes of catching a glimpse of the infamous undead hound. Gift shops sold magnets and other trinkets with the words "I <heart> vampdog" and "My vampire has 4 paws."

A few times Chad came across nefarious characters, both human and vampire, who were drawn to the idea of a vampdog— not out of innocent curiosity, but for sinister reasons. Nut jobs.

Perverts. Extremists. Heck, Lucy had disappeared under suspicious circumstances. Who knew what dark forces surrounded Chulie. Now he and Maggie were getting mixed up in it, too.

They decided to spend the day researching at the public library. They were determined to pour over every article and every photo relating to Lucy's disappearance and her family. There had to be something that was missed. As they stepped outside their apartment on their way to the library, Maggie and Chad halted in their tracks at the sight of white lettering painted on their front door: "Give up the search or else." Maggie gasped.

"What don't they want us to find out?" Chad whispered through clenched teeth, keenly aware someone could be watching them. Aside from his blog, he was a dime-a-dozen vamp fan looking into a missing person cold case. But this vandalism made him think that maybe they were pressing on a nerve. And it made him want to look harder, not stop. Was the gun shot at the rally a warning, too? This was both thrilling and frightening. Maggie grabbed his arm tightly. Chad knew she was unsettled, too, but also determined like he was. As they walked, Chad called the city's graffiti removal service for their door. They couldn't come out until next month. Great.

They set up at a table in the Main Public Library on Loyola Avenue and made a plan. Maggie was going to dig up some old yearbooks from Lucy's high school and Chad would use his investigative journalism techniques to skim the microfiche for the old society pages. A prominent family like the Broussard's was sure to make the papers.

After some time, Maggie pulled a chair up next to his at the microfiche machine.

"Found her." She opened a well-worn yearbook to a page of smiling senior portraits. There were signatures and scribbles everywhere. "Best Friends Forever." "Good luck at college." That sort of thing. Maggie pointed to the picture of Lucy. She looked like another pretty blonde girl-next-door.

"She wasn't in any sports or activities I could find, but look what someone wrote next to her photo."

Chad read the loopy handwriting: "Most likely to bang a fanger."

"Good girls always fall for the bad boys," Maggie concluded. "And Sister Eloise did mention Lucy being exposed to The Darkness through her dad and getting in with a bad crowd. Do you think ..."

"I do," Chad cut her off, but they were both thinking the same thing. Lucy's vampire boyfriend was a Darkness vampire.

"I'm Googling The Darkness vampires," Maggie said and started tapping on her phone until she hit pay dirt. She read it aloud. "This extremist coven of vampires and their zealous band of familiars view humans as inferior, making peaceful coexistence difficult. They believe it's a vampire's nature to kill. They organized at the turn of the century.

"In the 1950s, a group of militant priests called The Impalers broke off from the Church after three priests were killed by The Darkness. The Impalers made it their holy mission to eliminate vampires, sending most vampires into hiding. *Read more about The Impalers*.

"In the 1960s when more vampires started to live openly in society again, a group called The Light countered The Darkness and promoted peaceful co-existence. Today, Darkness vampires are vastly outnumbered by vampires who do not kill when they feed. _Read more about vampire supplements_."

"Interesting, Mags. Can you bookmark that page for later? Let's see what news articles we can find on the microfiche machine. I'll show you how it works."

Together they dug through thirty-year-old newspaper archives. They started with the date Lucy was reported missing: May 11, 1987, the Monday after the weekend of her debutante ball.

"I can't believe they were still having debutante balls in the late eighties," Maggie commented.

"You'd be surprised how common it still is in certain high society circles," Chad said.

"Jackpot, I found a photo essay of the event that year in _The Times-Picayune_. Look at all that feathered hair and blue eye shadow," Maggie mused. She giggled as she scrolled through photo after photo of the debutantes and their proud families. "Broussard's! Take a look at this, Chaddie. That fancy honey-colored hair-do?"

Leaning in to see Maggie's screen, Chad let out a slow whistle. "Indeed, that's Lucy. I believe that's the same photo of her that they plastered across the news when she went missing." They scrolled through several photos of Lucy and her family.

"Wait," Chad said. "Can you zoom in on that group shot? Recognize anyone?"

"Is that a younger Sister Eloise standing next to Lucy's mom?"

"I think so. She looks to be in her twenties there, which would add up since she's in her sixties now, I'm pretty sure. We'll have to ask her about that. She said she didn't know the Broussard's before Lucy went missing. She said she met Fiona at a prayer vigil for Lucy, but here she is before Lucy was even missing. Why would she lie?"

"Chaddie, look closely at the young man standing next to Lucy. At a glance I thought it was a brother. But look at their hands." Their hands were touching, each with a finger discreetly intertwined.

"That could be the vampire boyfriend. Where have I seen that face before?"

Maggie sat back in her seat, pausing to let this sink in.

"I'm going to take some screengrabs and print them out. Maybe it will trigger a memory for Chulie."

"Good thinking. Wait, I think I know where I've seen the vamp beau. He was in one of the portraits at the Krewe du Vampdog party house. Standing with his father. It was displayed in the hall of prominent New Orleanians from the turn of the century."

"Definitely vampires that go way back. I'd love to click in deeper on that and find out their story."

Oh boy, did Maggie love a good story.

"So Lucy's boyfriend was the son of a Darkness big shot," Chad pondered aloud.

Feeling energized, Maggie went further back in the society pages while Chad looked into the business and real estate sections. The library felt like a church. Hushed sounds, wood and paper smell, gleaming surfaces. Maggie sat cross-legged on her chair in front of the microfiche machine, pen behind her right ear, eyes glued to the screen. Chad could always count on Maggie and he was grateful she was geeking on this mystery, too.

"Look here at this photo from a Christmas party in 1980," Maggie said. "Patriarch Victor Broussard and his wife, Fiona, and only daughter, Lucy. The dad who just died, right before they closed the investigation, right? There were two younger sons. And see, a small girl peering out from behind her mom's plaid skirt. She's holding a stuffed animal." She stared at the photo. "Oh my God, that's Chulie before he was turned! Still an innocent mortal puppy," Maggie exclaimed. Chad could smell lavender soap when he leaned in for a better look. He inhaled, finding it difficult to stay focused. But a closer look at that photo snapped him out of it.

"Wow," Chad said staring hard at the grainy old photo. "A normal, happy puppy in the arms of a sweet girl. I just don't get it." Chulie was impeccably groomed in the photo but still looked similar to his current scrappy self.

"Don't get what?" Maggie asked.

"Why would anyone willingly turn their dog into a vampdog?"

Maggie pondered that for a moment.

"Could Lucy have been into goth or devil worship? Satanic Panic was an eighties thing, and Lucy is a child of the eighties. Plus, we know she was hanging out with a vamp."

"Odd enough for a pretty debutante to be mixed up with vampires, let alone Satan. I mean, a handsome young vampire is one thing …"

"You have a point. That would be a bit much. I'll stick to the vampire angle."

"Mags, what if Lucy and her vampire boyfriend wanted to become a little vampire family?"

They pondered that for a moment before Chad spoke again.

"But that still doesn't answer why Lucy would disappear and leave her beloved dog."

They continued to search the microfiche, pages whirring past in a gray blur. They combed through all the news footage after the story broke about the missing teenager who was Chulie's beloved owner. This was familiar territory. A plea from the worried parents. The father breaking down. The mother stoic as a statue. Then never the two parents together. One more glimpse of Sister Eloise near the family.

"I found something on an historic real estate registry site," Chad piped up, "The family home at 1020 Esplanade. The one Chulie still stares at regularly? It had been sold in 1987 after being in the Broussard family for three generations. It was only on the market for five days, priced for a quick sale. That was not long after Lucy was declared missing."

"How strange they would move at that time. Weren't they worried about her coming back and not being able to find them?" Maggie added. They agreed something was really odd about the timing.

"Do you suppose Lucy could have gotten pregnant so they hid her away somewhere? Wouldn't want to tarnish the family name, good Catholics and all that. Maybe it was all an act," Maggie wondered.

She had a great imagination.

"Maybe," he replied. "Or she died of an overdose or suicide and they swept it under the rug? Rich people do strange things." Chad paused on that last thought. He was hoping for Chulie's sake she hadn't died. "Strangest of all timing is how she vanished not long after Chulie was turned," Chad said. "What a cluster of strange events. We seem to be hitting more questions than answers. It would help to connect with Chulie on all of this."

"Mind meld?" Maggie asked.

"Mind meld," Chad replied.

They realized they had been at this search for hours and were now starving. They called it a day, just as the library was about to close.

CHAPTER NINETEEN:
Dinner Party

I was supposed to meet Chad and Maggie at the park to hear about their sleuthing. They had come to see our band the Plasma Casters on Frenchman Street and expressed a desire to mind meld again. I agreed to meet them after the set with a decisive bark. I wouldn't get my hopes up about their investigation though; not yet. But then Maggie showed me a photo of Lucy holding me in my mortal state at one of the many fabulous parties her family threw. It seemed they wanted to help me. They could be the familiars I've needed. But I'd be a fool to get my hopes up again. Then, that photo …

Humans were a selfish and complicated lot. Even the helpful ones like Chad and Maggie. I've had my share of "helpful" humans who have let me down. I was trying not to set myself up for disappointment again. The band's raucous musical set ended but the energy was still high. As usual, Strings was charming the crowd, looking for his next human snack. Beanie stuck close to his side, his faithful wingman. Glory was absorbed in her phone, ever lamenting the pain of her mortal life and seeking vindication. I could feel it building in her like a brewing storm. I slipped away from my nest mates while several people gathered around to contribute to the tip bucket and chat up the band. They noticed them at the concert but I didn't want my nestmates to know I was meeting up with Chad and Maggie. I'm not sure how they felt about Maggie's ruse. We looked out for each other in the nest, but they could be unpredictable when they were hungry and we weren't without our quarrels. Not that they would kill Chad and Maggie. That was just not the way of most modern vampires. Not with the supplements and other ways to acquire human blood. But with hurricane season upon us, the tourists would be fewer. The market for fresh blood would get sparse and desperate vampires do desperate things. I needed to see how useful Chad and Maggie could be before relinquishing them to my nest mates.

I scurried past couples strolling hand-in-hand, college students sitting on the neutral ground with po-boy sandwiches and beer. I jumped over discarded plastic cups and Styrofoam food containers, passed over the tiled street names on each corner and jumbles of broken concrete.

I decided to observe Chad and Maggie for a moment before revealing myself. They were sitting together on a park bench under a street lamp. Maggie wore a stylish hat but I could see her pink hair peeking out the sides. No more blonde charade. I was a tiny bit disappointed. Chad had his usual black get-up like it was his uniform as a Vampire Tour Guide blogger, both were sipping their P.J.'s coffees. They were chatting easily, but Chad's eyes kept darting about, looking for me no doubt. I wished they had been arguing. I am always more amused by people at odds. Conflict simply makes for a more interesting story. You might say the years have made me a little bitter and twisted. To my chagrin, these two were clearly content with each other. No conflict here.

I decided to have some fun. I used my preternatural speed to zoom over to them in an undetectable flash of fur, so that it appeared as if I had materialized out of thin air. It worked. They were both so startled they dropped their cardboard coffee cups. I flashed to the left to avoid the splatter. Once the commotion settled, I stood in front of them and stared.

"Hello, Chulie," Chad said to me. How nice to be called by my name. Maggie pulled napkins out of her bag to mop up the mess.

"Ouch," she said as she gave me an admonishing look. I laughed a little inside but gave them an innocent stare, mouth hanging open to air the tongue out. Once recovered, Maggie pulled papers out of her canvas bag. They were images of Lucy and her soap opera family. I saw her, my Lucy, in a beautiful gown. I hoped they knew I couldn't read, only recognize images and logos, all my awareness came from dipping into the minds of other people and extracting their thoughts. It wasn't like I attended school. Not even night school. Imagine me sitting in a desk. That's a laugh. Just the school of hard knocks for me.

"Chulie, do you recognize the people in this picture?" Chad said.

Maggie urged, "Can you do your mind meld trick to reveal more details about your last night together? The night when you were turned?"

What am I, a parlor trick? I thought sourly. Oh, the indignity. I'd again have to drag my heart across that jagged edge and feel the sting of grief and betrayal. If it would help, though, I'd do it. These two could be onto something. I recognized my former family and the boy standing next to Maggie. Obliging their request, I stared hard into Chad's face and watched as his eyes glossed over, receiving my memory images. An elegant dining room table was set for company with prominently displayed bottles of Broussard hot sauce lining the middle. A dog's eye-view moved to a kitchen buzzing with activity. Our cook, Miranda, was icing a cake and gumbo simmered on the stove. Lucy was trying to get me to take some medicine she had wrapped in cheese, but I wasn't falling for it and kept spitting it out. She was not happy with me. Lucy's parents came in to assess the progress in the kitchen. They instructed Miranda to bring out the cups of steaming gumbo at precisely six-thirty in the evening. I barked when I heard the doorbell ring just after the grandfather clock chimed six times and our butler Joseph grabbed a pitcher of icy green liquid from the refrigerator and placed it on a tray of crystal glasses.

Lucy held me in her lap as we sat out of the way in a bay window in the kitchen. I was slowing down, and didn't have all the energy I used to. But the show must go on. We would make an appearance for the guests, delight them, and then after a quick walk we'd hole up in Lucy's bedroom where she would play her music, talk on a phone shaped like lips, and scribble in her diary. Our usual, I thought blissfully. At some point Miranda would bring up a dinner tray for both of us. If only the night had played out so normally. If only.

Lucy's mom leaned her head in the swinging kitchen door to give us our cue. Show time. I walked into the dining room close at Lucy's heels. I bounced along excitedly because I could smell a treat in Lucy's pocket. When we entered the room, all heads turned in our direction, some still guzzling something green that smelled minty, some still cackling like birds, some with cigarettes bobbing on their lips. The young man from the photo was there. He and Lucy exchanged the briefest of looks. I don't remember noticing him at the time, but Maggie's photo made him stick out in my recollections.

The guests were all dressed to the nines. One guy was in an old-fashioned uniform. He was very pale, surely a vampire. Imagine, a vampire in Fiona's house. The women wore feathery fascinators on their heads and thick blue or green eyeshadow on their eyelids. The men had twinkly cufflinks on their wrists and wide multi-color ties on crisp shirts. Some had rainbow sherbet-colored silky shirts unbuttoned down low to show their chest fur. Lucy stopped and gave a pleasant greeting. The table exploded in high-pitched hellos and approving clucks. Tomorrow she would be a celebrated debutante. Tonight she was still a girl.

When they simmered down, Lucy looked at me. Our big moment. I spun in a circle and looked up at her. She made a circular motion with her hand, and I spun in another circle. Our audience chortled with glee. Then, she made jazz hands and flashed her fingers. I stood up on my hind legs and bounced around like I was dancing. The song "You Make Me Feel Like Dancing" by Leo Sayer started playing from Lucy's pocket cassette recorder and everyone started clapping while we danced together. (I only know the song title and artist now; back then it was just sounds to me.) After a moment, the music snapped off. The room erupted in applause; mission accomplished. This little exhibition totally wore me out. I saw tears in Lucy's eyes as she leaned over to give me a treat. The guy in the uniform jumped up and patted me on the head with his cold fingers. I noticed the tattoo on his hand as he reached for me. It looked like a bat on top of a sword. I know now this was the bouncer I encountered at the Krewe party when I freed the tributes! I made a point of conveying that image in our mind meld so Chad would pick up the connection, too. But back then in my head I called him Bat Hand. As I continued to play my memory of the evening from the late-80s in my mind, I saw Lucy and I darting out of the room so the guests could resume adult conversation. She'd have to carry me up the stairs that night since my energy was depleted. She chanced a final, yearning glance toward that young man, sitting next to Bat Hand. He was a handsome lad. Clearly a vampire I knew now. Back then, I knew no such thing.

When we were safely in her bedroom, I expected her to put on music or start gabbing on the phone. But instead she stared out the window. I was picking up a sad vibe, so I put my paws on her leg and looked up at her with my tail wagging. She scratched my head but was a million miles away. She gave me extra treats, that jumped out for me, and at some point we snuggled up in bed for the night's rest. I recalled something I hadn't thought about. We heard Lucy's parents fighting as we lay awake in bed. Her mother was saying something about a deal with the devil. Her father was saying something about how well the business was doing and vampires co-existing.

I relived the awful moments when the young man came into our room and Lucy offered me to him so Chad could see all the details of when I was turned and my mortal life was gone forever. That young man from the photo they showed me, the dinner and the late night intruder were one and the same. Lucy's boyfriend was my maker. It was as if a dozen gears clicked into place and a machine came to life. We were getting somewhere.

I looked away from Chad, ending our mind share session. It exhausted me, physically and emotionally. I laid down on the sidewalk at their feet and allowed Maggie to scratch my head while Chad shared with her what he saw in our mind meld.

"That was great, Chulie. I could see the whole affair," Chad said to me. His praise made me feel good. A dog can't help it. Part of me will always want to be a good boy.

"I know that tattoo," Chad continued. "The Darkness. We need to learn more about the connection between Lucy's boyfriend, his father, and her disappearance."

I didn't like where this was going. I didn't want to have anything to do with The Darkness. It seemed risky for these two amateurs and a dog like me.

"Chulie, is it okay if we meet again?"

But before Chad could finish his sentence, I was gone. Of course we'd meet again.

CHAPTER TWENTY:

I'm a v-a-m-p vamp

*B*loodlust, a Blog for Vampire Enthusiasts – August 15, 2023 by Chad Russo

Fellow Vampire Lovers,

A few juicy tidbits dunked in blood for you. Nicole G. from Slidell shares that she swiped right on a guy and went on a date with him only to discover he swiped something from her … as in a pint of O+! That's right, he stole a pint of her blood. After meeting for margaritas at Crescent City Cantina, Nicole saw her first red flag when her date ordered a drink but didn't seem to drink it. She even caught him pouring it into a plant in the courtyard. By her description, he looked like someone she could have met at a church picnic, with a collared golf shirt and a tidy haircut like a Ken doll. Halfway into her first margarita, as she was contemplating excuses to leave, Nicole started feeling as wobbly as a newborn calf. Her date, let's call him Ken Doll, acting chivalrous, took her by the elbow and escorted her swiftly to his pickup truck. She remembers Ken Doll opening the tailgate and then nothing else until she woke up with a cotton swab and bandage on her arm, curled up in the grass next to Crescent City Cantina. It was already morning. She checked herself and noted that she was unscathed except for the blood draw. Glad to know that, Nicole. She had her clutch and her phone. Looking in her purse to see if anything was missing, she saw a note that said simply, "Thanks for the pint." Of course, dear readers, we all know he wasn't referring to a pint of ale. What a quirky way for a vampire to take blood! Even in the age of human/vampire coexistence, this was an odd way to go about it. Perhaps a phlebotomist in his mortal life? We'll likely never know. But big thanks to Nicole for sharing this bizarre tale!

Over in Uptown, the 83-year-old Bailey twins, Vera and Blanche, claimed again to have been ravaged by a dashing pair of vampire twins in tuxedoes. When the police arrived, the two were drunk and dancing around naked in their parlor. These repeated claims have yet to be verified and it is the opinion of this writer that this may be a case of a shared delusion. But enjoy the fantasy and keep sharing!

Final note, I will be attending the next meeting of the Krewe du Vampdog Friday at midnight and will report back. I am investigating a few vampdog related topics, including a connection to The Darkness coven. Please share whatever you may know. Apologies for being a tease, but I am not at liberty to divulge anything more at the moment. Stay tuned, my blood brothers and sisters. Stay tuned.

Please like, follow and share. @Chadrusso #bloodlust #vampdog #findlucy

Look for my TikTok videos coming soon!

#

With his laptop closed, Chad hoped he'd provided enough details to satisfy his readers but not give too much away. He wanted to draw out any information they might have. The hive mind might know more about The Darkness and their connection to Lucy's disappearance. He could only hope.

It wasn't long before he heard the ding of an incoming message. He'd gotten a comment on his blog already. Someone with the handle LoveBites99 said simply, "If you want to learn more about The Darkness, you better talk to the Captain of the Krewe du Vampdog."

CHAPTER TWENTY-ONE:

Danger Dogs

Just before midnight I waited for Chad and Maggie at our agreed meeting spot in the Bywater, a place where a cluster of art galleries covered in brightly painted murals breathed new life into formerly deserted warehouses. Some were quite beautiful and it made me glad my vampire state allowed me to see in color. I sat in a pebbly lot with weeds poking through, admiring a giant painting of a girl with her arms stretched out the width of the corrugated metal warehouse. This was Studio Be. The Krewe du Vampdog held their meetings not far from here. The girl in the painting looked like an angel, with a serene plum-shaded face and halo of curls. I thought about heaven. My soul was now trapped in this monstrous body, so I'd never take that stroll over the proverbial Rainbow Bridge. Hybrid dog, human, monster, I assumed I still had the same soul I had when I was a mortal dog. My Lucy and I would take walks near this location as we lived several blocks from here. But the neighborhood had changed quite a bit since the 1980s. I'd seen the city endure hurricanes and a pandemic. The people here were resilient but even the strongest spirts could be broken. These dear souls helped each other when no one else stepped in.

Surely their spirits were heaven bound. Especially musicians and artists. Many of the murals depicted that "we're gonna make it" spirit. Here, people rallied for one another. The people who didn't share that generous spirit, or especially the people who harmed their fellow humans, were my midnight snack. I can't speak for my nest mates (or speak at all for that matter), but when I feed on a human, I am discerning. Never a child or any good-hearted human being. I go for the bullies, racists, the hateful. That's got to account for something, right? For any Higher Power who might be keeping score? I lingered to take in the beauty of the ethereal mural. That's when I heard a pitiful howling. The sound sent needles to whatever was left of my heart. The cry came from behind a metal fence made from old road signs and scrap metal.

"Aaaooooohhh," ripped through the night again. I tilted my head, listening intently. One more yelp and then a deep, angry voice, a thud, a whimper, silence. That can't be good. I sped toward the commotion. Through a small opening in the patchwork metal fence, I could see a dog chained up and cowering in the corner of the lot. He was a pit bull, with black and white markings like a cow. His skin was dotted with old pink scars and newer angry burn marks. I could do a mind meld with other animals but they were usually filled with simplistic, innocent images and didn't have the dark nuances of a human mind. I am able to meld with anyone, without their permission or cooperation, which has indeed been a learning experience over the decades. But I've learned to be selective. Otherwise I'm haunted with random anxieties, pettiness and negativity.

There was a hulking figure, a brutish lump of sinew and sweat, pale zitty shoulders bulging from a sleeveless T-shirt, with chopped black hair that looked like a kindergartner had cut it. The lug was stacking wooden pallets around in a circle in the empty lot. Weeds poked out from the gravel surface like nature was trying to make a break for it. He stopped to pull a phone out of his pocket and poked at the screen with his sausage fingers. He stood looking at the sky with phone to one meaty ear, then squeezed his eyes shut and nodded repeatedly. I stared hard at the fleshy slab that was his face. The images that came were white hot anger, swirled with pain, hate and annoyance. It was like someone was constantly poking him with pins. In his mind, I saw many dogs and heard a deafening barking and howling, like an ice pick to the brain. In his mind, I saw a screaming, bloodthirsty crowd, cash slapped down on a table, hundreds of dollars, a surge of pleasure, contorted demon faces in flickering torch light, then he was there. Could it be? A face that I remember from decades ago at the Broussard's party? Bat Hand. He must be a vampire to look the same after all this time. He was yelling at the brute whose mind I was dipping into. Clearly this guy disgusted Bat Hand. I felt my own heart pounding. I had to get out of this swirl of unholy thoughts.

I closed my eyes to break the mind meld with the brute and had trouble clearing the evil imagery. I shook my head around and scratched my ears with my hind legs. Then I rolled on my back in a patch of grass that smelled like another animal had peed there. What the blazes did I just witness in that brute's mind? I felt an urge to find Chad and Maggie. I needed to make them understand.

They'd help me fix whatever nightmare was happening here for these pitiful dogs. I was in a panic and feeling vulnerable and helpless. What I wouldn't give for the power to speak and the ability to stand upright and look some mother fuckers dead in the eye.

"Chulie!" a female voice shouted. I ran around in a circle before I got a fix on the direction it was coming from. Back over toward the art gallery, Chad and Maggie stood under a streetlight. I sped toward them.

CHAPTER TWENTY-TWO:

Krewe Pot Stirred

C hulie seemed more enthusiastic to see them than Chad had ever experienced thus far. Frantic might be a better word for his demeanor. Maggie called to him and he came over, almost like a mortal dog. He wasn't his stoic self. There was something different about him. Chad tried to stare at his eyes for some mind meld, but he shook his gaze away and gave his whole body a good shake.

After the tip had come in on his blog about talking to the Krewe Captain to learn more about The Darkness, Chad was anxious to attend a meeting. Chad and Maggie decided to bring Chulie in case he saw anything or anyone that helped trigger more details about Lucy. They were a team now, and Chulie held so many of the clues. Chad crouched down straining his black jeans to get to Chulie's level and make this as dignified as possible for him, holding his backpack open on the ground.

"C'mon, jump in, Chulie."

He got close enough to stare at Chulie's eyes, those deep pools of black rimmed in red. But faster than he could blink, Chulie grabbed the backpack in his mouth and was off like a flash, back in the direction he came, dragging the backpack, pens and papers flying out, leaving a trail behind. It was as if he wanted Chad and Maggie to follow him, so they did.

"Hey! The krewe meeting is the other way!" Chad shouted, wheezing a little, trying to keep up with Chulie. Maggie stopped to pick up papers and pens along the way. Chulie led them to a ramshackle building with a foreboding fence made from scrap metal and signs. He stopped here, dropped the backpack and looked up at them. Maggie caught up with him first. Chulie never really barked much, unless he had a point to make. But now he let out a sharp "ruff" and paced in anxious circles. Maggie looked around and found an opening in the fence at her eye level.

"It looks like an empty gravel lot. I see a couple of chains bolted to the ground. There's some sort of big shed at the back with the windows blocked with cardboard pieces. I can hear muffled barks coming from that direction. Maybe that's what Chulie is worked up about," Maggie said.

"What the hell is going on in there?" Chad asked. On top of this weirdness, he was starting to feel that familiar shakiness and confusion that happens when his blood sugars dropped too low. He told Maggie, and she grabbed the backpack and started digging around for the glucose tablets. The tablets would do for now but he'd need to eat soon. They'd have snacks at the meeting.

"We're going to have to solve this later, Chad needs some juice or food," Maggie stated with authority to Chulie. "The krewe meeting starts in ten minutes and they always have a buffet table."

It seemed as if Chulie understood in his super canine way. Chad and Maggie promised they'd come back to make sure the barking dogs were okay. Chulie let Maggie negotiate him into the backpack. She made sure he could see out just under the flap and off they went. But all felt lingering trepidation about this sinister-looking place and the barking dogs. Chad and Maggie both agreed it was smart how Chulie brought it to their attention. Clever vampdog.

As they hurried to the krewe meeting, Chad had the distinct feeling they were being followed. They'd be safe once they got to the meeting with dozens of people in attendance. When they arrived, Chad took the chance of looking back and scoping the street behind them. Sure enough, standing in the parking lot as still as a statue was a familiar-looking vampire—one he had seen in Chulie's mind. Chad hurried them inside.

The Krewe du Vampdog meeting took place in a former furniture factory that was in a raw state of renovation. The space was shared with several other krewes, such as the Krewe of Red Beans, a krewe who designed elaborate costumes decorated with the dried legumes that factor into so much of Louisiana cuisine. The space was also used by other culture bearers who needed crafting space, such as the Mardi Gras Indians and their stunning beadwork. Bean-work and beadwork, Chad thought as they tromped through the space.

Folding chairs were set up in concentric, semicircle rows, many filled already. Maggie grabbed a couple chairs and gently set the backpack down to hold the chair next to her. Chad headed straight for the food table and grabbed cheese & crackers, nuts, a bottle of water for Maggie, and a cup of pineapple juice that was intended as a bar mixer. Alcohol would not be good for him now.

He carried the items back to their seats, looked around the room, and saw the vampire standing at the back not far from Maggie and the backpack where Chulie hid. He heard someone address him as Bruce. Chad hadn't noticed before, but there was a dog laying at his feet. A brutish looking guy in a sleeveless T-shirt came up to Bruce and the dog and started yelling at him, trying to take the dog, but Bruce wasn't having it. He raised one hand, stared into the brute's face and the guy froze. Meanwhile, Bruce took hold of the dog's leash and slid along the perimeter of the space.

A few dozen krewe members and guests were still socializing until the krewe captain took the mic at the front and asked everyone to take their seats so the "business" portion of the meeting could commence. He sported a black sash bedazzled with vampire and dog symbols over a colorful Jazz Fest shirt and presented himself with an air of authority. Chad had his phone ready to record and brought a notebook in his backpack if it was still in there, but he didn't dare look. He didn't want anyone to get a glimpse of Chulie. If they knew Chulie was here, bedlam would ensue. Better to take notes on his phone.

Chad knew most of the krewe members, and most were just harmless enthusiasts of the undead canine and vampires in general. They even accepted vampires as krewe members and met in the middle of the night to accommodate them. There were many dots to connect; Chad just couldn't see all the lines yet. It was all woven into Chulie's origin story and what led to Lucy's disappearance.

Chad glanced around and saw several familiar faces. They spotted him and a few waved hello. Many were devoted followers of the *Bloodlust* blog and loved when he mentioned their krewe, even in kinky and sometimes unflattering ways. Like many fetishists, you would never know on the surface that these good citizens liked to have orgies with vampires and dress up like animals.

Chad's gaze landed on Bruce again. He had the stature of a vampire who has been around for a long time. Slim build and perfect posture, piercing eyes, handsome. He was the vampire in the painting with his son that hung on the wall at the Krewe party and the guest at the Broussard's dinner party that Chulie had called, Bat Hand. They locked eyes and Bruce gave him a nod. Had he followed them over? The dog with him was a sweet looking pit bull. Something had gotten the dog's attention, though, and it started pacing. Chad looked over at the backpack in Maggie's lap. Chulie. The dog might be stirred up because of Chulie. Luckily the meeting took focus.

"Welcome Krewe and guests," the Krewe Captain boomed, "this meeting is called to order. First on the agenda is the budget report. Treasurer Tanya?" An energetic woman with long grey braids and a flowy hippy skirt bounded to the front with her iPad and took over the mic. She announced the amount in their bank accounts, how much they had spent on their Blood Hounds Ball, and how much revenue they received from member dues and ticket sales. Tanya the Treasurer also mentioned the loss incurred by the escapade when the tribute dogs were released and animal control had to be called, resulting in a five-hundred dollar fine. There were murmurs of disapproval throughout the room, whether for the fine or for the terrible idea of having tribute dogs in the first place. Chad was glad to hear that it didn't sound like something they'd ever try again.

Chad's attention drifted back to Bruce and the dog on the sidelines. He was feeling much sharper after his snack. He poked Maggie in the thigh and gave her a look so she'd follow his gaze in a subtle way. He looked back at the speaker while she chanced a glance at Bruce and the dog. He could hear the dog making whining noises, clearly getting more worked up.

"Excuse me while I hit the Ladies Room," she said as she grabbed the backpack to whisk Chulie out of the way. Good thinking Mags, Chad said with only a small nod. They didn't need words. He hoped this would deter the dog's fascination. While Chad pretended to be scrolling his phone, he snuck a few snaps of Bruce and the pit bull. Bruce was doing his best to keep hold of the dog. The meeting rattled on as they shifted to the topic of membership.

As Maggie walked over to the restroom, Bruce took notice. Before Maggie slipped into the Ladies Room, a tiny brown nose peeked out of the backpack flap. Bruce caught on. He actually looked surprised and turned toward Chad. At that moment, the leash slipped from his grasp and the dog bolted toward Maggie.

The krewe members were oblivious to this dog drama as they argued about what band should play at their next event, Bonerama or Honey Island Swamp Band. The focus of the room shifted to a krewe member vampire who was also a drag queen as she spoke passionately about trombones. Maggie had slipped inside the Ladies Room just before the dog reached the door. Chad look over to see Bruce at the Ladies Room door with the poor doggy scratching to get inside. Chad's phone dinged. One quick word from Maggie: "window." Bruce was trying to act nonchalant.

Drawn by the commotion, a few krewe members went to see what was happening and the crowd started murmuring and pointing at the door. Bruce tried to charm a few krewe members as a distraction. Bruce couldn't just burst into the restroom without raising suspicion, but Chad knew they only had moments before he worked his way in. Chad dashed out of the room and over to the exterior restroom window.

Chad's heart pounded. He reached up to the frosted window as Maggie carefully hoisted out the backpack with Chulie inside. Chad eased the backpack out of the window. Mad barking and frantic, muffled voices talking about the locked door came through the window.

"Try standing on the sink, Mags!" Chad called to her. The window was high and narrow. He saw her hands reaching out of the edges of the window.

"Where's a stunt double when you need one," Maggie moaned.

After a few meaningful grunts, Maggie's head and torso stuck out of the window. Chad reached up to grab her arms. After a few painful pulls, Maggie fell into a heap on the ground.

From inside, they heard Bruce speaking on the microphone to the room, "The vampdog is here among us!"

Maggie quickly brushed herself off and said, "let's get out of here."

Amazing Maggie.

The crowd erupted in gasps and murmurs and shouts. They needed to get Chulie as far away from this mob as possible.

CHAPTER TWENTY-THREE:

Maggie Meld

I was jostling around in the knapsack that Chad gripped firmly. If only I could conjure myself into human form, I'd surely flee this scene on my own volition. It wasn't long before I figured out Chad and Maggie had haled a pedicab and were bouncing gaily over the cobblestones, heading to the opposite side of the Quarter toward the Central Business District or CBD. Now it was my turn to feel shaky due to the need to feed; I hadn't had any blood since the night before.

As Chad and Maggie hustled me away from the meeting, from what I could hear and sense from inside the knapsack, the jig was up and the crowd somehow discovered I was there. I heard a lot of noise from a mortal dog who I wouldn't have minded getting to know. I know that the vampire with the Bat Hand was there, too.

Once the poor bike driver was paid for our super long ride, we found a dark stoop across from Lafayette Park and huddled together on the stairs out of sight to catch our breath. It was the first fresh air I had in over an hour and I sank down as flat and long as I could make myself against the cool cement.

"Chulie," Chad addressed me respectfully, "I've got some photos on my phone for you to look at. It's Bruce, Darkness vampire and I think he's the one you call Bat Hand from the dinner party." I tilted my head to indicate curiosity.

Chad held his phone screen where I could get a good look. But the screen blurred and I felt dizzy. I put my head down on my paws.

"You listening, Chulie? Chulie?"

They were so wrapped up in their little investigation, they hadn't noticed my lethargy.

"He needs to feed," Maggie said.

"We should get him back to the nest. But first I have an idea," Chad said. He pulled a little blue case out of his knapsack and unzipped it. Inside were three grey tools. He took one and touched it to his finger. Then he squeezed his finger and a big, juicy glob of blood bloomed on the tip. He held it in front of my snout and I greedily lapped it up. It wasn't much and I'd need more before the dawn came, but it was a refreshing pick-me-up. Chad had sweet blood, probably from being diabetic, and I felt grateful. I could get used to these two lunatics. I wondered how they knew they could trust me not to drink more. Of course they couldn't. But for now I wanted to see if they could lead me to my Lucy. The very thought of her made me ache.

While I had the snack, Maggie shared what she learned by eavesdropping on conversations at the meeting.

"It seems as though the dog with Bruce was from that big empty lot. They host dog fights there. Bruce and other krewe members were adamantly against the dog fights and fawned over the poor beat up pit bull. Bruce said something about how his son, Adam, loved dogs. One krewe member said something about not needing kibble after they were turned and I realized, they were talking about making vampdogs."

I perked up. Maybe Chad and Maggie could stop this abomination.

"Horrible," Chad said. "What is wrong with people?" He shook his head and let loose an aggravated sigh.

I could tell him what was wrong with people. I've listened to enough human thoughts. They're greedy and hateful and some are energized by violence. Sometimes people are just dumb. But sometimes they are both dumb and hateful. Those were the types I had no qualms about feeding on. Good to the last drop.

"Okay, Chulie, now look here." He held his phone screen to my eye level. The first picture was close up on a vampire. No question a vampire. He was indeed the vampire from the Broussard's party long ago, as well as the Krewe's recent shindig. I put my head down and whined a little. It was Bat Hand.

"Good boy, Chulie," Chad said as if I were a common pet.

"It's him." Maggie said. "Do you think he followed us from that empty lot Chulie took us to?"

"I do," Chad replied. "But I don't really know why he'd want to follow us."

I did a whole body shake. I wanted to tell them something. I'd need to do a mind meld, but I wasn't sure I had the stamina for it. I stared hard at Maggie this time. I didn't want her to feel the full assault of horrific images I saw in that brute's head, but I tried to focus on enough to get the idea across. The ramshackle fence. The dog cowering in the corner. The waste of human skin who hurt the dog. From her I got images of Chad, distinct love vibes, the vampire at the meeting and fear.

"Jinkies!" Maggie said. "I've been mind melded."

"Who are you, Velma from Scooby-Doo?" Chad quipped.

"More Daphne I'd say," Maggie said shakily, coming out of the grasp of the mind meld. I laid on the ground and crossed my paws.

"Well?" Chad said.

"The dog with Bruce was an abused dog from the dog fight ring. I saw the creep who runs it. Bruce was saving the dog."

I was on my feet, tail wagging, staring back and forth expectantly at Maggie and Chad.

"We've got our work cut out for us," Chad said.

"Can it wait until tomorrow, or I mean later today? It's got to be almost three in the morning." Maggie yawned, drained by the mind meld.

"We should get Chulie back to the nest," Chad said.

But I was gone before he could finish his sentence.

CHAPTER TWENTY-FOUR:

Bait

Chad and Maggie swung by Chulie's nest on the way home to make sure Chulie made it. They watched the place for a while, contemplating their next move. Willingly stepping into a vampire's nest was a risky move. But they were mostly concerned for Chulie. He had seemed so weak when they saw him.

They decided to knock. The vamp clan welcomed them in, reassuring them they had fed already. Chad and Maggie obliged but kept their eye on the door in case they needed to make a quick exit. They wanted to make sure Chulie made it home and hoped the nest would appreciate their concern. Foolish? Perhaps.

"Where are your tarot cards, Maggie," Beanie joked about her ruse, breaking the tension and giving everyone a chuckle.

Chad took his chances and filled them in on The Darkness connection to Chulie, as well as the dog fight ring. He wasn't sure why, but he thought they might be vampires that could be trusted. He'd find out soon enough if he was wrong. They seemed appropriately appalled. It was a relief to learn they weren't associated with The Darkness.

"I abhor The Darkness and their disregard for life, but dog fighting is worse," Glory said.

"You really think this could help solve what happened to Chulie's Lucy?" Beanie asked with genuine concern. They all knew Lucy was Chulie's forever quest.

Chulie showed up while they were all commiserating. He ran from Glory, to Maggie, back to Glory and then over to Beanie. He seemed excited they were all together.

"I have an idea," Strings announced. From the way the other two deferred to him and gave their full attention, Strings was clearly their alpha.

"What if we draw The Darkness and their minions out through our show and your blog and lure them to see our band? Then we can face them head on. See if they are the ones who made Lucy disappear."

Strings explained to them that like most things that had a yin and a yang, there was a counterbalance to The Darkness. There was a group called The Light. Chad had definitely heard of this, but it was great to get the vampire perspective. The members of this nest leaned more toward The Light. The vampires in The Light and the humans who supported them believed in a peaceful co-existence, not the same powerplay that fueled The Darkness. The Light far outnumbered The Darkness in modern times. Blood supplements and non-violent access to blood had come a long way. Learning to feed without killing was key.

"You can count on support from The Light to help with the investigation," Strings assured them.

Strings, Beanie and Glory all stood together before them to recite the creed of The Light: "I pierce the darkness with a light, vampires united to do what's right."

This was amazing, Chad thought. A first-hand view into vampire code of conduct. At least these vampires. Even as scary as he found Strings to be, it helped to know they had moral boundaries.

Maggie and Chad agreed to the plan. It may have been the late hour, or even Strings' charms, but they were all in on this plot to draw out The Darkness, including Bat Hand. The cretins who ran the dog fighting ring were another matter that would be dealt with. Chulie's nest mates would stay on high alert at their shows, and even bring reinforcements from allied vampires of The Light. They would join forces to protect Chulie always and support his quest to find Lucy. Chad wrote the blog post as agreed almost as soon as he got home, and he and Maggie didn't go to bed until almost dawn.

CHAPTER TWENTY-FIVE:
Charm

My new human friends and my nestmates were in cahoots now. This should have made me happy but doubts started creeping in. Chad and Maggie would surely get in over their heads. Strings, Beanie and Glory could get on the wrong side of a dangerous group of vampires. Why was I the connection point for all of this? What did it have to do with my Lucy? I wondered. I was also skeptical about all this focus on The Darkness. After all, Bruce had tried to rescue a dog.

I was out and about again, wandering the Quarter on St. Peter, just passing the apartment where Tennessee Williams lived when he wrote *A Streetcar Named Desire*. How would I know that? There was a plaque on the side on the building that I'd witnessed hundreds of tourists stopping to read. Some appreciated it, some could care less. On this occasion, a middle-aged couple stopped there with their dog. I stood by a lamp post and watched them.

"Tommy," the woman gasped, putting a hand to her heart. Clearly she was a fan of Tennessee Williams. Tommy smiled at her and they marveled together, pinching themselves to be standing on this hallowed spot. Their dog, a poodle mix, sat patiently, staring up at them adoringly, head swiveling back and forth as each spoke.

I knew exactly how that dog felt. Domesticated dogs were unfailingly loyal. That is why I suffer the relentless devotion to my Lucy, a bond I can never break.

Combine our loyalty with being highly trainable and undead and it's no wonder there are humans that want to exploit me. If you were to train a vampire dog to be a ruthless killing machine like they do in dog fighting … well, then, you've got yourself a stealthy assassin. Who would ever suspect a cute little lapdog? Imagine how easy it would be to get in places. It made sense, their obsession with me. It all swam around in my head. Maybe Chad and Maggie could help me sort it out.

I was so wrapped up in my thoughts that I had hardly noticed when the couple with the dog had moved on … and when someone came up behind me.

"There you are!" a voice shattered my thoughts. The jolt sent me like a brown furry streak to the nearest courtyard.

"Wait! I finally caught up with you, you lovable little demon!"

I recognized that voice. It was my friend Sister Eloise. I shook my body and walked back in her direction.

"Hello, Chulie," she said as she patted my head. Before she pulled her hands back into the sleeves of her cloak, I smelled Murphy's Oil Soap, the same soap they used to clean the pews in the Church. Where did I smell that recently? It would come to me. Ah yes. It was the same scent I detected after the shooter fled from the rally. *Could the shooter be connected to the Church?* I wondered, maybe even those scary priests who hated vampires? Her gray, traditional habit hung on her like drapes. I had seen her age over the decades and now in her sixties she moved a little slower but was still spry. I gave her my full attention.

"It's been a while, Chulie. I wanted to make sure you were okay."

I tilted my head to the side, and then tried to make eye contact with her in case she wanted to mind meld. But she had her thoughts on lockdown. She turned her face away from me.

"I've heard some troubling news about some very bad people who are interested in you."

Was she referring to The Darkness? Or the dog fighting ring? I wondered. I noted she didn't specify vampire or human, just people.

"I have something that could help you, my little dog friend. It's a talisman."

Sister Eloise had always been into charms and talismans. It wasn't the first time she'd attached a talisman to my collar. She even once gave me a charm blessed by the pope after he visited the States. I'd lost them all over the years.

She leaned over and put her fingers through my collar. The big gold cross she wore around her neck dangled in my face. Contrary to popular belief, a crucifix does not repel me or have any ill effect at all, as long as it's not made of silver. Silver burns our skin. My collar was so old it was no longer pink and I was amazed it still held together at all. It was just frayed leather fibers now, all the rhinestones popped off. Hardly any point to wearing it except it made me look slightly less wild. Sister Eloise snapped a small religious medal onto my collar. How quaint, I thought, she's calling upon some saint to protect me, no doubt. Maybe the patron saint of dogs? I doubted there was a patron saint of vampires, although I used to think maybe that's who she wanted to be.

"There you go. Godspeed, little demon."

With that Sister Eloise was off. I was a bit sad she was gone so abruptly. Sometimes she brought me a bag of fresh blood from the hospital where she volunteered. But not this time. I marched on.

Around the corner on Charters Street, I heard an altercation.

"Did you give my girlfriend beads?" an alcohol-soaked voice slurred.

I made it around the corner to see a drunk, pink-faced, mullet-head screaming at a terrified Black waiter still in his uniform shirt and name tag.

"Boyd, please," urged Mullet-head's girlfriend, go-cup in hand and at least twenty beads slung over her tube top.

"You must have me confused …" the young waiter tried to explain. But Mullet-head wasn't having it.

"I see a dude hitting on my girlfriend," slobbered Boyd. "I can't have that." Boyd cracked his knuckles. "I'm going to teach you some respect." The cretin lunged at the waiter. The waiter was so frightened, he tried to turn and run but his foot caught on a tree root and he stumbled but caught himself before falling. The brute took full advantage, cocking his fist back as he loomed over him, spitting out slurs.

This brute had no spirit of our town. Before Boyd's right fist hammered down, my fangs were around his left wrist. I sank in hard, immediately tapping the radial artery.

"What the fuck?" he spewed as he tried to punch at me. A swing and a miss. I heard his trashy girlfriend scream. She threw her neon plastic cup at me. They hardly knew what was happening. In my periphery, I saw the young waiter scurry away. I sucked extra hard until I brought Boyd to his knees from rapid blood loss. He crumpled into a nasty heap. I turned to the girl. Truthfully, I was full and Boyd's alcohol-filled blood was making me a little tipsy. But if you can't overdo a little in New Orleans, where can you. Her face drained of any color beneath her garish make up as I clamped onto her ankle. I took a few meaningful gulps, enough to make her weak but not pass out. She sat down next to her blob of a boyfriend who was gasping weakly. I sincerely hoped neither of them would be visiting again any time soon.

CHAPTER TWENTY-SIX:

Plasma Casters

*B*loodlust, a Blog for Vampire Enthusiasts – August 20, 2023 By Chad Russo

Fellow Bloodsucker Groupies,

I am with you when I say I cannot get enough of the vampires in this town, in every variety, shape and form. I am your kindred spirit in this obsession. But the frontrunner for me right now is a vampire band called the Plasma Casters who play on a corner near Frenchman Street. After consulting the OffBeat music calendar, my partner and I decided to stay and listen for a set late last night. We had an ulterior motive, which was keeping tabs on their mascot who lays by the tip bucket with soulful (or soulless?) eyes and a cute furry face.

Even though the moon was high and the sky was black, the August heat hung like a veil. The drummer cracked his sticks together three times and the music exploded. The one they call Strings started with an electric guitar riff so intricate it was beyond a mortal's dexterity. The female vampire they call, Glory, tore open the night by reaching notes that would make wolves howl. Her body swayed to the rhythms of the drummer pounding at preternatural speeds. The effect was spellbinding and the crowd erupted in dance as if their bodies were possessed by a voodoo ritual. My friend and I also were swept up in the groove. The music was so intensely satisfying at one point I thought I saw smoke coming out of their portable amps. James Singleton sat in on a few tunes on the upright bass. He was coated in sweat trying to keep up. A shimmer of Glory's tambourine signaled a drum solo, giving the other musicians a break. The drummer, Beanie, was entirely a blur to my human eyes and the crowd was enthralled. When the drummer stopped, Glory gestured toward the tip bucket. On cue, the dog raised his head and green bills rained down into the bucket. Dozens of phone cameras were aimed at the band.

To all the vamp hags and fang bangers out there, I highly recommend catching a late night set of the Plasma Casters for a mind blowing experience. But I do regret drawing so much attention to the fact that they keep company with the one and only elusive vampire dog. It seems that he is less elusive all the time and this worries me. For your safety and his, never forget he is not an ordinary dog, even though he looks like one with the exception of his red-rimmed eyes.

Now on a different note, for the well-being of all of our four-legged mortal dog friends, I'm going to ask one last thing of you dear readers: we are seeking information about an illegal dog fighting ring in our fair city of New Orleans. If anyone has any information, please email me at: Chad@bloodlust.com. Dog fighting is unacceptable. Period. If you disagree, please unfollow, unfriend and unsubscribe. @Chadrusso #bloodlust #vampdog #plasmacasters

CHAPTER TWENTY-SEVEN:
Captain's Table

A few things had been niggling at Chad's brain about this mystery, and one of them was the post from his reader that said if he needed to know more about The Darkness, he should talk to the Captain of the Krewe du Vampdog. Having been unable to connect at the krewe meeting given the vampdog drama, he made some one-on-one time. Captain Dean Langham was a fan of the blog, so it wasn't hard to set up a meeting. They met on the patio at Basin Seafood & Spirits on Magazine Street for their fifty-cent oyster happy hour special. You can feast like a king there on a pauper's salary. Because of his krewe's fandom for Chulie, Chad was hoping Dean would be willing to help him connect some of the dots. He started by setting his phone on the table to record the conversation.

"You mind?" Chad pointed to his phone.

Dean shook his head. He wanted this off the record, so Chad slipped his phone back in his pocket.

"Let's start with your favorite topic. How did you first become aware of the vampdog?"

Dean gave him the whole backstory. "We had been hearing about sightings for probably ten years and there were stories that dated back even longer. After the news stories about Lucy's disappearance and her dog turning vampire, the sightings took on mythical proportions. Over time, they became better documented thanks to the proliferation of cell phones. Smart phone cameras improved and suddenly there was proof everywhere on social media of Chulie's existence. That's really the spark that started our group. There was a Facebook site with a growing number of followers. People had a thing for the vampdog, Chulie. So, we decided to transform the thread into a more formalized krewe community and charge dues for a big party every year. Hence *Krewe du Vampdog* was born."

Chad just nodded; he knew all of this. "I can relate to the fascination," Chad replied. "Why do you think so many people are intrigued by vampdog?"

Dean thought for a second and said, "Have you ever lost a beloved pet? I have. It's like losing a family member, an innocent one at that. The idea of a dog who is immortal is irresistible. At least that's the motive for most of us. I can't speak for everyone. We are exceedingly open-minded and welcome people with all kinds of, shall we say, passions?"

Chad flashed back to the bizarre goings on at the Blood Hounds Ball. He laughed a little. "I think I got a taste of some of the krewe's passions at your party." They shared a laugh just as the waiter slid a full tray of raw oysters in front of them. They adorned the slippery contents of the shells with lemon and hot sauce and indulged in these fresh gems from the sea.

Chad tried to probe deeper. "Have you ever come across anyone who would want to harm or capture Chulie?"

"Harm no, capture yes. Some krewe members just want their own vampdogs, dogs that could live forever. But I've recently discovered some with darker motives," Dean said in a hushed tone.

"Really?" Chad pressed.

"A dog fighting ring, for one. We've also had several members from The Darkness over the years. That gets tricky. Currently, though, we have a vampire member who is trying to modernize The Darkness. Bruce. They were trying to get him to participate in turning aggressive dogs into vampdogs but he wanted no part of it. In fact, he exposed them at the meeting you attended…after you left. Is it true you had vampdog with you?"

"No comment," Chad said with a wink. Dean smacked his hands on the table and laughed. Chad paused for another oyster, giving Dean some space together his thoughts.

"Let's just say there was an incident."

"Incident?"

"Before we get to that, you need to know a little more about Bruce. He is an older vampire who is especially zealous about the vampdog. He and his grown son had turned vampire in 1883 to avoid dying of yellow fever."

Chad was intrigued. "Go on."

"His son met an untimely final death the same night Chulie was made into vampdog in the late 1980s and Lucy disappeared. That is how his story is intertwined with our krewe. But his obsession centers around avenging his son's death and finding who is responsible," Dean said. "And apparently, his son loved dogs."

"Does he know how Lucy's disappearance connects to his son's death?" Chad asked, his curiosity dialed to eleven.

"Nah. But he believes the creation of the vampdog is at the heart of it. His son had been the one long trying to convince his father to adopt more modern and peaceful vampire ways and so he has honored that after his son's death, which makes it easier to have him as a krewe member of course. Can't have members being murdered by vampires. But Bruce blurs the line between vengeance and justice, so we still use caution in our association with him."

Chad agreed that was prudent as they both went in for another oyster.

Lucy disappears. Chulie becomes a vampdog. Adam son of Bruce is murdered. Chad mulled this over as he scrolled through his phone to the photo they took of Lucy's vampire boyfriend.

"Is this the son of Bruce, your Darkness vampire?"

"Yes, that looks like Adam. He was friends with Lucy. Strange little mystery. And Adam meeting the true death. It's crazy no one has been able to solve it."

"Indeed," Chad replied. "Well you've helped fill in some blanks for me. Thank you for that."

"Oh man, happy to help. I love your blog. Especially when you mention the Krewe du Vampdog."

"So what was the incident you mentioned?"

"Vampire Bruce found the goon from the dog fight ring. Turns out they were experimenting with making vampdogs aggressive for fighting. But the dogs were so mean they killed each other or went mad. It wasn't working. They wanted to profit by creating undead fighting dogs."

" Horrifying," Chad said.

"It totally crossed the line for most krewe members and they are banned forever from participating in the krewe. Bruce might be Darkness and a bit dangerous. But he too has moral limits. He follows the vampdog because he thinks vampdog and Lucy hold the key to what happened to Adam."

"Are there any other Darkness vamps in the Krewe? Any who aren't as moral as Bruce maybe?"

"Not anymore, just some human minions who openly support The Darkness. Some of them are local entertainers. The adult variety."

"Do you mean strippers?"

Bruce smiled and nodded as he sipped his beer. "They all bear the mark in one place or another. That bat and sword thing. Can we talk about the oysters here? Outstanding."

Chad could tell he wanted to change the subject. He had divulged so much and Chad wanted to maintain their relationship. So they moved on to other topics, and conversation paused for a lot of hot sauce and slurping.

CHAPTER TWENTY-EIGHT:

Breach

After the night's gig, Glory sat at the table in our nest counting our tips with her long, alabaster fingers. I lay comfortably under the table, a good distance from her feet. If it was a good take, she would kick her feet up and down. If it wasn't so good, she'd stomp and kick. Either way, I didn't want to be near her combat boots.

Several weeks and many gigs had passed since Chad had amplified his fandom for the Plasma Casters in his blog. It certainly helped draw a crowd, but no sign of The Darkness. Still they all kept watch. Chad told me, Maggie, Strings, and the others what he'd learned about Bruce. I was no longer sure The Darkness was who we needed to worry about, though Bruce was definitely drawn to me for answers he thought I held. Did he consider me responsible in some way for his son's death? I couldn't imagine.

"Four. Hundred. Sixty. Dollars!" Glory shrieked and started kicking her feet. She noticed me under the table and tried to make me dance with her. She was my favorite nest mate.

Funny thing about Glory from what I've heard in whispered conversations between Strings and Beanie, she was really unhappy in her human state. She was what is known as suicide by vampire. People like her were so clinically depressed, they just wanted to shed their mortal life and join the ranks of the undead. You would never guess that from her exuberance as a vampire. I've heard them say she was just eighteen when she was turned, the age of consent according to the vampire moral code … at least for those who follow it. There are no rules in the code for dog vampires, they are simply a freak of nature. Lucky me. I'm still the only one I've ever met.

Of course we knew other vampires. Ever since the Vampire Ordinance of 2005 was instated, after the devastating flood associated with Hurricane Katrina, more and more vampires came out of the shadows to intermingle with humans and vampire kind. The ordinance prohibited discrimination against vampires as post-Katrina was a time everyone had to pull together.

Vampires played a critical role in the city's renewal and recovery. I guess we knew something about transformation. The New Orleans Vampire Association (NOVA) performed many good works to help see that people were fed and cared for. I remember my nest mates unloading supplies from a truck in the middle of the night. I met a mortal dog named Underfoot who amazed both vampires and humans with his ability to survive the Katrina flood disaster and aftermath and still act like a house dog. I could relate to being underestimated. Underfoot was a wiry terrier with a sharp bark. A survivor. Humans found him cute, some even held his front paws to dance with him in the bars on Frenchmen Street. I wondered if he could possibly still be around. That would be really old for a mortal dog.

Just after the flood waters receded, many dogs who were once pets ran in packs through the streets, surviving like their ancestors once did. I wished I'd made Underfoot into a vampire companion. But I didn't know how and failure could be gruesome.

Of the New Orleanians who self-identified as vampire, only about twenty-five percent were actually immortal, sanguine feeders or blood suckers. The rest were humans who drink blood for energy or kicks. There were also glampires who had the appearance of vampires but were not immortal and didn't drink blood. For them it was more of a fashion statement. And sexual vampires were mortals who derived energy from the danger of having sex with vampires. It was a colorful collective. I was glad people can be themselves here. It's worse when you suppress it. I wonder if that's what has turned some vampires and humans dark, all the pent up energy. I was in a ponderous mood about our vampire kind.

"Did you all fricking hear me?!" Glory shouted until Strings and Beanie paid attention. Glory cradled me in one arm and gripped the wad of money in the other. Strings snatched the money from her hand so quickly I barely saw the transfer of funds.

"Glorious, Glory!" Strings proclaimed. "Let's go celebrate. I have a taste for a blogger and his gal pal from Iowa."

A low growl rumbled in my chest. I wanted the nest to know they were mine. I rarely asserted myself this way but I needed Chad and Maggie to help me find my Lucy. Mind melding with other vampires isn't possible for me, so it was hard to know when they were kidding.

"Easy, boy, I'm just pulling your leg," Strings said much to my relief. Glory set me down on the couch.

"Hey, doggy, one of those weirdo krewe folk left you another bag of blood by the tip jar. O+. They wrote Vampdog on it so I guess that's you," Beanie offered, trying to calm me. "I only had a little sip." He plopped a half-full bag of blood on the couch next to me.

Glory hissed, "That was for the dog, you imbecile!" She was on Beanie in a flash. "He can't feed as easily as we can!" Strings broke it up. I was used to them bickering like siblings, always trying to win favor with Strings. In our own way we were a family. Glory squeezed the dark red liquid into a bowl for me and Beanie plopped down on the couch.

Before I had a chance to lap up any blood from the bowl, we heard a loud thump upstairs in the wig shop, followed by pounding footsteps. Beanie, Strings and Glory shifted into high alert and began circling the edges of the room, monitoring every doorway to the main living space. The wig shop had long since closed so no one should be up there. It was close to the time we would each retreat into our sleeping chambers, which were comprised of well camouflaged trap doors set into the floor, impenetrable by light. The chambers were each coffin-deep, just enough for us to comfortably sleep and each was cushioned according to our individual preferences. Mine was similar to a mortal dog's bed and even had a plush toy chicken Glory had given me on my Deathday. Glory would set me in my hiding place, close the hatch and then cover it with a throw rug. The others were undetectable within the natural floorboards. No one came down here and it was locked from the inside, but we took precautions, nonetheless.

We had a plan in place for a breach but only had to enact it one other time, and that turned out to be a false alarm—just a cat that got in the vents. My role in our breach protocol was dependent upon Glory. I would go to her so she could quickly put me in my sleeping compartment, close it up and slip the rug over it before getting into hers or going into battle mode. The others would either lock themselves in their chambers hoping to be undetected or stand ready for a fight. But this breach was no false alarm and happened so fast, there was no time for debate. Glory scooped me up from the couch and had me in my compartment in a flash. She was still standing on my rug after tucking me away. Beanie and Strings were fighting with each other over what to do, hide or fight, when beastly shouting interrupted them. Others were in our chambers.

"Where's the vampdog?" a deep voice growled.

There was hissing and banging and a huge commotion—then a gunshot. I heard Glory shriek and then a *thud*. I wanted to wail but I didn't dare. Footsteps shuffled madly overhead. I heard Strings roar like a lion. Then suddenly the room went quiet.

Hours passed with no sound at all in the room above me. After a while I lost all sense of time. It had to be dawn by now. I hoped Beanie, Strings and Glory had found their way to their sleep chambers. The cellar was pretty dark, but even the slightest sliver of sunlight through a crack could leave a horrible burn or worse. Then I had a terrible thought. What if they were all dead? I mean dead again … the final death. How would I get out to feed? I cursed my helpless canine body. I tried to sleep as I wondered if vampires who experience final death go to heaven. At least if they are good enough vampires. The vampires who murder probably don't pass the pearly gates. But Beanie, Strings and Glory didn't kill, and they were good to me. I've heard the thoughts of humans wondering if their beloved pets have souls and go to heaven. Now, I was wondering the same about my vampire pals. I sure hoped my nest mates weren't about to find out. I wished I could make myself big. Eventually I fell into a fitful sleep, images swirling in my mind, dreaming that I was running away from a monster, maybe a vampire, my feet kicking as I slept on my side.

Footsteps above woke me. I didn't dare move. A moment later my hatch creaked open. It was the face of Strings, not Glory. Standing next to him was Chad. I heard Maggie's voice.

"Hey, Chulie. So glad the bad guys didn't get you," Maggie said with forced brightness. Strings lifted me out. My legs felt stiff at first but I worked them out. How long was I in there? I stretched my body. Once my legs were in order I scurried about. Where was Glory? Beanie? Strings, Chad and Maggie just stood there looking at the floor, silent. I jumped up onto the couch and stared at Strings. Finally he sat next to me and spoke.

"Glory and Beanie were hurt real bad. A militant religious sect of vampire haters called The Impalers broke in and tried to take you. We wouldn't let them get you." I froze, feeling numb. What exactly did he mean by hurt real bad? Religious vampire haters? That reminded me of those scary priests who tried to catch me at the jazz funeral parade for Lucy's father. They must have been Impalers, too.

I wondered how they knew where to find our precious nest. And strange that we were so worried about The Darkness and they weren't our biggest threat after all.

Strings continued once he thought I understood. It was like he knew what I was wondering about. "We fought them off. But one of them had a silver chain and another a gun with silver bullets." He paused to let that sink in. I started shaking. Strings put a hand on me. Maggie slipped onto the couch on the other side of me.

"I was so focused on The Darkness I hadn't thought about The Impalers," Strings admonished himself. "They broke off from traditional Catholicism decades ago and are some of the most militant vampire haters on the planet. Countless vampires have met the true death at their hands. They have a twisted belief that a lesser known rogue apostle of Jesus named Josiah made a deal with the devil to become the first vampire in order to experience his own resurrection. According to their beliefs, that plan backfired, unleashing evil and terror rather than peace and hope."

"What people won't do in the name of religion," Maggie added.

I felt panic but also confusion. What would these demented vampire killers want with me? And why would Maggie and Chad be here with Strings?

Chad picked up on my worries and said, "We're here on your behalf, Chulie. Strings asked us to help."

I looked back and forth at all of their faces, afraid of what I'd find out if I mind melded Chad or Maggie.

"They wrapped Beanie's leg with the silver chain and he's slowly healing from severe burns. He'll be able to come out in a few days or weeks. But Glory, she took a bullet to the heart. She had to go to ground. Her recovery will take much longer." I tipped my nose up and unleashed a long, piercing howl. Maggie was crying softly. It hurt the same way as losing Lucy. An ache in my chest.

"At least she's not dead, Chulie," Strings said coldly. It was almost comforting that he was his old hard self. He was in survival mode. There was a reason he was the alpha. "I have to guard Beanie in case they come back. He's too weak to defend himself. When he's strong enough, we will find a new nest. We will come for you. Now you will go with the mortals."

I noticed that Chad had opened up a hard-sided tuba case on the floor that was lined in soft blankets. I started to run away from them, but faster than a human eye could see, Strings snatched me up. I wiggled out of his grasp and darted about.

"Chulie, this is just for now. We need to throw them off the trail. They know you nest here." Strings was all business about what must be done. "You can focus on your search for Lucy in the meantime. Oh yes, I've been aware." Strings rolled his eyes. "I think you will be safer with the humans."

I had stayed with humans in the past. I'd spent time with my friend Sister Eloise at the convent. She hid me in the sealed off third floor. It was a handful of years later I met Glory and her bandmates and the rest is history.

Maggie picked up what was left of the bag of blood that someone had left for me earlier.

"I looks like this blood is starting to crystalize on the edges," she said.

"It won't be good for much longer. Leave that here for Beanie," Strings commanded and Maggie did as told. "Chulie can find other food."

I paced in circles over every inch of our cellar home, wanting to take it in, knowing there was about to be a change. Over the decades, I'd experienced many changes and a variety of living situations. But I'd really miss being here. I'm not great about measuring time; I don't keep a calendar or a smartphone for obvious reasons. But it had to be twenty years that we'd been here. To me it's all just a strand of moonrises, strung together like cafe lights.

"We best get going," Chad said. "Morning is fast approaching."

Maggie turned to Strings. "Are you sure you'll be alright?"

Strings brushed off her concern, "Of course. You have the items I'm sending with you?"

Maggie nodded and lifted a huge duffle bag.

"Into the case, Chulie." Strings scooped me up and plopped me in the tuba case unceremoniously. So long to you, too, I thought.

CHAPTER TWENTY-NINE:

Protest

C had sat at the bar in Sanchez, comforted by the sounds of pinball but not quite up for a game. He was hoping to bump into his retired cop buddy, Frank, to fill him in on all that had transpired over the past few weeks, but it was late. Probably too late for Frank. He pictured the old guy asleep in his Lazy Boy with a late-night talk show glowing in the background. It was the hour that restaurant workers would stream in after work. Back at the apartment, it would soon be time to let Chulie out for his nightly stroll. But Chad needed a little space to think. The break-in at the nest was beyond unsettling. All this time they had thought The Darkness were behind all the wrongdoings. Then they were attacked in the name of religion. And clearly, the freaky priests were after Chulie.

Chad tried to piece it together. On the one hand, The Darkness, namely Bruce and Adam, were intertwined with the events the night Lucy disappeared, as well as with Broussard hot sauce business. Could the final death of Lucy's beau, Adam, be a motive for her disappearance? Bruce was clearly following them, but why? Did he think he and Maggie were on to something? He'd hoped his fixation with the case and public blog hadn't drawn the wrong kind of attention. Nothing was a straight line to Lucy's disappearance. She'd likely know who was responsible for Adam's true death. Could Bruce possibly think she or Chulie had anything to do with his son's death? Who knows what Bruce would do if he found Lucy first.

Chad stared down into his Sazerac for answers. He was glad to provide sanctuary for Chulie in partnership with Strings. He truly hoped Glory could pull through but it didn't look good. They were pumping her with ancient vampire blood. Ancient blood held healing properties and boosted strength. From what Strings told him of the process, it's grueling and painful with no guarantees. But what he knew of Glory gave him the impression she was tough.

A loud racket grew on the street outside the bar. Chad heard shouting and chanting and the clanging of metal and drums. He stayed glued to his barstool but swiveled to see outside the small window to the side courtyard. A group of hipsters stood and watched the commotion. Curiosity got the best of him. He settled his tab and slipped through the front bar and out the door. In the street, dozens of vampires were marching in protest of yet another vampire murder. Chad joined the group of hipster humans standing in the Sanchez courtyard to see what he could find out.

There in the group of young men and women was the waiter from Café Amelie, the night someone had paid for Chad and Maggie's dinner and sent the disturbing photo of the bloody gown. What was his name, Justin? Jason? Chad wondered if he'd remember him and then remembered his name.

"Hey there, Jordan," Chad ventured a greeting. Jordan looked a little rattled. "I was a customer at Café Amelie the other night."

"Oh yes, you were with the lady with pink hair and someone paid for your dinner."

"That's right, good memory."

"I don't forget a tip like that. No problem making rent this month."

"So, the vampires are protesting another murder?"

"Yes, it's awful," Jordan said with eyes wide. "Some of my best friends are vampires. We keep similar hours in the restaurant industry."

"I'm sorry, did you know the vampire who was killed?"

"Not this time, but it's hitting a little too close to home," Jordan said, adding, "you can probably relate to being close to vampires since a vampire paid for your dinner that night?"

Now it was Chad's turn to stare at Jordan with wide eyes. He didn't know what to say.

"Oh, I guess I wasn't supposed to say that," Jordan replied. "Ooops."

Chad thought about that for a second and got an idea.

"Jordan, do you think you'd remember what the vampire looked like if I showed you a photo?"

"I'm pretty good with faces." Jordan paused, thinking, "Oh, why not, I already slipped, what could happen?" Chad scrolled through his photos until he found the ones of vampire Bruce from the Krewe meeting and the old portrait at the Bloodletter's Ball.

"Yes I'm sure that's him," Jordan confirmed. "It's so strange sometimes to see vampires from decades ago and then in their modern state. He must be pretty old."

"I'm sure that's true. I'll have to find a discreet way to thank him for dinner. No worries, I won't tell him you slipped."

"Thank you," Jordan said. Most of the marchers had passed and Jordan's group of friends decided to head inside Bar Sanchez. Chad took that as his cue to head home to Maggie and Chulie.

So vampire Bruce bought them dinner and left the photo of Lucy's bloody gown. He felt both excitement and trepidation. Here they were, harboring the vampdog, consorting with vampires and evading vampire killers. They'd wanted to draw The Darkness out, but Bruce had been following their investigation all along it seemed, likely to avenge his son's murder. Maybe it meant they were on to something. If only they could find something to make the authorities open the case again. Or better yet, solve it themselves.

CHAPTER THIRTY:
The Vulnerable

When they let me out of the tuba case, we were in a kitchen, the same room where I once spied on Chad and Maggie through a window. I hoped they were smart enough not to have led anyone here. The shades were drawn tightly and my senses told me it was nighttime, feeding time. I was feeling the shaky-hungry feeling more strongly than usual. I was sure it was because of the trauma of last night. Was it just last night? No one was talking, which was fine by me. I wasn't interested in their thoughts right now either.

Chad sat at the table with the kit he used to check his blood. He squeezed a drop of blood onto a strip and I heard a little beep. Then he poked a different finger and held it out for me. He squeezed and a big goopy drop of blood blossomed on his finger. I lapped it up but knew it wouldn't be enough. My fangs popped out and I sunk them into Chad's meaty palm.

"Yeeeeowwww!" Chad yelped in pain but pulling away only made it hurt more.

I took a long draw, then stopped and looked up at him calmly, licking my chops.

Chad held his hand, wincing. Maggie rushed to his aid.

"Talk about biting the hand that feeds you," Maggie said.

"Some Neosporin and I'll be fine," Chad told her. "I need some juice, too."

Chad's blood was a sweet treat. But I stopped well short of my fill. While Maggie and Chad were fumbling with his love bite, I searched the perimeter for a way out. I succeeded with a hard push on the screen door.

As I slipped into the blackness of the night, I heard Maggie calling my name after the door slammed. I was out of sight in a blink. I headed for the hill across the street where I observed them in Chad's kitchen, the same place I watched them the first time when Maggie removed her lovely blonde curls. That seemed a long time ago. I never thought I'd be cohabitating with them. I was acting out because I missed my nestmates and being with my kind. I stood in the same spot, watching Maggie tend to Chad's hand and pour him juice. I thought about how they were researching Lucy's disappearance for me and felt bad about biting Chad. Once I fed I would return here and be more agreeable. I was their guest, after all. But first, I needed to find a safe place to feed without attracting attention from the vampires and humans who were after me.

I walk along the edge of the sidewalk nearest the buildings where the streetlights didn't reach. To the average human eye, I merely looked like a ripple in the shadow, hardly noticeable at all. But to a vampire, I still might be vulnerable. Luckily, it wasn't long before an opportunity presented itself.

I heard the child crying from somewhere near a bar. The sobbing was gut wrenching and persistent. I was there in an instant to help not harm her. It was a little girl of about five or six human years. Her yellow hair was a beacon in the haze of the security lighting. She was alone in a tiny patch of grass between the buildings. What in heaven's name was going on here? She was holding a headless stuffed rabbit. My stomach growled, wishing it was a real rabbit. I crept up slowly to the little girl, doing my best to look harmless, whining a little. She stopped crying and stared at me.

"Doggy," she said in a tiny voice. She held out her headless bunny to show me, her big wet eyes pleading. I took a step closer. I licked the bunny and that made her smile a little. What sort of dope would leave a small child alone outside at night? I could wait here and find out. Or perhaps I'd go inside the establishment next door and see if I could identify the perpetrator.

First, I'd do a little mind meld with the child to learn more. I'd start by cuddling up next to her like a mortal dog would. Mind melding a child can be a bit of a carnival, mixed with cartoons and imagination, but I could sort through that and be careful to extract her thoughts without sharing mine. I'd spare her the horror of things I've seen. She put her tiny hand on my back to pet me and I flashed on a memory of my Lucy. She was clearly comforted by my presence. I stared at her face as she made cooing sounds while petting me.

I saw in her mind her mother reading to her. Then there was a man, a man who made her feel scared. Her mother left her with the man, which made her cry. Her mom exchanged indistinct angry words with the man, gave a last hug to the girl and left upset. The girl started wailing. The man paced, agitated. He grabbed the bunny out of her clenched hand to get her attention and somehow the head ripped off. This made her screech. He picked her up roughly and the next thing the girl saw was the backseat of a car. The car stopped and she was carried briskly through a bar and deposited in the grassy area outside where I found her. Lovely behavior on that man's part. I got a good look at him. His blood would taste delicious.

I would see what father-of-the-year was up to now inside this place. One of the many nice things about New Orleans was they didn't mind a well-behaved dog wandering into a bar. The child wasn't crying anymore and even dozed off. I nudged her awake and coaxed her to follow me. She did willingly.

At the entrance to the bar, the door was propped open hopelessly optimistic for a breeze. We walked into a chaotic scene.

"Goddamn you, Larry! I knew I couldn't trust you with her. Fuck the courts." It was the mother I'd seen in the little girl's mind, but a different side of her, a ferocious lioness. There was a female police officer by her side.

"What was I supposed to do? She wouldn't stop screaming the minute you left. I needed a drink to calm my nerves," the worthless deadbeat said. He was belly up to the bar and the head of a bunny was sitting next to his nearly empty beer.

"You could have been a parent to her," Mama growled. "You did the right thing calling me, Mable," she said to the bartender. "Where's my Ruby? Where is she?"

"Mommy!" the little girl lit up and ran to her mom as we entered the bar together.

The patrons turned to watch and it was the distraction I needed. My mouth was wrapped around the man's ankle as quick as lightning. I sunk my teeth in deep and sucked hard. He was so shocked he didn't really know what was happening at first. Then he started yelling and kicking his leg, trying to get me off. I dug in deeper and hung on. He started staggering. It happened so fast the patrons didn't understand what they were witnessing. I was gulping. I was locked onto the Great Saphenous vein that runs from the inside of the ankle to the groin. I could tell he might be a good candidate for gout or a blood clot, probably from drinking his worries away. I felt him start to sway, so I let go and was a flash to the door before he hit the floor. Most people didn't even notice me.

"And you're drunk. Nice, Larry," Mama said.

"Bye, doggy," said the little girl, Ruby. I turned to give her a quick nod and saw that her mother held her toy bunny's head.

As I passed the bar I smelled that familiar cleaner smell. They probably used the same cleaner to clean the wooden bar as Sister Eloise used to clean the pews in the Church. Something strange was going on with Sister Eloise. There was also the charm she gave me for protection. She'd been popping up more than usual. I'd make a point of visiting her to see what was in her head.

Since I had eaten, it was time to make my way back to Chad and Maggie's apartment. As I trotted along, I thought about that little girl, Ruby. Why did my dark little heart feel for her? I could relate to feeling small and vulnerable. Despite my peculiar abilities and the danger I posed to other creatures, I was still vulnerable, especially during the day while I slept. Before I met my nestmates and aside from the time with Sister Eloise, I used to dig deep holes and tunnels in the soft, sandy earth. It's a wonder I survived as long as I did. A wonder, just like Underfoot the Wonder Dog who survived Katrina.

I reached the apartment and saw a soft glow in the kitchen, so I went to the back screen door. It was a good thing they were still awake, otherwise I wasn't sure how I'd get back in. It was well past midnight from what I could tell by the moon.

Maggie let me in and they both acted glad to see me. To my astonishment, the third person in the room was none other than my nest-mate Strings.

CHAPTER THIRTY-ONE:
Bad Blood

It was harder than they thought waiting for Chulie to get back. After Chad had returned home from Bar Sanchez, he and Maggie were doing their best to distract themselves from worry by playing cards. Chad told Maggie all about what he had learned from Jordan the waiter. She was as floored as he was about their dinner benefactor.

"Why would Bruce want us to find Lucy and why give us the bloody dress photo?"

"Maybe he thinks Lucy killed his son."

"If that's the case, I wouldn't blame her for disappearing," Maggie stated.

Maggie had always been more self-assured than he was, Chad thought, and better under pressure. But now she was jumpy, too. This must be something close to how parents of teenagers felt waiting for their teen to get home with the family car. They heard someone at the door and felt a momentary surge of relief. But it wasn't Chulie. It was Strings.

It surprised them when Strings showed up before Chulie. It was weird, Chad thought. After all his years of vampire fandom, he had never really envisioned having a friendship with one. Friendship may be too strong of a word, but there he was, Strings, dropping by and casually hanging out at the kitchen table—a blood-sucking vampire.

In another moment, Chulie returned and as soon as they let him in, he jumped into Strings' lap. Strings sat stroking his back like one might do with a mortal dog. The dynamics of the nest were a bit dysfunctional. One minute adversarial, the next co-dependent. Strings could be harsh, and he was cold when Chulie departed the nest to stay with Chad and Maggie. But he too had a soft spot for the vampdog and Chulie knew it. Chulie kept his head up, tongue wagging, and looked back and forth at their faces as they chatted, seeming to understand what they were saying.

"Chad," Strings started and Chad felt it weirdly satisfying to have a vampire speak his name. "I discovered something about that last bag of blood that one of the vampire enthusiasts left for Chulie," he continued, his voice emphasized "vampire enthusiasts" with disdain. It was clear he didn't suffer fools gladly, fools like vampire fanboys. *Ouch*, thought Chad.

"It seems there was a tracking device in the metal clip attached to it." He pulled the empty bag out to show them.

"You brought it here?" Chad asked.

"Yes. Don't worry, it has an off switch. I was disposing of the empty bag when I noticed a tiny light. I had a friend come by and analyze it and sure enough, it's a micro tracker."

Well that solves how they found the nest, Chad thought. He was relieved he and Maggie hadn't been the ones to give them away.

"Okay, no more bags of blood from strangers," Maggie chimed in.

He stared at Maggie for a moment with his smoldering eyes. "That's not all," Strings said in a hushed voice for dramatic effect. Chad was aware that at any point he may try to charm Maggie. "The blood was tainted," he went on, "it was laced with juniper, which is poisonous to vampires. Not enough to do much harm to Beanie but enough to put him out for a while. If Chulie drank from the bag it could have been enough to do him in. He almost drank it before we were interrupted by the breach of religious zealots."

Chad and Maggie let that sink in. Chulie put his head down on Strings' knee. Strings continued.

"It was likely a part of the plot to get to Chulie. Maybe they thought they'd need to subdue him to capture him. Do you think it's possible they wanted Chulie to lead them to his long disappeared Lucy?"

Chad shook his head. "It's my opinion that The Darkness might want Lucy found to exact revenge or find answers to Adam's death. But it seems The Impalers cult who breached the nest are motivated to keep the truth hidden. I'm still trying to figure out why. I'm afraid they'd benefit more from doing Chulie in. That's my hunch."

How on Earth did he and Maggie get tangled with both The Darkness and The Impalers, Chad wondered to himself. They were way out of their depth.

"A hunch, huh," Strings said unimpressed. He gave Chulie a last pet as he announced his leave. "Well, things to do, people to drain." Strings set Chulie on the floor. He froze when he noticed something. He fixed his stare on Chulie.

"What the hell is on your collar?" He grabbed something stuck on Chulie's collar under his fur and pulled the whole collar off. "Shit, it looks like another tracker. How the hell did you get that?"

Chulie bounced around in circles, shaking his head, appearing annoyed that Strings took off his collar.

"Sorry Chulie, this has got to go," Strings said.

"We can take care of that," Chad offered.

Strings handed him the collar and tag, nodded, and was gone in an instant. He clearly wasn't from Iowa like Maggie and Chad, land of the twenty-minute goodbye.

They turned off the tracker on Chulie's collar. It looked like a religious medal with a tiny switch that lit up in the on position. Strange. Maggie, Chad and Chulie went to the living room and sat on the couch for a while, contemplating their next move. Someone knew Chulie was here if they'd followed the tracker. How long had Chulie been there? Hopefully not long enough for anyone evil to have noticed. A mind meld with Chulie could tell them how he got the tracker on his collar. Chad was too tired to pursue it now but would revisit it first thing tomorrow. They decided to call it a night, maybe he should say call it a day since their hours were starting to sync up with vampire hours. They locked up tight and activated the motion sensor alarms. They had Strings on speed dial. Tomorrow, they could do more research. A mention of that got a wag from Chulie's tail. So the plan was unanimous.

Maggie and Chad took Chulie to where he would sleep during daylight. Just off of their laundry room, there was an interior crawl space where not a speck of daylight got in. Maggie had even crawled in there yesterday at high noon to make sure no light seeped in when it was closed up. They added a well-sealed doggy door so Chulie could get in and out, along with the blanket and toy from Chulie's hiding place at the nest. They lifted Chulie into place and closed the door to the crawl space tight. Then, they hugged each other, feeling a bit overwhelmed and seeking each other's comfort. They were just a B-list actress and a Vampire Tour Guide/blogger. How the heck had they gotten in so deep?

CHAPTER THIRTY-TWO:
Dog Fight

I have to admit, I slept well in the cubby Chad and Maggie made for me, despite Strings' warning and everything else on my mind; I must have been exhausted.

I had the strangest dream while I slept. I was a mortal dog again and my mistress and her mother took me to a man in a white coat who liked to poke at me. That was the last time I'd taken a ride in a car with Lucy. I remember standing on her lap and leaning my head out the window to feel the breeze. There were extra treats and cuddles after that, almost worth all the pokes, but also some new yucky food I didn't want to have anything to do with. My people took good care of me. Until, well, they didn't. But the dream left me feeling strangely refreshed, as if I forgot for a moment about my lot in life, or rather in death.

But when I awoke, I was still uneasy that Strings had taken off my collar. I felt naked without it. I was also disturbed that the charm Sister Eloise had given me was a tracker. What was up with that lady?

Maggie was the one who opened the hatch and lifted me out of the crawl space into their peaceful nighttime house. I heard someone swear and stomp upstairs.

"Chad's on deadline for another blog article. It's trickier now that we've got secrets to keep."

I liked how she talked to me like she was aware that I could comprehend. She didn't use a baby talk voice either. Points for Maggie.

"C'mon, let's go upstairs and get Chad out of his funk for a bit."

I scampered after her because that's just the way I move. No sauntering, no swagger, just scamper. Sigh.

"Wahoo!" Chad shouted as soon as we got into the kitchen.

If that's a funk, I want to be funky, I thought.

"What happened? Five minutes ago you were swearing at your laptop and cursing your muse for abandoning you," Maggie asked.

"You won't believe what I found when I was going down a Google search rabbit hole on old families in New Orleans. Oh hi, Chulie!" He seemed genuinely glad to see me.

"Someone has an antique desk still filled with papers that used to belong to a famous hot sauce magnate who lived in the Quarter until the 1980s," Chad explained. "That would have to be the Broussard's!"

Now they had my attention. That sounded like a description of my mortal family. Sometimes it was hard to even remember my former state.

"Holy hell, what are the odds of that popping up," Maggie exclaimed. "Those papers could be bills, letters, documents, a treasure trove of clues."

Chad was already on his phone leaving an after-hours message at the antique shop, asking them to hold the Mid-Century Secretary Desk until the morning.

"New topic," Maggie started when Chad was off the phone, "we need to get rid of this collar tracker thing, right?" Chad nodded. They were anxious to have this thing out of their house, even if it was off. "But I was thinking," Maggie went on, "what if we used it to throw them off our track?"

Chad pondered the idea. "Mags, I think you're on to something."

All this plotting and scheming was making me hungry. To be fair, I'd be hungry anyway. I started circling near the back door. Chad and Maggie caught my meaning and opened the back door so I could slip into the night. Chad's hand was still wrapped up from the night before, so I didn't think he'd offer a finger again. I heard them continue to talk about the tracker and the antique desk. I liked where this was going but a puppy's got to eat.

Weighing on my mind were the scary priests who came after me, invaded our nest and harmed Beanie and Glory. It had me ultra-vigilant, looking over my shoulders every five minutes for threats. I wished I had the power to exact revenge on creatures like them. But I didn't. Just my speed, my fangs, my mind meld and my immortality. At least that's all I had discovered in the past few decades. I didn't know another of my kind who could teach me. I guessed it was a good thing I didn't always have the power to make bad things happen because I'd grown cynical and had a bad temper. I'm sure I'd misdirect my anger and regret it at times. With the powers I do possess, I can stop certain bad characters from doing more harm. That makes me feel good in a way, like I'm dropping little bits of light into my dark world even though I'll never see natural light again. If I can stop someone from harming an innocent, maybe there's something good left in me. Something redeemable. But other times, all I feel is anger and loathing.

As I walked through the Quarter jumping from shadow to shadow, that abused dog in that vacant lot came to mind, the one that Bruce brought to the krewe meeting. It was as if he was trying to tell me something that night. I wondered if Bruce was able to get him to a shelter. Maybe I'd take a quick detour that way to see what was up at that empty lot. There was plenty of nighttime left.

I made it to the Bywater neighborhood quickly and could tell a big event was in full swing at that strange lot. I went up to the patchwork metal fence where I had seen the poor abused pit bull. I crouched near a small opening between two metal road signs. The place was packed with beer-swilling, wild-eyed, grisly men, arguing, laughing, gripping wads of money. Savage heavy metal music blared from speakers. Way in the back by the building were six crates holding snarling, agitated dogs. Someone blew a whistle. It was that wretch I'd seen in the dog's mind. I wondered if Bruce was here to protect the dog, too.

The men cleared to the edges of the yard, opening up a circle in the middle. This was terrible. I felt helpless and horrified. A voice over a P.A. announced that betting was closed. The men opened two of the crate doors. Two dogs flew out, all snarls, muscle and aggression. Their teeth were filed to sharp points and someone tossed milk onto them. That's when I noticed the more docile dog I'd seen the other day. Damn, he was still in danger. He sat hunched near the building and had many bite marks. He was favoring a front paw that looked injured, possibly broken. I realized he must be one of the weaker dogs they used as target practice to train the fighting dogs. Standing in the shadow of the building behind the docile dog was Bruce. Bruce looked displeased. The dog looked up for a second and sniffed; I wondered if he could sense my presence again like at the krewe meeting. Bruce noticed the dog's reaction and motioned to two thugs I didn't recognize. One grabbed a dog-catcher's stick with a loop on the end for catching a dog around the neck. He looked to be coaxing the docile dog out of the dog fight arena. Was he helping the poor dog escape? Or were they after me? Maybe both. They ran toward the exit. That was my cue to get the hell away from there.

I turned to run and smacked into the legs of a hulking figure. I wasn't sure if the legs belonged to human or vampire, but I sunk my fangs into an ankle and heard an anguished hiss. Definitely vampire. My only hope was to make a break for it and get as far away as possible. I was a blur of dog fur and two blocks away in the blink of an eye. I headed upriver. I was pretty sure I wasn't followed. Maybe I shouldn't have bitten that vamp. I still felt bad about biting Chad, too.

I was back at Chad and Maggie's apartment in moments. I ducked around a corner and waited a long time to make sure no one had followed me. Once satisfied, I flew up the steps to scratch at the door. No one answered. I was dying to send the images of the dog fight to Chad. Time was of the essence for those pitiful dogs. I heard footsteps behind me. Then the bubbly voice of Maggie and the deep laugh of Chad.

"Leaving that collar and tracker in the pedicab should keep those Impalers busy for a while," Chad said. He stopped when he saw me. "Chulie, good to see you." I think he meant it, even after I bit him. Interesting.

I spun in a circle and made some yipping noises to convey my urgency.

"We sent your collar on a wild goose chase, Chulie," Maggie said, thinking this would please me. "We got the bad guys off your tail." Chad took a moment to really look at me.

"I think something has Chulie worked up," Chad said as he opened the back door to the kitchen.

Yes finally! What I wouldn't give for a voice box that could accommodate complex human speech! Chad and Maggie sat at the table and stared at me. I stared hard into Chad's face and he closed his eyes. The images of the dog fight bombarded him. He grabbed handfuls of his own black hair and groaned. I knew this was a lot to lay on him, but I needed him to understand the magnitude of this horror.

"Chad!" Maggie exclaimed.

"Maggie, call 911. We need to report an illegal dog fight at that old yard we saw in the Bywater near the Krewe meeting. Now!"

"The one on Royal and Piety. Got it."

Maggie called the police and reported the dog fight. I only hoped they got there in time to save some of those dogs if they weren't already lost causes.

CHAPTER THIRTY-THREE:

Dirty Deeds

*B*loodlust, *a Blog for Vampire Enthusiasts – August 26, 2023 By Chad Russo*

Friends,

These were the results of a wretched illegal dog fighting ring in the Bywater. Three dogs were badly injured, one is in critical condition and five others had to be euthanized. A few were brought to a shelter, including the gentle pit bull they used for sparring in case any of my readers are able to give him a home. As part of their greedy operation, dogs were badly abused and malnourished in order to make them aggressive for fighting. The authorities rounded up three men and two vampires associated with this heinous operation and seized over $10,000 in illegal betting money.

This is no way to treat dogs or create vampdogs.

While I can't reveal how I am connected to this, dear readers, suffice it to say this has me shaken to the core. The depths to which man and vampire alike can fall, the pain they are capable of inflicting, disturbs me greatly.

Please, if you suspect dog fighting or see anything, report it.

This will be a short post today. Still processing.

Be well.

Please like, follow and share. @Chadrusso #bloodlust #vampdog #humanesociety

#

Chad posted this edition of the blog and shut his laptop. Though he and Maggie were meeting up with Strings, all he could think about were those poor dogs. It was clear who the real monsters were. He was also sorting in his mind the image of Bruce leading one pit bull out of harm's way. Had he been trying to save it?

Their next meeting with Strings was at Checkpoint Charlie, a twenty-four hour laundromat, bar and music venue. Only in New Orleans, as they say. Per Strings' request, Maggie and Chad arrived at Checkpoint Charlie at one in the morning. Chulie remained at the apartment, safely tucked away after his nightly feeding.

A crowd had gathered in the front bar to listen to a male and female duo playing original pop songs in Cajun French. The lively music bolstered the boisterous crowd. Glasses clinked, blenders whirred and the smell of stale beer permeated from the soaked floorboards.

Maggie and Chad held hands as they snaked through the crowd to the laundromat in the back. Strings waited, sifting through a basket of clothes and popping them into a washer.

"Strings," Chad announced, his voice swallowed up by the chugging and buzzing of washers and dryers. But Strings heard and turned to glare at them with his piercing blue eyes. Chad felt a chill.

"Someone has to have the clothes ready when Beanie is strong again and Glory comes back above ground," Strings explained as if embarrassed by tending to this menial task. "When Glory comes back, she's going to be ferociously hungry. She has also been receiving blood from very old vampires, so her strength and powers will have intensified tenfold. Fair warning."

Strings' shame at this mundane domestic task was almost endearing. It was a different side of him.

"Someone has to do it," Maggie agreed.

"Why did you ask us here?" Chad jumped in, wanting to get to the point and feeling uncomfortable with this awkward version of Strings.

"Well, it's not to help fold laundry," Strings sniped. "I got a tip and I need some daytime work from you. Checkpoint Charlie is a safe spot for vampires and humans to intermingle late at night." Strings dialed the knobs, poured in detergent and slammed the lid before continuing. "I've learned things about Bruce and his position with The Darkness. Intriguing things that may give us insights into Lucy's disappearance and the Impaler's efforts to harm us. It seems since he lost his son, Bruce has been more progressive in his beliefs about vampires and other creatures. His teenage son was always trying to convince him that peaceful co-existence was worth it. The loss of his son affected him deeply. In his honor he had become more pro-peace and anti-violent. He was trying to stop the dogfights and explore humane ways to create more vampdogs. I believe there is something in this shift that is key to this mystery."

Maggie and Chad were intrigued too and didn't dare interrupt Strings as he paused to toss in a dryer sheet. "This is where you two come in," Strings continued. "The Darkness has a league of familiars. They do their bidding during the day and guard them at night. Some have been charmed, some just willing. They aim to make more vampire dogs humanely. But there is a rift in the Darkness between these more progressive followers of Bruce and the more traditional faction. The conservatives have been tragically unsuccessful in making vampire dogs through the dog fighting network since the dogs are so mistreated. Many have died from the abuse, malnutrition, shock. My hypothesis is Chulie was made differently. Chulie was made from love."

Chad and Maggie let that sink in.

"What can we do to help?" Chad offered.

"We think someone from that vampdog krewe you are so chummy with may be one of those in servitude to traditional Darkness vampires. An inside source."

"We?" Maggie asked, "You said 'We think.'"

"Beanie and I have been chatting. He's well enough for conversation, not quite up to the nightly hunt," Strings explained. "He knows people who know people."

Chad wanted it spelled out. "So you want us to gather intel from a Darkness familiar during the day to see where the connections are to Lucy and Chulie?"

"Yes. I need to know how the pieces fit together. I need to know why they need Chulie. I need to know how we can work together to stop The Impalers from wiping us out."

"What makes you think the familiar will tell us anything?" Maggie asked.

Strings explained, "A vampire would be too clever to divulge such information. But a human in their servitude could be tricked. I've seen you two be clever, like the ruse you pulled on the Plasma Casters."

"Do you have someone in particular in mind?" Chad asked.

"Indeed. There is a burlesque dancer in the Quarter called Mimi. You must connect with her without drawing suspicion."

Chad and Maggie exchanged a look. Well this would be fun.

CHAPTER THIRTY-FOUR:
Miz Mimi

My human roomies and I were getting quite cozy. While I'd been out feeding, they were out chatting with Strings, so we had a lot of mind melding to catch up on. It seemed Strings was becoming domestic, which was disturbing in itself, but I wasn't sure what to make of him plotting with Chad and Maggie. Granted, they were not horrible as far as humans go.

The three of us were curled up on the couch, comfortably exchanging mental images. I knew the burlesque dancer they were talking about. She was bubbly and beautiful and I never would have pegged her as a familiar of The Darkness coven. You just never know about people. Her hair was platinum blonde, three shades whiter than Lucy's honey-colored hair. We were all getting sleepy. I wished to go to sleep and dream of my Lucy. Lucy. Lucy.

Maggie scrolled on her phone with long, graceful fingers, her brows knit together as she studied the screen. I caught Chad staring at her with puppy dog eyes. What a sap.

"She teaches a burlesque fitness class at eleven-thirty tomorrow morning. I'm signing up."

I got the impression that Maggie was pursuing an acting career and was really getting into this cloak and dagger stuff. It combined her proclivity for taking on a character with her love of solving puzzles. As to whatever was going on between Chad and Maggie … I chalked it up to the maddening human complexity of emotions when you lead with your heart.

"I'll wear another wig and glasses," Maggie went on.

Chad nodded, slipped his arms around her, and yawned. They both giggled.

"Sleepy time?" Chad whispered to her.

"I'll put our furry baby to bed," Maggie replied.

Furry baby? The indignity. I was three times older than them. As Maggie scooped me up, I let one of my fangs scratch her arm enough to draw a tiny line of blood. She yelped. I looked at her with innocent eyes, then licked the dots of blood from the scratch.

Yummy, midnight snack.

"C'mon you little vamp scamp," she said.

I'd take that.

I settled into my cozy sleep spot and the dreams came right away as they often did, usually images from the night I was turned, that fated night everything changed so completely. Lucy and I performed for the party guests. Bruce was there with his strange tattoo and his son Adam would show up in our room later. Miranda gave us treats to take back to our room. My tail wagged the entire time, doggy bliss. And then the fateful visit from Lucy's sweetheart. When I woke up I wasn't in our bedroom anymore and would never be again. I was in a dark place with Adam who was overseeing my transition. Bruce came to visit me when I was being watched over. I had forgotten that part.

CHAPTER THIRTY-FIVE:

Shimmy, Shimmy Fake

The plan for the day was a little sleuthing at the burlesque studio and then Chad and Maggie would swing by the antique shop to see the desk once the shop opened in the afternoon. They decided that while Maggie took her burlesque dance class with Ms. Mimi, Chad would rummage through Mimi's office to find anything connecting her to The Darkness. If he found anything, they would figure out how to call her out and get more information. Just a couple of Super Sleuths. Like Sherlock Holmes and Watson, but with vampires instead of Moriarty.

The studio occupied a storefront space. Sexy, jazzy music pumped out of it into the street, inspiring a few passersby to bump and grind. Inside, seven women and one man milled about the dance studio and Maggie joined them, while Chad hung back in the waiting chairs in the hallway reading a Where Y'At free circular. Ms. Mimi came out and clapped her hands, all business, commanding attention. She was petite yet curvy, had a beautiful, perfectly made up face and a perky ponytail. She wore a bustier, a ruffled skirt, tights and black dance shoes. She lined up the group and paced in front of them, giving them the rules of the class.

"Burlesque is an art form in New Orleans. It is not stripping, and we won't refer to it by that crude term. It is the art of the tease, and can be quite physically demanding, which is why it is great exercise. In this class, we make burlesque accessible to all. That means all body types, all genders. We enter this room with respect for all, and we honor each other as desirable, sexual beings," Ms. Mimi instructed her pupils. She shut the door to signal the start of class.

That was Chad's cue to begin searching her office. Just off the foyer at the entrance where he sat, there were three doors—the studio where the class was, a bathroom, and at the end of the hall a small office. He looked inside to make sure it was empty and tip-toed into the room. Music blared from the studio where the students were enthusiastically learning a burlesque routine, so he wasn't too worried about making a little noise. He flipped on a pen-sized flashlight to avoid using the overhead light, though. The walls were full of photos of Ms. Mimi in all sorts of festoonery, sequin costumes, big feathery fans, French maid, Betty Boop, even an old fashioned bell hop. She was an impressive performer, her whole persona sparkled. It was easy to see why she was considered a New Orleans treasure. The desk had a laptop that was left on, a pile of signed waivers to take the class, some utility bills, and lots of post-it notes with inspirational reminders in bubbly handwriting like, "You've got this," "It's okay not to be okay," "Believe in yourself and you will be unstoppable" and "Positivity is a choice." Go Mimi. She had a huge following on Instagram and TikTok and Chad and Maggie had already stalked her posts. She was delightful and it was truly hard to believe she had anything to do with The Darkness.

Chad's flashlight bounced a white circle around the room. Where would she hide something sinister? He opened a few drawers and slid his hand under the ordinary contents to check for false bottoms. He tapped on the sides of the desk looking for secret compartments. He even looked in the file cabinet under "d" for Darkness. No dice. He started taking a closer look at all the photographs lining the walls. In her colorful costumes, she posed with celebs like Brad Pitt and Angelina Jolie, Big Sam, John Goodman, Mayor Cantrell. That's when he saw it. Mimi standing in front of the Broussard hot sauce factory in Abbeville with Bruce. The patio lights were lit and there was a banner behind them under the Broussard logo that said, "Hot Sauce Festival." South Louisiana loved its festivals. You could probably find a festival on any given weekend throughout the year. In the photo, Mimi wore a sash that said "Queen Hottie" over her ball gown with matching tiara. They were both grinning, which was weird to see from a vampire. He was wearing a short-sleeved plaid shirt and the tattoo on the hand he had around Mimi was visible, the sword and the bat.

Chad took a photo of the photo with his phone to show Maggie and Strings. So many thoughts swirled in his mind. What was Mimi's relation with Bruce? Was she one of his minions? Could be. Seemed like more than a coincidence that they'd all be at the Broussard hot sauce factory. He noticed this frame was different from the others. Instead of a dusty, thin black frame, this one was shiny silver and pristine except for two fingerprints on the lower right edge. He pushed gently on the fingerprints and the frame sprung open, revealing a small, magnetized door. Behind it was a safe. Now his heart was beating in his ears. He was so absorbed in what he was doing that he didn't notice that the music in the studio had stopped.

"You triggered my silent alarm, you goth goon. Tell me one reason I shouldn't shoot you." Mimi stood in the doorway pointing a pearl-handled pistol directly at him.

CHAPTER THIRTY-SIX:

Nun the Wiser

My last encounter with Sister Eloise left me with many questions. Why would she have put a tracker on my collar? If anything, she was probably trying to protect me. Chad and Maggie weren't the first humans to help me. Sister Eloise was always welcoming to me, even if she was a little odd. But smelling that wood cleaner aroma after the shot went off at the rally and two people were running away had left me feeling uneasy. Something was off.

I also felt like Strings, Chad and Maggie focusing on The Darkness was all wrong. The Impalers were far more dangerous. Bruce wanted to find out what happened to my Lucy, too, certainly. But they had different motivations of course, which meant we had to find Lucy first. If Bruce thought she killed his son Adam she'd be done for. That is if she wasn't already, but in every fiber of my being I felt she was still alive.

I thought about the night I escaped from my maker, Adam. Who could have murdered him that night? Could it have been The Impalers? After I had escaped the place where I transitioned, Sister Eloise let me sleep in a wooden box under her bed. She told me how back in the early days of New Orleans, they had sent a bunch of young women from France to be brides for the men who were building the colony. They were called Casket Girls because of the wooden boxes of their belongings they brought over on the ship. They were also accused of either bringing vampires to New Orleans (because of the boxes) or being vampires themselves because they were so pale from the sea travel. Sister Eloise had inherited one of the boxes from an ancestor. It was just right for me.

I'd go see Sister Eloise and insist on doing a mind meld with her to learn about the tracker. There had to be a good explanation. She was a complicated character and had more inside scoop on New Orleans culture than anyone I knew. She was obviously religious and The Impalers were a twisted type of religious, so perhaps she had some ideas. Plus, she might have a bag of O+ in her fridge like she used to. She had a source at the hospital where she volunteered. Since this blood was sourced from live humans, it was edible for vampires and was one way we could live with humans less violently. Blood from things already dead was not desirable.

The museum was way past closing time. I scratched on the door that led to her quarters. While I was standing there waiting, I sensed a movement behind me. I turned around to see Strings across the street on the sidewalk. He tipped his hat at me but didn't walk away. I had a feeling he had been following me like a vampire security detail. I was glad for that given my limitations. I nodded back at him. Sister Eloise opened the door and greeted me enthusiastically. I slipped inside.

"I was going to come find you and now here you are. You're in for a treat tonight, Chulie. I'm working the night mission in the mobile blood donation unit."

I couldn't imagine this tiny middle-aged woman driving that massive RV. This could be harrowing. But at least I could get quality time with her and a mobile blood bank had its obvious perks. Sister Eloise told me she loved being able to help and use her old phlebotomist license. She took the mobile unit to where people hung out at night. Bourbon Street, Frenchman Street, St. Claude. She had to catch them before they started drinking. She partnered with the local pubs for free drink coupons and cookies, and made the donors sit and have juice and cookies before they went on their merry way. Some people called it Blood Donation before Libations. It intensified the buzz. Only in New Orleans.

We climbed aboard the van. I sat on the passenger seat and was glad I was already dead so that I didn't have to fear for my life while Sister Eloise did her best Mr. Toad's Wild Ride impression. We made it to the corner of Decatur and Esplanade in one piece and parked where we could intercept people on the way to Frenchman Street. Frankly, I thought there were about a hundred flaws in the logic of this approach to blood donations. But what do I know, I'm just a vampdog. While she set up shop, I tried to perform a mind meld. She was one of my favorite subjects, her head was an ocean of stories, mostly the vampire legends of New Orleans.

"Are you in my head again, Chulie?" she called me out playfully.

I stared up at her and did my best head tilt, which delighted her into soft laughter. I saw so many colorful images of street performers, carriages, brass bands, fortune tellers, tourists, Casket Girls and nuns. There were ghosts and pirates and vampires. It was as if she was a library of New Orleans lore. I sent her back an image of the scary Impalers priests. She immediately shut me out.

"Oh my, I need to sit down," Sister Eloise said as she plopped down on a stool. She shook her head. I continued to probe and saw only a closed door. Strange. She was actively closing me out of her mind. This took a level of mental strength I didn't know she'd be capable of.

There was a pounding on the door.

"Y'all open yet?" Came a voice along with the sound of other voices and people gathering.

Our first customers had arrived. Good, I was famished, and this conversation was confusing.

"Need to get the cookies and juice!" Sister Eloise said with a bit of panic in her voice as she darted about gathering things. I wondered how she could sound more alarmed about cookies and juice than vampire killers. She reached up high on a shelf for the cookies and the sleeves of her grey tunic slipped back on her arms. On one arm I saw the mark of The Light, the same one Glory had. On the other arm, I saw the mark of The Darkness, the one I'd seen the night I'd been turned and at the Krewe party. I sat very still staring at her, my head tilted. She noticed my inquisitive stare.

"Oh, yes Chulie. I've been unceremoniously bounced from coven to coven. A familiar in search of a master. Not unlike the legacy of my French ancestors who were treated so poorly because of vampires. Nuns, prostitutes, dark, light. Enough to make your head spin. Until Fiona and I found our calling. Our holy mission."

Now that gave me pause. Fiona was Lucy's uber religious mom, vampire hater, and a major party pooper. What could they be up to?

"And funny enough, Chulie. It all started with you." She had all the supplies ready to go now and opened the door to a line of donors already forming. But I was dying to know more.

She mumbled to me under breath as she set the snacks out, "The Light is delusional thinking there can be harmony, The Darkness is ruthless in pursuit of wealth and power at any cost. But we found our goldilocks when we started to engage with The Impalers. Fiona runs The Impalers now."

I felt a chill through my bones. Maybe she didn't know what they did to Glory and Beanie, how could she? I sent an image to her mind of Glory going to ground.

"Oh dear," Sister Eloise gasped. But the corner of her mouth turned up.

She knew.

My mouth opened and my tongue flopped out. It was a perfectly inappropriate response but that's just what my mouth did sometimes. I felt a wave of sadness thinking of our noble Glory and her association with The Light. I whined a little and poked around for a way out.

Sister Eloise logged in the donors who were lined up and made sure they answered a questionnaire about their lifestyle habits. She also drew a blood sample first to test for AIDs, COVID-19 and other ailments that would render their blood useless. Once the first two volunteers were hooked up, she poured a tiny bit of the blood into a small bowl for me. Once I had a full belly I'd find a way to get far away from this psycho.

But Sister Eloise bolted the door to keep me in.

The donors had no clue the sinister underpinnings at play. The mood was light and lively and people chatted freely like it was a social event. Sister Eloise had that effect as she chatted up a storm; the people came as much for her stories as for the free drink tickets and cookies. I was reminded why I once liked her. No surprise she'd been part of The Light. Now her crazy religious fanatic side had taken over like an alter ego.

Abruptly, Sister Eloise announced to the crowd that she'd finish the last two people in line and that would be it for the night. I needed to get out of here and back to Chad and Maggie. Of course I had to warn them about Sister Eloise and find out what they had learned from the Burlesque dancer, Mimi. They'd surely be back by now.

Sister Eloise had the door open now as she brought in the last folding chair. I saw an opening to flee and was about to go for it, but then a hulking figure filled the doorway.

"I'm sorry, we're clo…"

Sister Eloise couldn't even get the last word out before the hulk knocked her to the ground.

CHAPTER THIRTY-SEVEN:
Chamber of Truth

" Who the hell are you?" Mimi asked. Chad froze in place with his hands up. Maggie came running up behind her.

"Ms. Mimi, no! This is a huge misunderstanding. He's with me," Maggie blurted out.

"Chad Russo, of Bloodlust blogger fame," Chad said, voice shaking. He held out his hand.

Mimi didn't reciprocate or take her gun off him.

"Let's go where we can talk." Mimi motioned with her gun toward a bookcase. She hip checked a shelf and the bookcase opened to a reveal secret parlor. The parlor had a black and red motif and there were more pictures of Mimi on the walls, but these featured Mimi with vampires about town. The focal point of the parlor was a circle-shaped bed with fuzzy pink handcuffs hanging on a post. Assorted sex props hung on the walls. Mimi invited us to sit in a grouping of armchairs on the side. She noticed Maggie eyeing the array of kinky sex toys.

"Cute," Maggie commented.

"I run a dominitrix business as a side hustle. You'd be surprised how many prominent titans of business like to be tied up in this town. Any other secrets you pervs want to know?" Mimi sniped as she continued to hold the gun on Chad.

"I can tell you why we're here, but can you please set the gun down?" Chad asked politely while sweat beaded on his brow. He was experiencing a significant sugar low to make matters worse. He could kick himself for leaving his backpack in the waiting area.

"I'll listen," Mimi replied lowering the gun only slightly.

"We are trying to find a connection between The Darkness coven and the disappearance of Lucy Broussard, for Chulie the vampdog," Maggie stated plainly. Chad felt she was wise to leave out the part about Strings putting them up to it.

"Oh that little vampire dog. I do have a soft spot for that creature," Mimi said mellowing and lowering the gun to her side. "What do you think I know that can help?"

Chad ventured a response, "You are a Darkness familiar, are you not?"

Mimi's eyes narrowed, and her pretty face got harder. "Who wants to know?"

Chad held up his hands in a gesture of surrender. "I'm not trying to pry. We just want to find Lucy. Chulie's never given up on her."

"The vamp dog?" She softened a little. "I was a Darkness familiar. Past tense." Mimi sat in the chair behind a small table and gestured toward the guest chairs. Chad didn't want to picture the transactions that happened at this table so he avoided any contact with the surface. He was fixed on Mimi's every move. Her smile was knowing but her eyes were a million miles away. She set the gun on her lap. They gave her a moment to gather her thoughts. Maybe she was deciding how much to share.

"Classic story. I fell for a bad boy who just happened to be a vampire. His name was Bruce."

"I can relate," Maggie said tilting her head toward Chad.

"Oh please," Mimi said amused. "He's not even in the same league of bad, sweetheart. Behind his Halloween fascination with vampires, goth garb and tattoos is a total marshmallow."

Maggie smiled. She knew this was true.

"You know me?" Chad asked amused.

"I read your blog. Makes me laugh."

"Thank you, I think?" Chad replied. "You dated vampire Bruce?" Now that was interesting, Chad thought.

"Dated, yep. You might say he left his mark on me," Mimi stood up and twisted around. She pulled down her tights just enough to reveal The Darkness tattoo on her right hip. Maggie and Chad stared. The places that tattoo kept popping up!

"That tattoo seems intertwined in Chulie's origin story and Lucy's disappearance," Chad said.

"You know I'm also a member of the Krewe du Vampdog, too. We all just love that critter. He represents the misfit in all of us. I saw you one night when it was my turn to follow him."

Mimi touched Chad's arm. Maggie made a face.

"It was the night Chulie fed on the abusive boyfriend on Esplanade and then you wrote about it in your blog."

"That was you? The mysterious witness?" Chad asked and Mimi nodded.

Maggie jumped in, "You said you *were* a Darkness familiar. Boyfriend or not, how did you get out? I would think that would be near impossible to quit The Darkness." Chad was thinking the same thing.

"I had help. I couldn't take the coven anymore. Bruce and I decided mutually to split, no hard feelings. Have you ever heard of The Light? As you'd guess, it's the opposite of The Darkness." Mimi pulled the left side of her tights down to reveal a tattoo on her left hip of a sun intersected by a quill pen.

"We made an exchange. One person going from The Darkness to The Light for another person going from The Light to The Darkness."

Chad and Maggie just stared, hoping she'd go on and tell them what Strings wanted to know about why the The Darkness wanted Chulie. Strings had told them about The Light and that Glory was a member, too. He had to have known about Mimi. What had he gotten them into?

"It goes way back," she continued. "Long before my time, The Darkness started getting more and more powerful and they were in cahoots with some of New Orleans' most powerful humans—other people who craved power, titans of business. Politicians. Pillars of society. Law enforcement. With their vast stores of money, they became investors and shareholders in local businesses. Locally, there was a powerful businessman who worked his way into the inner circle. He wanted to go international with his hot sauce business. He made a deal with The Darkness in order to take his enterprise to the next level. He needed their venture capital. Now his hot sauce is wildly popular in Japan and fun fact: Guam consumes more New Orleans hot sauce than any other country."

"Hot sauce?" Chad said, feeling like the combination on a safe was clicking into place. "Was the hot sauce magnate's name Broussard?"

"Yes. He was indeed the patriarch of Chulie's mortal family. The business deal with vampires was top secret and caused a major rift in his family. And everything got dialed up after Bruce lost his son. I wasn't around then of course but that's the story I've been told. His son was always trying to convince his dad of co-existence with humans. His dad was only interested if they could monetize the relationship."

Maggie and Chad exchanged a look that said *Are you hearing this too?*

"What, you didn't know that?" Mimi asked. "Well, I guess once they all moved away from New Orleans, their story became murkier."

"Do you know what became of their daughter, Lucy?" Maggie asked.

"Not sure, but she went off the grid after Chulie was turned. From the stories I've been told, the whole thing was a cluster of disappearances. Lucy vanished, the family moved out of town, Bruce lost his son, Chulie was in the wind. That is the tale I heard amongst The Darkness coven, but I always had a feeling there was more to it. Victor Broussard, rest his soul, and his wife, Fiona, haven't really been together since. She went from religious to ultra-religious and fervently anti-vampire. Lucy, if she's still alive, must be middle-aged by now."

Chad was feeling the rush of finding another piece to the puzzle. Victor Broussard had been in business with Bruce. He could tell Maggie was feeling the same way. They knew Broussard Hot Sauce had a vampire investor, but this was interesting. Mimi, on the other hand, looked drained. She twirled the gun on her finger and stared into space.

"I have to ask you a strange question," Chad ventured, "was it you who fired the gun at the courthouse rally?"

"Good Lord no," Mimi replied.

Chad believed her.

"Well, you've been very helpful." He couldn't wait to share this information with Strings and Chulie. He started to rise, hoping they'd reached an understanding.

"Hold on. Don't think you'll get off that easy for trespassing," Mimi said focusing once again.

Maggie pleaded, "We need to get back to tell Chulie and we were supposed to look at an old desk belonging to the Broussard's …"

Mimi cut her off, "You can communicate with that vampdog? Interesting. I'm not going to interfere with your geeky Sherlocking. But you owe me now. I am thinking you have skills that could benefit my business."

"I didn't think I was that good of a dancer…" Maggie started.

"You're not," Mimi cut her off again. "But I could use some social media to promote the next show." Mimi turned to Chad. "It's called Nymphs of the Enchanted Garden District."

Maggie and Chad stared at her.

"I'm going to lock you in my dominitrix lair for two hours while you come up with a social media campaign that will dazzle the beads off of everyone. Ta ta!"

Mimi moved quickly toward the door. Chad knew there was no stopping her and she still had that pretty little gun.

"Wait," Chad said, "just one more question."

"I will allow one more."

"Who was the exchange, when you came from The Darkness to The Light? Who became a part of The Darkness?"

"It was a psycho nun named Sister Eloise."

CHAPTER THIRTY-EIGHT:

Light or Dark

The huge man had Sister Eloise pinned to the floor of the RV and I growled, unsure if he wanted to harm me, too.

"I'm here to help you, Chulie," the guy said. How did he know my name?

Sister Eloise moved quicker than I would have imagined. She pulled a hand loose to free a knife from her pocket and without hesitation stuck it in the guy's neck. The man let out an agonized groan. Sister Eloise pushed him off. The man turned to me and said, "Run! Chulie, run from here!" I wanted to run but Sister Eloise wasn't having that. As the guy lay bleeding, he reached out a hand and I saw the mark of The Light, the plume and the sun. I gave Sister Eloise an imploring look. At least I thought it was imploring. I made my eyes wide and whined a little. I hoped there was still a part of her that remembered when we were friends. Maybe it was that dog part of my brain that was trusting to a fault.

"Oh get over it, Chulie," Sister Eloise said suddenly hard. So much for friends. She moved quickly to bolt the door again. I'd lost my opening. *What now?* I thought nervously.

Sister Eloise rushed about the RV opening up all the window shades wide. The man on the floor was still out cold. "They threw me out like the trash. Traded me," Sister Eloise explained, the hurt still in her voice. "After all I'd done for The Light. It was part of a transaction to save a high-ranking vampire's human girlfriend. She went to The Light. I went over to The Darkness. It was pointless because they broke up soon after. But the hope was also to pave the way for peace. As if one could make peace with devils!" Her voice had gotten shrill. "Fools! Thank goodness Fiona and I found The Impalers to cleanse the evil from the world. They valued my inside knowledge of both The Light and The Darkness. And I've been getting blood from the vampires we kill to make me stronger and younger than my years."

I was doing my best to process this. Fiona was Lucy's mother. I knew she hated vampires. But enough to kill them? I remembered the fight I overheard between Fiona and Lucy's dad the night I was turned. He did business with vampires. No wonder there was a riff.

Sister Eloise got behind the wheel and turned on the motor. She didn't even collect the sign and table from outside before peeling out and spitting up gravel beneath the wheels. I slid across the floor and into the pool of blood formed around the guy. I detected a very faint heartbeat.

"We can't let anyone know what really happened to Adam and Lucy that night. Your Chad and Maggie are bumbling a little too close to the truth. You and those mind melds, Chulie. I've had to stick close to Chad and Maggie. Fiona and I tried to warn them off with the gun shot at the rally. I also painted the warning on their door. They should have dropped it. But now, they'll suffer the consequences."

Oh Chad and Maggie, I truly hoped they were okay. *Nothing would stop them from helping me find Lucy.* Not even a psychopath Sister.

"We're going to the lake to wait for the dawn, Chulie," Sister Eloise said with an eerie brightness. "That will be the end of you and for me as well. I brought arsenic for me. The sun will be your executioner. We'll enter our heavenly reward together, Chulie." She started laugh-crying, a sound like gasps and squeaks trying to one-up each other.

"After you're gone, no one will care about tracking down Lucy."

She knew something about Lucy and I realized now why she opened all the window shades. I wondered how long I had before the fierce Louisiana sun would pierce through the windows. I let myself think about the Sister Eloise I once knew. So dedicated to her vocation and the uniqueness of New Orleans. She once had compassion for vampires, including me. Getting swapped into The Darkness, her legacy of rejection, must have been the last straw that destroyed her fragile mind. I almost felt sorry for her, but now she was doing awful things. I needed to survive this somehow. Chad, Maggie and I were getting closer to knowing what happened to Lucy. And I wasn't about to give up now.

CHAPTER THIRTY-NINE:

Faux Review

*B*loodlust, a Blog for Vampire Enthusiasts – August 31, 2023 By Chad Russo

SPECIAL ENTERTAINMENT EDITION: Must see performance! Five stars!

Greetings Vampire Lovers and Friends,

This edition is going to be a little different than the usual dish about vamping in New Orleans. Today we are reviewing the world premier and latest tour de force of New Orleans' own Ms. Mimi and her burlesque beauties in "Nymphs in the Enchanted Garden District."

I was fortunate enough to catch a preview and let me tell you, this is a show you won't want to miss. So tear yourself away from reruns of Dark Shadows and get out for some good old-fashioned T&A. Ms. Mimi and her troupe are word-class masters of the art of the tease and not even a 500-year-old vampire would be immune to their charms.

This bouquet of blossoming burlesque beauties shook what the good Lord gave 'em and left me screaming for more. Get your tickets today and prepare to be dazzled! This reporter gives it 5 sequined and tasseled stars.

Please like, follow and share. @Chadrusso #bloodlust #vampdog

#

Chad felt a little dirty about faking a review, but he held his nose and posted the article. He'd never even seen the show of course, but at least it would get them out of Ms. Mimi's lair and back on track with their mission. He'd have to think of a way to make it up to his readers. He didn't consider himself an important journalist or anything, but he had an integrity threshold. Unlike Mimi. She didn't let them out of her dominitrix chamber or return their phones until midnight. So much for their visit to the antique store to go through the desk. He wondered how angry the shop owner would be at their no-show. He had no way to even call and cancel.

They were bursting to share what they'd learned with Strings and Chulie, but their hunger and Chad's blood sugar became more urgent. Luckily, they found some gummy bears in Ms. Mimi's desk drawer to tide Chad over. It seemed a weird thing to find gummy bears in this sex dungeon, but he wasn't going to be picky. By the time Ms. Mimi let them out, they had constructed an entire social media and digital campaign in addition to Chad's blog post for her new burlesque show. All Ms. Mimi would need to do was hit post on the social ads. Maggie had taken some graphic design courses and helped whip up gorgeous digital flyers for the show, filled with flowers and female body parts. Talk about putting the graphic in graphic design, they joked. But the pattern was subtle and tasteful. New Orleans was the last place for puritanical censorship.

Maggie and Chad were both disappointed at missing the appointment to see the desk at the antique shop and hoped they could reschedule, that is if someone didn't already snag the desk or they weren't too pissed off about the blown off appointment. But they had other things to deal with now.

"I am having a strong urge to get back to Chulie," Maggie said as they left the burlesque studio.

Chad agreed. They were deeply connected to the little guy now. Plus, they were both weary from the strange day. They thought it best to report back to Strings tomorrow night. That is until they arrived home to find him eagerly waiting in the alley by their side door.

"Took you long enough," Strings said as a greeting.

"Ms. Mimi locked us in her kinky sex room until we created a social media campaign for her new show. She didn't take kindly to us snooping around."

Strings reacted in a way they hadn't seen before; he busted up laughing.

"She's something, isn't she," he said delighted.

"You knew she had switched over to The Light," Chad accused. "Well c'mon in, we'll tell you what we learned," he offered.

They all went up to the flat like three chums and Maggie offered Strings some chicken blood she'd been saving for Chulie in a pinch. He declined. Most vampires didn't like blood from something dead.

Chad made sandwiches for Maggie and himself. Maggie loved the way he made a toasted PBJ with the crust cut off. Chad was so relieved to be home and now that it was well past one in the morning, he was hoping Chulie would be home, too. But there was no sign of the vampdog. Hopefully he was having a better night than they'd had so far.

In between bites of their sandwiches, Maggie and Chad tag-teamed the story of what they learned about Broussard's doing business with The Darkness, and the swap. Strings just sat and nodded.

"Did Ms. Mimi say she had broken up with The Darkness vampire?" Strings inquired.

"Yes," Chad confirmed, looking at Strings quizzically.

"Did you know Ms. Mimi was also a member of Krewe du Vampdog?" Maggie asked.

"Of course, it's all about her devotion to Chulie."

Chad interjected, "I still don't understand exactly why they are so bent on getting Chulie and why they can't make their own vampdogs."

"I think the reason no one has been able to successfully make a vampdog is that Chulie retained his devotion to a human. The vampdogs created by The Darkness were uncontrollable," Strings explained. "The Darkness is also fixated on amassing wealth. And Bruce on avenging the destruction of Adam."

"I'm not sure this ruse got us any closer to answering the million dollar question. What happened to Lucy and who killed Adam," Maggie ventured.

"I really can't see Lucy killing Adam like apparently Bruce believes."

"Aren't you eager little investigators," Strings said slyly, tapping his long slender fingers on the arm of his chair as if he longed to feel the neck of a guitar. He let them hang a bit while he pondered this information.

"I do know the Broussard's hot sauce business benefitted greatly from rich vampire investors like Bruce all those years ago, so Victor Broussard was no stranger in the vampire community," Strings continued. "But the family was sharply divided on vampires. Fiona Broussard is a known anti-vampirist. Maybe his family wasn't too happy with Adam after making Chulie one of us?"

"Could Lucy have run off to get away from her family?" Maggie inquired.

"It's possible," Strings considered it.

Chad was already cleaning up and about to administer his nightly insulin when Strings asked, "Tell me again how Ms. Mimi switched from The Darkness to The Light. She's not dating anyone else now?"

Chad was starting to believe Strings had an ulterior motive to sending them to Ms. Mimi. Chad explained again how it was a trade. "She has both tattoos, and I don't think she's dating anyone."

"How on Earth did she get away with that?" Strings was downright amused. He actually seemed smitten.

"She joined The Light and someone from The Light went to The Darkness," Maggie reiterated while Chad finished his injection. Strings had an eye on what Chad was doing and licked his lips. "It's someone we know," Maggie added.

"Who was it?" Strings asked with an edge to his voice.

"It seems impossible, but Mimi said it was a sweet old nun we happen to know. A friend. She's harmless, though," Maggie looked at Chad to see if it was okay to reveal her name. Strings looked a shade paler than he already was.

"Her name's Sister Eloise," Chad said.

"We have to go. Now. Chulie is in grave danger. We'll take my car," Strings urged. He moved at vampire speed and Chad and Maggie did their best to keep up. They were barely inside his blood red Mustang when he hit the gas.

CHAPTER FORTY:
Mobile Confessional

I mulled over my options, which actually was just one option—die a slow painful final death at dawn. It was hard to say how soon dawn would arrive, but I knew we were in the wee hours of the night. I tried to see if the sky was lightening. I looked around for some place to crawl into, but every cabinet door was secured. Damn my lack of fingers.

Meanwhile, I watched Eloise completely unravel.

"Your Lucy was no saint. I'd say she had her share of the devil in her. She thought she was in love with Adam, the vampire who turned you," Sister Eloise scoffed.

"I was going to help Adam get away from The Darkness and his father's influence. But he refused to let go of Lucy," she explained. "So Fiona and I had no choice but to end him."

The air brakes squeaked as Sister Eloise pulled to a stop. I wasn't sure but I caught a faint whiff of lake water so assumed we were on the road near Lake Pontchartrain. She jammed the gas pedal and we turned onto a bumpier road.

"I'm sorry, Chulie but it has to be this way. It's God's will. By joining The Impalers and their crusade against vampires, I can atone for my life and my Casket Girl ancestors with their whoring ways. I led The Impalers to your nest to do their good works."

Sister Eloise was quite hysterical now. Her voice was manic.

"My end is near, too, Chulie. I am confessing to clear my soul before we both leave this brutal world. It was me who left the juniper tainted bag of blood that poisoned your nest mate Beanie. It was meant for you. That would have been a less painful way for you to go, Chulie." She was shaking her head. Her rambling confessions continued.

"Holy Father forgive me, it was me who fired the gun at the rally. Me who painted a warning on Chad and Maggie's door, even while I pretended to be their friend. But still they persisted. Fools."

I hoped Maggie and Chad were okay. Would they come find me? How would they ever know where Sister Eloise has taken me? I felt the depths of despair. The Impalers and Fiona were after them now.

Eloise continued with renewed energy. "I've been serving penance for my sins in every vampire I destroy in your name, Holy Father! I've killed dozens of vampires and taken their blood to make myself invincible. Fiona now runs the Impaler's cult and calls all the shots. But she won't drink the unholy blood so she has weakened while I've gotten stronger. I'm the one who does her bidding to perform the executions while she keeps her hands clean."

I stared at her in disbelief. Sister Eloise executing vampires? Fiona calling the shots? I tried to go in her mind again. Now, it was a tangle of anguish, guilt and fury. I just couldn't believe this was the Eloise I thought I knew. I felt the same sting of betrayal after my family had abandoned me. I tried not to slip into depression, because if I did I would surely give up. I held tight to the notion that somehow Lucy did actually love me. Somehow, we would find her, however old she may be and wherever her life has taken her.

"Your Lucy didn't betray you, Chulie," Sister Eloise announced as if she knew what I was thinking. Did I project that thought to her unknowingly? "You may as well leave this world with some peace. You had a fatal disease and your Lucy wanted you to be a vampdog so you could live forever."

What? I wanted to believe Lucy would never betray me, although I had my doubts. But I hadn't thought she'd been trying to save me. Now I felt more determined than ever to find her. All this time I had wrestled with the idea of her leaving me or worse betraying me. While my devotion never wavered, this was a jolt of added purpose. I had something else to live for, if you could use the term "live" for my vampire's existence.

"Have you heard about the casket girls, Chulie?"

Of course I have you withering old bitch, I thought. You told me that story a million times. I used to sleep in one of the boxes. The French girls who were shipped here from France as imported brides and everyone thought they brought vampires. Sister Eloise was truly losing her shit not to remember our conversations.

"You know I inherited that box from my ancestors. They were persecuted by the colonists when the colonists thought they were associated with vampires. They shunned them and treated them like they were cursed. They were adrift in a foreign land. In deep despair, one of my ancestors killed herself when her daughter was only three. The daughter grew up to become a whore like the rest of them. She had a daughter from one of her johns and so the legacy continued, generation after generation. My mother followed in their footsteps when she had me out of wedlock with one of her customers. I tried to break the cycle and make up for their sinfulness by becoming a nun. But it's impossible to shake all the dirty details about vice and vampires in my family history. It only consumed me."

The legacy of Sister Eloise's tragic life hung between us. The pain of being disregarded, rejected and made to feel invisible. I felt bad for her but my fear and desperation outweighed any sympathy I could muster. She was distracted by her own yammering and nearly missed a turn. As she tugged hard on the steering wheel, it felt like the RV would tip over. I slid across the floor, paws flailing helplessly. What I wouldn't give for some Air Jordan's with gripping power.

"Almost there, Chulie," Sister Eloise said as if we were taking a joy ride to a park, not our death site. "Fiona insisted we destroy Adam. He and Lucy were so young and smitten and determined to run away, but it would never be. And you, of course, complicated things." She was sobbing a little bit now. "Turning you into a vampdog saved you from certain mortal death. But was it worth the price of becoming one of the devil's own?"

I never liked Fiona much but I had no idea she was capable of such carnage. Again, it was like Sister Eloise knew what I was thinking. It must have been the vampire blood from her victims sharpening her powers of perception.

"Fiona was a force to contend with. It was impressive how she could sit through all those press conferences and pretend she didn't know what happened to Lucy and Adam."

What the blazes? I thought.

"I once thought there were so many like Adam I could have saved. But eventually Fiona and I began to see eye-to-eye. I realized she was right. The only salvation for vampires is the final true death."

The mobile blood unit screeched to a halt and once again I slid across the floor. The almost-dead man who attacked Sister Eloise groaned softly. Sister Eloise swiveled her chair around to face me. "We're here," she announced brightly like we'd just arrived at the dog park.

I watched the demented Sister Eloise exhibit her freakish strength as she hoisted the man who served The Light. She picked him up under the armpits like he was a large rag doll and out the door they went. A big splash a few minutes later told me she deposited him in Lake Ponchetrain.

CHAPTER FORTY-ONE:
Pulling Some Strings

S trings had tentacles in every corner of the city and beyond. His vampire and human informants were widespread throughout the Quarter and he was going to tap into his network to find where Sister Eloise had taken Chulie. He pulled up alongside a group of vampires sitting at an outdoor café in the French Market. All of the vendors were closed at this hour and the three vamps sat lazily in the darkness like cats. Strings told Chad and Maggie to wait in the car. As soon as he stepped out, striding toward them with purpose, the vampires sat up a little straighter.

"Leo!" Strings growled. If he were Leo, Chad thought, he'd be terrified. In an instant, Strings had a vampire who must have been Leo by the throat. Leo's eyes were wild and he struggled to speak.

"It was your turn to keep watch on Chulie. Where has he gone?" Strings released Leo in a heap on the cement. Leo gagged and hissed, showing his fangs.

"What the fuck, Strings. Chulie was at that nun's mobile blood bank near Frenchman. I watched the whole time until they closed up. At that point, a human familiar from The Light showed up and I figured he had the next shift. They let him inside, so I took off."

Wrong answer.

"You what?" Strings said in a low tone that was three times as frightening as his growl.

"I …"

Strings had him back in the air before he could utter another word, toes dangling ten inches off the ground. Leo choked again but this time Strings was not touching him. He just held up his slender hand. Chad and Maggie had never seen this power of telekinesis before and were in awe. The other two vampires didn't move a muscle to help their friend. Probably wise. Strings let him fall again.

"Did you see where they went?" Strings asked.

"I didn't. I'm sorry, Strings. But there were dozens of people around."

Strings seemed calmed by the apology but didn't acknowledge it.

"Tell me immediately if you spot the vampdog." And with that he was back in the car with Chad and Maggie.

They zoomed through the Quarter and stopped for Strings to grill a few more vampires and humans who happened to be near the convent or in the vicinity of Frenchman Street where the mobile blood bank had parked. They needed to figure out where Sister Eloise took Chulie. They gathered enough information to know a human in service of The Light had been deployed to help Chulie but they'd need to figure out what happened to him, too. According to a teenage busker, the unit sped away heading North. Strings, Chad and Maggie combed the site where the mobile blood donation unit had been parked in the neutral ground, the tire marks heading North and the discarded folding table and chairs with juice and snacks left in the dirt. They must have cleared out in a hurry.

"The Light was onto her," Strings said, turning things over in his mind. "They have been probing after the attack on Glory, seeing as she's one of their own."

"If Sister Eloise was swapped to The Darkness," Chad said, building on his line of thinking, "why wouldn't she run to them for protection and deliver the vampdog they so desperately seek?"

Maggie piped in, "Maybe she's had a change of heart and is going rogue? She has a complicated relationship with vampires, twisted with religious devotion. According to Mimi the trade between her and Sister Eloise was a contract shrouded in secrecy."

"In New Orleans there is a thin veil between religion and the supernatural. Sister Eloise was tangled in both," Strings offered.

"Sounds like a recipe for a crisis of faith. Or worse," Maggie added.

"I think she hated people for what happened to her Casket Girls ancestors, but ended up hating vampires even more," Strings added.

"I'm curious about the involvement of The Light," Chad interjected. "I know you said Glory was a member. Bruce may have blamed Lucy for Adam's death. He wants to find her, too." He told Strings about Lucy's bloody dress in the photo.

They continued to poke around the neutral ground for any sort of clue as to where Sister Eloise and Chulie might have gone. They came across liquor bottles, condoms and dog crap. They knew that wasn't from Chulie. A woman came running toward them. Strings was immediately on guard, stepping in front of Maggie and Chad.

"That's close enough," Strings said in a voice that would have made Chad tremble. But the woman persisted.

"You're the blogger and the vampire musician, right? I need your help," she said as she kept moving forward. In an instant, Strings had her by the throat, her feet dangling off the ground. Not wise to be so aggressive with a vampire who's already on edge. The woman wiggled an arm to allow her sleeve to fall back revealing the mark of The Light on her forearm. Strings dropped her and her frail frame crumpled on the dusty ground. She had a long auburn braid that she flung back in place and carefully stood. She started by reciting the Creed of The Light:

"I pierce the darkness with a light, vampires united to do what's right," she recited the same creed the vampires had recited at their nest not long ago. Strings acknowledged with a nod.

"I'm Stephanie, sorry not to be more polite, but we're wasting time," she said with trembling voice. "I heard you've been asking around about the nun and that vampire dog."

"What do you know?" implored Maggie as she helped Stephanie dust off her flowy skirt and denim shirt.

"My boyfriend and I were deployed to save the vampire dog. We caught wind of the nun's dangerous intentions and association with The Impalers. That crazy nun wants to destroy the vampire dog so no others can be made and the truth about Lucy remains a secret."

They were stunned about The Impalers remark. How could Sister Eloise pretend to be their friend and follow The Impalers?

Chad was puzzled about the other part too. He asked, "Why do you think no one has been able to make a vampire dog?"

"I don't have time to explain fully, but they are messing with the nature of things, there is a certain order. When trying to force the outcome, the vampire dogs made by The Darkness are deadly aggressive and destroy each other. Chulie the vampdog was an exception to that rule because he was made out of benevolent intent and retained his devotion to his owner. If he loses that devotion he might go mad, too."

"Benevolent intent?" Chad questioned.

"Love," Stephanie stated simply.

"Enough of this, what do you know that can help us find Chulie?" String insisted.

"That's what I'm trying to tell you," Stephanie said, "I had a tracker on my boyfriend's phone. Kevin."

"Where is it tracking now?" Chad asked.

"The signal just disappeared near Lake Ponchetrain."

CHAPTER FORTY-TWO:

The Power and the Glory

I could hear Sister Eloise singing church hymns from the driver's seat. We hadn't moved since she dumped the young man into the lake. I was hoping that somehow he had woken up and was able to get out of the water. But I doubted that was the case. I pondered how much vampire blood Sister Eloise must have feasted on in order to be so formidable. How many vampires had she killed?

I wondered if her affiliation with The Impalers made her snap or if the crazy had been brewing all these many years. I probably should have seen it coming. Not important now, staying alive with dawn looming, that was all that mattered. I was running out of time. If I were to bite her and incapacitate her, I'd still have no way to open the door and get out.

"Be not afraid, I go before you always, come follow me, and I will give you rest," Sister Eloise sang. Her voice was high and sweet. It seemed completely out of sync with the death metal scenario about to happen to me if the sun started stabbing through these windows. With little else to do, my dog instincts had me pawing and scratching on the particle board flooring as if I could dig a hole.

Maybe if I used my speed on my digging paws? Worth a try, but it didn't get me anywhere.

I wondered if the undone nun would off herself first or wait to make sure she had actually destroyed me. I heard a screech from far away, maybe some other dying creature. I thought about Beanie who was still recovering from the attack on the nest and Glory who was still underground. Of course Strings and his alpha persona were always in my thoughts. Would he save me? I thought about Chad and Maggie too, and realized I had grown fond of them. Would I ever see any of them again? Would I actually have people who would miss me when I was gone? What a concept. And what of my Lucy? I couldn't stand the thought of never knowing what became of her, especially since we'd been making progress in the investigation.

There was a soft thump on the roof that made Sister Eloise stop short. I heard the screech again, now above us. The screech turned into a roar and the thumps turned into pounding.

Sister Eloise jumped out of the driver's seat, her eyes were wild as they darted around the ceiling, trying to figure out what was happening.

"Chuuuulieeee!" a monstrous voice roared. I recognized it right away. Glory. Glory had come out from underground. If the past told us anything, a vampire who returns from ground is ravenous, ferocious and ten times as strong after being pumped with ancient vampire blood to heal, which Glory certainly had been.

I howled to let Glory know I was there. Sister Eloise tried to kick me with all her freaky strength, but I used my speed to dart back and forth. When she almost lost her balance I sunk my teeth into her calf, piercing her sensible black stockings, instantly soaking them with blood. Sister Eloise made a sound like a cow giving birth. She grabbed for a long silver chain in her pocket. I released her quickly, but not quick enough to miss the silver chain she wrapped around my torso. I wailed and was immobilized as I watched Sister Eloise come for me again.

The deafening sound of ripping metal pieced our eardrums and Sister Eloise and I looked up to see Glory, in all her glory, ripping a hole out of the top of the mobile RV like it was a can of sardines. She peered in, her eyes glowing red, dirt caked in her hair, looking like the fiercest, most beautiful thing I'd ever seen.

Sister Eloise began chanting prayers in Latin like they were an incantation. But she was cut short as Glory pounced on her and had her throat ripped out in seconds. Sister Eloise flopped like a dog toy being flung around by a puppy. Glory took a gluttonous drink, with Sister Eloise's esophagus hanging from her mouth and blood streaming down her chin.

"Chulie," Glory turned to me. She was now half monster. But I knew she'd eventually get back to her old self. She ripped the gear shift clean off the vehicle and used it to fling the silver chain off of me. I could see burn marks through my fur. Glory grabbed me so quickly, I barely knew how I ended up in her arms. I started licking her hand madly, something I hadn't done since I was a mortal dog. She looked down at me and her gruesome faced turned lovely for a moment as she smiled, revealing her fangs. We heard a bird sing, a sign of impending dawn. That was a terrible sign for both of us and I wondered how we could possibly get to safety in time. Glory cradled me a little closer and flew through the door.

Then of all the fantastical things, she actually flew! I'd only heard of supremely ancient vampires with the ability to fly. But sure as can be, we were soaring through the air. Looking down, I saw Strings' red sports car. Glory screeched again and flew a quick circle around the red car. The car spun around sending a spray of gravel and sped in the direction we were headed. The sky was lightening to a purply blue and I felt the burns from the silver chain stinging. Glory soared downward until we landed in what I recognized as the Private Estate area of the Metairie Cemetery. My nest mates and I had crashed here before. In a flash, we were at a crypt that was shaped like a pyramid. Had we survived?

Glory moved the rock at the entrance aside as if it were a screen door and we plunged into the cool darkness. She tucked me into a small coffin, and I heard her pulling one out for herself. Just before I drifted off, I heard Strings' voice inside the crypt. Oh, thank goodness he made it, too. I do know he has a way to make his car sun proof if needed but I was glad we could be all together. Then I heard two other voices.

"Is Chulie safe?" It was Maggie.

"Shall we close this stone door for you all?" Chad asked.

Yes please, I thought before I slipped into a dark-side-of-the-moon oblivion.

CHAPTER FORTY-THREE:
The Desk

Maggie and Chad were exhausted after running around with vampires all night. But after a few hours of sleep, their alarms went off. Despite their sleep deprivation, they had work to do. They needed to follow up on the desk from the Broussard estate. They felt some peace knowing that Strings, Glory and Chulie were resting safely after such a harrowing night. Chulie would need time to heal from the silver chain burns. But they were safe for now. They were still numb in their grief for Sister Eloise. What a shock and what a brutal way to go, even for a psychopath.

More pieces were starting to click in place but they were still far from knowing for certain what had happened to Lucy. Chad thought about what his brother would think if he saw what they'd gotten up to. Oh how he wished they could discuss it. What would his theory be?

Time to get to that antique shop before the old desk was gone. There was more to learn about the Broussard hot sauce connection. They scraped themselves out of bed and made a beeline for the coffee maker and two steaming mugs of Community chicory coffee black. As soon as they were dressed and feeling human, they made their way to the antique shop on Magazine Street.

The shop owner, Boris Brum, greeted them lukewarmly, probably still miffed about them missing the last appointment.

"You two look like you've been enjoying our famous New Orleans nightlife."

"Something like that," Maggie said.

"I'm sorry to tell you this especially after you finally made it here. But someone snagged that old secretary desk last night just before closing. They'd kept *their* appointment," he sniped.

Damn. They were too late.

"Can you tell us who bought it?" Maggie urged.

"I respect my customer's privacy." Boris replied smugly.

Chad had a sense that Boris loved keeping secrets and was enjoying this.

"Can you at least give us a hint? We are working on behalf of Chulie the vampire dog." Chad offered. Boris thought a moment, savoring his secret.

"Well, you didn't hear this from me, but it may have been someone in that krewe obsessed with the undead pooch."

Let's see where this leads, Chad thought, pushing for a bit more. "Can you tell us anything about how the desk came to be here?"

With an eye roll and a huff, Boris Brum gave them an, "oh please"

They followed the shop owner as he kept moving through the store, too busy to stand in one place and chat. They made their way through rows of dishware, figurines, lunch boxes, jewelry and assorted nostalgic trinkets.

As he moved, the shop owner breezily relayed that inconvenience and information came at a price. Chad caught his drift and handed him a five dollar bill. The shop owner just stared without taking it and Chad handed him a twenty. He smiled. There crammed between rows of antiques and collectibles, Boris enlightened them about the desk and how it was miraculously left undisturbed.

"There was an estate sale at the old Broussard mansion on Esplanade. The current owners, no relations to the Broussard's, had been there thirty years but wanted to retire to Florida quickly since the husband was diagnosed with cancer. They left and didn't take much. They let their adult children go through what they wanted and then an estate sale company took over. The kids didn't want the dusty old desk, so we snagged it. It was untouched in the attic, there since the Broussard's moved out decades prior. It hadn't fit the new owner's decor and they had forgotten about it. The Broussard's had also left in a hurry decades ago, too. Must be a thing with that house."

He stopped at the back of the store where there was a pile of boxes he needed to sort through. "Will there be anything else today?" he said without hiding his impatience.

"Just one more question and we'll get out of your hair," Chad said then cringed as he realized the shop owner was as bald as a cue ball.

"Um, did the buyer happen to take the contents in the desk? You mentioned old papers?"

"No, I pitched those before they came to pick it up."

Maggie and Chad thanked him and scurried out, hoping garbage pick-up wasn't that morning.

CHAPTER FORTY-FOUR:

Chasing Lucy

It was night again and I slipped out of the pyramid-shaped crypt to stretch my legs. Strings and Glory would see that I got fed. I was very weak and would not get far. The eerie calm of the cemetery was comforting to me, while it might feel spooky to mortals. My heightened sense picked up the heartbeats of other small creatures, stirring my hunger. As I wandered among the tombstones, I caught a glimpse of something that made my vampire heart swell. Ducking behind an enormous angel statue was a female in a blue dress with a cascade of honey-colored curls. Lucy! Could it be? I mustered up a bit of energy and used my super speed to reach the angel statue in an instant. But alas, she was no longer there. Could it be a trick of the eyes? No, there she was not twenty yards from me, face forward this time, bending lower to my level, beckoning. She didn't have to call twice. Again I flew to her side. But when I looked up at her, it was Adam my maker.

He was pale and sad. His brown eyes were damp, and he bent to scratch my ears as he talked. "I miss Lucy so much, Chulie," he said. "We were supposed to have forever, but we only had a few nights." He rose, a few tears dripping down his cheeks. Did this mean Lucy wasn't with Adam? Or was it just wishful thinking on my part?

As I tried to wriggle away, I felt his long cold fingers and sharp fingernails wrap around my mid-section. I turned my head back as he lifted me off the ground and he changed once again, to Bruce his father. What the shape shifter? I felt so helpless and defeated and saturated with grief, that I cried and yelped and whined pitifully. I squeezed my eyes shut but couldn't stop the noises I was making.

I heard a familiar scrape and opened my eyes to see I was still in the coffin Glory had placed me in last night. I had been dreaming. Of course, how else would I have gotten out on my own? But the dream was so real; was someone projecting it into my mind?

"Such noises you poor precious creature. You were crying something awful," Glory said as she gently lifted me with hands so strong now they could rip out a man's heart. "You're okay. You're safe with me now. No more demented nuns."

Sister Eloise. Such a disappointment. Behind Glory stood a beautiful, raven-haired vampire. She must have joined Glory last night. Glory always had desires for both sexes and perhaps now in her reborn state those desires had been stoked.

I wagged my tail and pranced about their feet with less energy than my normal self. I wished they could have seen the images in my dreams.

Glory filled me in, "Strings had some unfinished business. Beanie is nearly well. We have a lead on a new nest. For now, the safest place for you will be with the vampire fan boy and his gal pal."

Chad and Maggie. They were part of my rescue crew once again. I wouldn't mind so much spending more time with them. Maybe another mind meld so I could share all the craziness that Sister Eloise had revealed before she died. But first, I needed to rest again. I still wasn't one hundred percent after my Sister Eloise encounter.

Glory and her beautiful friend started making out and it was clear I was a third wheel. It was good to see Glory back and better than ever. I knew she would always be a powerful protector. I rubbed my furry body on her ankles to express my gratitude and took my leave.

The cemetery felt as still as it did in my dream, minus my Lucy of course. I was aware of so much more now than when I was a mortal pooch. That was a blessing and a curse.

The heartbeat of a squirrel beckoned me to my midnight meal.

CHAPTER FORTY-FIVE:
Dumpster Revelations

The dumpster for the antique store was on the sidewalk by the side of the building at the cross street. Unfortunately, it was also shared with a hair salon and a taco stand, overflowing and baking in the mid-day sun. Chad and Maggie popped into a nearby hardware store to grab some gardening gloves and masks.

They stood in front of the mountain of garbage, feeling daunted and discouraged at where to start.

Maggie turned to Chad and said, "For Chulie?"

"For Chulie," Chad responded.

They began by pulling out some of the bags on top and piling the ones that were obviously from the taco stand or hair salon to the side. There were assorted loose items, too, like Styrofoam go containers of rotten rice and beans, dog poopbags and great clumps of freshly cut hair from the salon. The smell could knock someone over. The flies were loving it, though. Chad and Maggie had pulled out everything they could reach, opened several bags, but did not come across anything that looked like papers from a desk.

"We're going to have to get in there," Chad told Maggie. Maggie gagged a little.

"Okay, I'll go in there and hand stuff out to you," he told her. Getting in was quite a production. Maggie cupped her hands and Chad tried to step in to get hoisted up, but Maggie lost her balance and they both toppled over. Then Maggie got on all fours and Chad stepped on her back. He tried to hoist himself over the side but he wasn't a guy with a lot of upper body strength. That's when they noticed a bunch of plastic milk crates outside the back door of the Mexican restaurant. They stacked them up high enough for Chad to climb over the side, but they made a big commotion.

"Hey, what's going on back here?" An employee from the restaurant stuck his head out the back door.

"I dropped my phone in the dumpster and he's trying to help me find it," Maggie lied. The guy offered to help but Maggie said they had it under control; he went back inside the restaurant and closed the side door.

After another ten minutes of slogging around in garbage and filth, Chad threw a box over that was filled with papers. He stood on a bunch of bags and hoisted himself out awkwardly but didn't hurt himself. Much.

"Jackpot." Maggie was already going through the box. Chad leaned in. "Oh god you stink, honey," she told him.

"You don't smell too great yourself. What's in here?" The box was crammed with papers, receipts from haircuts, groceries, and household repairs, letters, Mardi Gras trinkets, pens, paperclips, general desk stuff. Maggie and Chad pulled things out one-by-one and placed them in neat stacks to sort through like they were CSIs at a crime scene. It was strange looking through someone's life this way after so many years. There was an invitation to tea at the Columns Hotel dated April 1, 1982. Ordinary things that felt like relics.

Maggie found ledger papers from the hot sauce business and sat on the ground with one of the ledger books in her lap, occasionally taking photos with her phone.

"It looks like things were taking a downturn for Broussard's hot sauce in the early eighties. Entries as red as their hot sauce. Huh, that's strange. Not long after there seems to be a huge investor who came on the scene. There are large deposits made under R&D."

"That might track with vampire Bruce partnering with Victor Broussard. What could they have been developing?" Chad added. "Surely his wife Fiona was not on the same page. Given her hatred for vampires."

Chad kept muttering his thoughts out loud as he shuffled through more desk contents. There were several Sunday bulletins from St. Louis Cathedral. Must be Fiona who saved those, he thought.

"Not sure how the business connected to Lucy's disappearance," Maggie offered. "She was a teenager, probably unaware of her dad's financial woes. But maybe that's how she met the vampire Adam?"

"Likely," Chad agreed.

They sifted through almost everything in the box. Ninety percent of the contents were trivial stuff. Then Chad pulled out a piece of paper stuck under one of the box's flaps at the bottom.

"Oh my god," he said as he read it and realized what it meant. It was an invoice from a veterinarian. It was for the mortal version of Chulie.

"What is it?" Maggie asked trying to get a look at it. Chad put one gloved hand over his mouth and handed the paper to Maggie. It was a summary of service from a vet office visit, along with a diagnosis: "Terminal kidney disease. All known treatment options explored unsuccessfully. Suggested treatment euthanasia." It had a scheduled date: May 25, 1987. Just weeks after Chulie was turned and Lucy disappeared.

They sat there dumbstruck realizing what that meant. Chulie was already dying before he became a vampire. This changed everything. They decided that Chad would put together a summary of everything they'd learned to send to his cop buddy Frank. Sister Eloise's confession, Fiona's role and now this revelation. This might be what they needed to convince them to open Lucy's case again. That was worth some dumpster diving.

CHAPTER FORTY-SIX:

Sir Blogsalot

*B*loodlust, a Blog for Vampire Enthusiasts – September 9, 2023 By Chad Russo

Apologies for the delay since my last post. My assistant and I have been up to our necks in drama. There has been so much vampirical activity since we last met fang-to-fang. I have gotten all of your messages. Thank you for your patience.

Quick posting today; A new nest has moved into the suburb of Metairie. Take note, suburbanites, this is a nest of gardening enthusiasts who have been beautifying lawnscapes for over 200 years. So if you don't mind the hum of a lawn mower in the middle of the night, reach out on their Green Fangs Facebook page. All your yardwork done while you sleep! Bonus pest removal, no extra charge, but they ask you to please keep your own pets indoors. Chaining dogs outside at night is not cool anyway.

Please like, follow and share. @Chadrusso #bloodlust #vampdog #findlucy

CHAPTER FORTY-SEVEN:
Dancing With the Devil

I had given myself a week of recovery time, not venturing far from the pyramid crypt where we gained refuge. Strings and Glory visited me daily and made sure I could get in and out and feed. But they didn't stick around long. They both had distractions of the heart. Glory was spending a lot of quality time with her beautiful gal pal. And Strings? Well let's just say he had his eye on a different prize. I knew Strings had been stalking the burlesque dancer. He sent Chad and Maggie on a fool's errand. They visited me at the crypt, too. Strings was clearly attracted to Mimi and amused by her antics. He actually laughed at the tricks she pulled on Chad and Maggie.

After my recovery week, the Nest moved to a temporary new nest. It was in Uptown off of Freret Street, which had its own nightlife with restaurants and a club called Gasa Gasa where the Plaster Casters could perform, minus me. I visited but mostly stayed with Chad and Maggie.

I scratched on the new nest door and Beanie let me in. I listened to Beanie and Glory go at it like nothing had changed. Glory was clearly living her best undead life. Beanie was back to his old self. The new nest was cozier, security tighter. Located in the vegetable cellar of a grand estate owned by a very old vampire family, it smelled of onions and okra even though it hadn't stored vegetables in a hundred years. It was still assumed I was safest with Chad and Maggie who could guard me in the daylight hours, but we liked to convene together, my nestmates and I, before our hunts and haunts.

"Hey little dude!" Beanie greeted me in all his warmth and quirkiness. Next, Glory came over and scratched behind my ears. If vampires have hearts, mine was glowing. I walked around sniffing everything.

The central gathering space was small but comfortably furnished with a stereo system and walls lined with bookshelves. There were four stalls that stuck out from the center like spokes. That was where the coffins were kept. A laptop was strewn on the couch. Beanie picked it up and started tapping on it. I stopped patrolling and curled up in a circle. It would be nice to settle in for a bit before the evening meal.

As I was drifting off to sleep, Strings burst in from the outside. His energy was electric, he seemed really excited about something. He also looked like he had made an effort to look extra dashing. He wore a crisp blue shirt that matched his electric eyes and his hair was styled with gel. I may have smelled cologne. I lifted my head up and he patted it, but he was clearly preoccupied. He found his cell phone and keys and was off. I decided I would follow him. I was getting hungry and needed to go out anyway. So off we went out into the night. Strings was so distracted he didn't even notice I was on his trail.

I used my speed to duck around corners when he glanced back and followed him at a distance. It was not a great surprise when we ended up in front of Ms. Mimi's burlesque studio. But what he did next was something I had never witnessed in the decades since I became vampire.

Instead of watching her window from across the street, Strings went right up to her door and knocked. I felt a chill. Ms. Mimi opened the door looking radiant in a white satin gown with her hair pulled up in a fountain of platinum curls. She was beautiful. She welcomed Strings in with a smile and it wasn't clear to me if he had charmed her or if she truly consented. I was afraid for her. I had paid her visits before because she gave excellent belly rubs and I knew how to sneak in through a window she left cracked. Sure enough, the window was still cracked open and in I went silent as a ninja. Ms. Mimi didn't concern herself too much with security since she was handy with her pistol. I padded through the kitchen as quietly as I could, but my long nails made noise and I froze in the hallway to watch them in her parlor. They stared silently at each other. Ms. Mimi gave Strings a half smile and pulled the bow behind her neck, sending her satin dress down her torso like water. She was obviously good at this and she was definitely into Strings. He took in her naked breasts hungrily with his eyes for a moment, then in a blur he was on her. I felt ashamed for watching. Ms. Mimi moaned as Strings covered her with gentle kisses and stroked her with his long musician fingers. I tried to back away toward the door. Suddenly, Strings looked up. Damn nails on the tile floor. I ducked into a broom closet, trapped.

"What was that?" Strings said.

"What was what?" Mimi asked. "Don't get distracted on my last fuck as a mortal woman." Strings laughed and dove back into lovemaking. I curled in the corner and hid my face. I just couldn't watch. They both made all sorts of noises, like animals. But I'd say even dogs are more dignified. It seemed forever until it was silent again. Then Mimi let out a piercing cry that made me peek out to see if she was okay. She lay back in Strings arms while his fangs were inserted firmly in her neck. She smiled at him, totally compliant in this transformative experience, before she went limp. I watched him wrap her in a cloak and carry her away. Given the process, I knew he'd have to watch over her for a rough couple of days. I cleared out of there as fast as I could, feeling empty and remembering my hunger.

CHAPTER FORTY-EIGHT:

Getting Somewhere

M aggie watched Chad as he tapped away at his laptop. "More pieces are starting to fit," she said.

"Indeed," he replied, half distracted as he wrote an email. It was twilight and they would have a bite to eat together before it was time to get Chulie up, as soon as he finished correspondence with his followers. He'd been so wrapped up in the drama surrounding Chulie that he'd been neglecting his duties as the Bloodlust blogger like answering DMs and emails. He couldn't take a chance at having his followers lose interest, this was his bread and butter after all, and there were many wannabees nipping at his heels—Queen Vampira, Love Bytes, and Ren Field Notes to name a few. If his followers were to decrease, so would his sponsors. Chad wasn't rolling in riches, but as a content creator he made enough to stay comfortable and enjoyed being a minor local celebrity. He once got chosen to help grease the poles on Bourbon Street before Mardi Gras, a ritual to prevent revelers from climbing the poles onto the balconies. The city selected local notables to do the deed every year. It was every bit as raunchy as you would imagine pole greasing might be.

As he scrolled through his inbox he came across a message from Fiona Broussard, Impaler leader, Lucy's mother and partner in vampire hatred with Sister Eloise. It had arrived a few days ago. He kicked himself for missing this.

"Looks like our activities have landed on the radar of the reclusive Fiona," Chad told Maggie. "I didn't think anything could penetrate that force field. Aside from Victor's funeral, no one in that family has made a public appearance in ages. Not even when they closed the case."

Maggie jumped to his side to read the screen with him.

"Dear Chad, We've learned that you have been continuing the inquiry into the disappearance of my daughter, Lucy. I am writing to save you the trouble of pursuing it further. All efforts to find her have been exhausted and we have come to terms with not having Lucy in our lives. Through strong religious support, we have found peace.

It is true, dark forces may have been at play. But we ask that you honor our wishes to let it rest. We prefer not to focus on the darker, inhuman elements that exist in our world.

Please cease and desist any further pursuit of this investigation into Lucy. The case has officially been closed. Failure to heed this request will result in legal action. Please respect our privacy and the memory of Lucy. The Lucy we knew no longer exists.

Sincerely, Fiona Broussard."

"Whoa, we must have hit a nerve," Maggie voiced what they were both thinking.

"What do you make of it?" Chad said as they studied the words together.

"I find this part odd...*we prefer not to focus on the darker, inhuman elements...*" Maggie said.

"Fiona and Sister Eloise the vampire killers, together with The Impalers. Who knows what they are capable of next?"

"Chilling." Maggie shook herself at the thought.

"Do you think vampires are evil?" Maggie asked Chad.

"I think evil exists in both humans and vampires. Maybe it doesn't have anything to do with mortality." They both mulled that over. They'd seen a lot of vampire and human aggression lately and it was beyond unsettling.

"Did you notice how she said 'Let IT rest?' Not let HER rest. Odd," Chad said, getting back to the note from Fiona.

"I wonder what prompted this. The desk at the antique shop, maybe?"

"Maybe when Sister Eloise was killed?"

"Maybe Sister Eloise told her about our conversations? Or maybe she follows your blog, too?"

"I've been careful about not including too much about Chulie. I've never mentioned Chulie staying with us."

"Thank goodness. She probably considers Chulie a darker, inhuman element that needs eliminating," Maggie said.

Maggie moved to the stove, stirring some tomato soup and flipping a couple of grilled cheese sandwiches in a pan until they were golden brown. She ladled the soup into two mugs and positioned the triangles of gooey grilled cheese onto two small plates that she set on the table. The deep red soup made Chad think for a moment of blood, and the vampires who existed amongst them. Ever since the vampire ordinance went into effect after Katrina, there had been an uneasy coexistence.

"What would you think if we were to take a trip out to the Broussard hot sauce plant and see if we can call upon Fiona, too?" Chad suggested. "It's only a few hours' drive."

"I'd be willing. I'm just not sure if we'd find anything," Maggie replied. "The modern factory is run mainly by robots and the family is said not to live on the grounds. Who knows where they could be."

"Wait, weren't there some letters that we dug out of the dumpster that you took pictures of?" Chad said.

Maggie started scrolling through the photos on her phone. "None have a return address, just the Broussard Hot Sauce logo."

"But look at the postmarks, Maggie."

"Ah, we have letters mailed from New Orleans, New Orleans, New Orleans … oh wait, here's one from Abbeville, LA, 70510."

"That's where the factory is located."

"I'll pull it up on a map." Maggie was getting into her sleuth mode. Chad loved her when she got like that. He could feel her energy. It struck him how deeply he loved her. Childhood playmate. Best friend. Co-conspirator. Lover. He was crazy about her. So why didn't he make it official already like she wanted? Maybe it was time. But first, they had a mystery to solve.

"Just shy of a three hours' drive says my map app," Maggie stated.

"Abbeville is deep in the heart of Cajun country," Chad added. "The Broussard hot sauce factory has been located there since they expanded in the eighties. Just a few years before Lucy went M.I.A."

"Road trip?" Maggie bestowed her big, beautiful smile upon him.

CHAPTER FORTY-NINE:
Emotional Gumbo

I had settled back in at Chad and Maggie's once I was feeling well enough. Ms. Mimi now a vampire, psycho Sister Eloise, near-death experience—it was all a bit much and I craved some normalcy. It was Maggie who opened my sleep compartment my first night back. She smelled like tomato soup. As soon as she set me down on the floor, I stretched my body out in a downward facing dog pose. Then I took a few steps and shook my whole body; I felt ready for action as I scampered at Maggie's heels. I was picking up on an excited vibe from her; she had a certain spring in her step. I anticipated a mind meld would need to happen before I went out to feed. I knew Strings wouldn't have my back since he had bigger, curvier fish to fry. To steer clear of The Impalers and The Darkness, I'd feed close by the apartment and come back for the company of Maggie and Chad.

"Hey, there Chulie dog! Who's a good boy?" Chad greeted me when we got upstairs. Okay, I'll admit, I didn't mind that. It stirred memories of being a mortal dog.

"We've got a lot to catch up on, Chulie."

Now you're talking. The three of us settled in on the couch, me between Maggie and Chad. I decided to start with Chad. I stared intensely into Chad's face. He was unable to look away. The mind meld joined us like an electric current. I sent him the image of what I saw through the opened closet door—Strings biting Ms. Mimi and carrying her away. I wasn't sure I was okay with that and Chad gently stroked my back. Then, I mustered up the strength to share more of Sister Eloise's ranting confession. The gunshot. The graffiti. The vampire murder club. I saved the biggest revelation for last. I projected Sister Eloise's bizarre proclamation that I was already dying when I was turned.

We paused at that point. Chad took a deep breath before filling Maggie in on all that craziness.

Then, I cleared my mind screen and dove into Chad's. I saw the antique store and Chad and Maggie digging through a dumpster. I wished I could have smelled that. Chad's mind was fixated on some business charts from the hot sauce business, neither of which I could read. But I could read his reaction to both. The hot sauce business had a big spike after a big investor stepped in, presumably vampire Bruce. And the other paper was from the veterinarian's office saying that I had a terminal kidney disease. They knew about my illness, too. I was turned vampire as an act of love, to save me from death.

Chad also shared that he was sending the new discoveries to his retired police officer friend in the hopes of reopening Lucy's case.

I wondered how much time I'd had left as a mortal dog when Adam the vampire came into our room that fated night. Maybe Lucy and Adam had planned this together. I started to tremble and Maggie put her arms around me. This was all so much to consider.

If that was the case, why did Lucy abandon me after that? Why wouldn't she have stuck around for her little vampire dog? Unless somehow she couldn't. I couldn't let my mind go to the place that said Lucy had ended that night, the same night that Adam was staked and her bloody dress had turned up. I could not accept that.

Maggie walked over to the turntable and announced that she was playing Alex McMurray's record, "Here at The End of the World." The imploring lyrics felt strangely appropriate. Then Maggie took me in her lap and I looked up at her, locking our gazes. I was ready for more. I needed to know. Her mind was fixed on maps and a destination. They were planning a road trip to a place called Abbeville. It was connected to my mortal family and the hot sauce business … and Fiona. I didn't have much use for Lucy's mom. But I could tell Chad and Maggie thought this was important.

We would leave in a few days after Chad was done with some appearance he had committed to. Halloween was just a few weeks away after all, prime vampire season. Spare me if I were to see one more pair of plastic fangs in the gutter on All Saint's Day. I put my head down on my paws and closed my eyes. We were officially caught up and I needed to ponder this new information. I was fine leaving town for a short trip, having no desire to bump into Strings at the new nest right now. I'd get word to Glory somehow so she didn't worry. But I had a feeling she wouldn't give it a thought anyway. She was likely preoccupied, too. The idea of being off the grid for a few days was appealing after all that we had endured recently. I let myself sink into the music, smells and sounds of Chad's apartment. Dinner could wait a bit.

CHAPTER FIFTY:

Vampire Sensitivity Training

*B*loodlust, *a Blog for Vampire Enthusiasts – September 30, 2023*
By Chad Russo

Dear Readers,

If you are interested in bonding in-person over vampire culture, I will be making an appearance at Vampire Fest this coming week at the Convention Center. Streaming options are also available. I'll be speaking about the History of the Vampire in New Orleans. After looking at the roster, there are several topics being discussed that may be of interest to you. Here are the ones I've highlighted:

- *Vampire Sensitivity Training for Law Enforcement*
- *Mental Health Resources for the Undead*
- *Know Your Rights: Hiring Accommodations for Vampires*

Those topics seem especially timely in light of what happened in Aribi recently. Aribi residents, the Morgan family, go all out with their Halloween decorations every year and this year was no different. As early as Labor Day, they had skeletons crawling over their roof, ghosts hanging from the trees and witches dancing around a cauldron on their patio. Most prominently near their front door stood a coffin that would open to reveal a mechanical vampire who would open his cape, a vampire in the most cliché attire, high collared black cloak and slick-backed black hair with pronounced widow's peak. Most vampires would have found it rather campy but harmless.

But not poor Evan, a fairly young vampire at 80-years. Unfortunately, Evan suffered from a deep form of vampire depression. His friends report he was in despair at the notion that his eternal existence would be based on draining blood from mortal beings. Just before dawn he ransacked the Morgan family's outdoor display and carried the mechanical vampire away screaming, "Free My Soul." He made it as far as a nearby schoolyard before the sun came up and the authorities arrived. Although, they did not arrive soon enough to save the troubled vampire Evan. Luckily, it was too early for the school children to have arrived, otherwise they'd have seen the smoking, charred remains of a real vampire with a melting plastic vampire on top. Rest in the final death, Evan.

So my fellow fang fans, please remember – vampires are people, too. Please like, follow and share. @Chadrusso #bloodlust

CHAPTER FIFTY-ONE:
Road Trip Slip

I was back in the sousaphone case and we were on the road. I could hear birds, so I thought it best to sleep until nightfall. But my mind was racing. My Lucy wanted me to live forever. But why didn't she stay with me? I pictured Lucy, a middle-aged woman by now. Not the teenager with the honey-colored hair and fashions from the 1980s who I remembered. Although, funny enough, she would be vintage chic if she had the same wardrobe today.

I was also thinking about her other family members. Her father, who was a serious businessman, ambitious and tightly wound. Her mother, who was content in her husband's shadow and fiercely religious. Who knew Fiona could be the biggest villain in all of this?

Of course I didn't have these insights when I was a mortal pet, living in their home and lapping up attention and kibble. This was a retrospective of impressions that now had more meaning. A series of other people's thoughts viewed and turned over in my own mind to inform what I knew now. The intelligence I've gained through decades of mind melds was a mixed blessing. I understood the human condition, in all its wonder and complexity, better than I ever wanted to. A rift between Lucy's parents had been there a long time—a conflict about vampires. The late Victor Broussard was in cahoots with Bruce, father of my maker Adam. Meanwhile, Fiona and Sister Eloise harbored a hatred for vampires to the point of genocide, or vampocide. When I thought about how close I had come to the final death, it made my whole body tremble.

I must have drifted into a dream, where I was having a conversation with Adam. It seemed so real I wondered if he somehow entered my mind again. He was telling me that he had left this plane of existence long ago. In my dream, I was begging him to tell me where she was now.

It was several hours later when the sousaphone case opened in a dimly lit motel room. Through a gap in the curtains, I saw the neon hotel sign and heard Maggie say, "Welcome to the Huckleberry Inn." Maggie and Chad were there, seated on the bed and a guest chair as they watched me stretch my limbs and shake off the sleep. I'd wished they'd left me to the dream so I could learn more from my maker, even if it was only a dream. Maybe it was just pieced together from information in my subconscious that I haven't processed yet.

"We're in Cajun Country, Chulie," Maggie said sweetly. I tilted my head at her to let her know I understood.

"Ready for some hot sauce sleuthing?"

It didn't take long for the three of us to gather ourselves and get back in the car. But this time I was in the backseat on a pile of towels we snagged from a housekeeper's cart. The sky was inky black with a sliver of a moon that looked like a human nail clipping flung into the sky. The sparse moonlight left the bayou in shadows. It didn't take more than fifteen minutes before it looked like we were in the middle of nowhere. Then fifteen minutes more, and the hot sauce factory loomed out of the swampy abyss like the castle in the Emerald City. This was the modern, working hot sauce factory according to Chad and Maggie's conversation. The Broussard residential estate wouldn't be far from here. We'd start with the factory. Operations would probably be at a minimum in the middle of the night, Chad and Maggie guessed. It appeared a few lights were on for a small crew to watch over the twenty-four hour hot sauce makings. Chad had read up on it and was explaining that the pepper mash was aged in barrels and then went to the mixing room where it would be transformed into hot sauce.

"Well aren't you the hot sauce expert," Maggie teased him.

We drove into the visitor parking lot slowly with our headlights out. We parked the car in a dark back corner under an oak tree. The plan was, we'd peek in some windows and try to sneak into the office to see if there was any useful information about business dealings with vampire Bruce or any information about the whereabouts of Fiona. If Chad and Maggie were unable to get in, I could potentially slip in and use my speed to go undetected. Whatever I observed, I could share with Chad and Maggie in a mind meld. It was all a bit Scooby-Doo, that vapid cartoon my Lucy used to watch, but I'd go along with it if it gave us some clues.

After watching the building and seeing a few people walk past the windows, we decided it would be too risky for all of us to poke around, so I was on. Chad turned off the dome light so it wouldn't light up when he opened the car door. I slipped out and was at the side of the building in an instant, which looked like a big country estate with a massive barn behind it that was actually the hot sauce processing and bottling facility. I positioned myself behind a shrub at the employee's entrance, letting my brownish-blackish fur blend into the shadows. There I waited, my eyes never veering from that door. In about ten minutes, I was rewarded for my efforts as someone burst out of the door and over to the side for a smoke. The door took only a moment to close, but it was enough time for me to slip in.

I was in a fully lit hallway and felt terribly exposed. I heard voices down the hall coming from an open door, either an office or a break room perhaps. I searched desperately for a hiding spot before the smoker returned, but the hallway was bare. I zoomed past the open door hoping I was fast enough to go undetected. My nails made a swoosh noise on the polished tile floor.

"What was that?" a voice from the room asked.

"Sam went out for a smoke," replied another.

I heard the outside door open again and Sam trudged down the hallway with heavy footsteps, leaving a smoky odor in the air that made my nose tingle. I pressed myself up against the wall just behind the open door to the room where the men were talking. My heart pounded. Why had I agreed to this ridiculous plan? Through a crack near the hinges of the door, I saw that the men were in an office/break room with a desk, filing cabinets and a large sitting area with table and chairs and a small kitchenette. One man sat at the table. The other had his back to me. Parts of the room were out of my view as I peered through the opening between the door and the wall. I saw the man turn when Sam came back into the room. The third person present was Bruce the vampire. What on Earth was he doing here? The guy who went for a smoke, the one they called Sam, addressed him.

"Bruce, what's eating you?" Sam asked. Funny question to ask a vampire, I thought.

Bruce replied, "I followed the humans out here, the ones who have been digging into Lucy's disappearance. I think they know who killed Adam. I'm not so sure anymore if it was the bitch hot sauce princess."

I held back a growl at hearing Bruce talk about Lucy that way.

Bruce continued, "I need the scoop they got from that rogue nun who nearly killed the vampdog."

"Do you think they know about our side operation here? Fiona would have a conniption fit if she knew what her husband was up to all these years. Especially your involvement."

"Fiona is a force I don't want to tangle with," Bruce confided. "That's why I steer clear of her."

"For real," the other man said. "She'd stake you in a heartbeat."

The three laughed as if this were impossible. *Guess again, boys,* I thought.

"Well, we better not let her know about my involvement in Sanguine Sauce, then, shall we?" Bruce said. "I don't think she'd take kindly to hot sauce for vampires being made at her own factory."

Sanguine Sauce for vampires? Now that sounds awesome, I thought.

I wondered how this had anything to do with Lucy's disappearance. I had been hoping Bruce knew the answers, but he had been following *us* to find out. At least he no longer thought Lucy killed Adam.

The lingering smell of Sam's cigarette started to tickle my nose again and before I could help it, I sneezed. Damn. The two men and Bruce ran to the doorway to see where the sneeze had come from.

Before I could make a run for it, I felt a frigid bolt through my entire body.

"Well, if it isn't Chulie the vampdog. After all this time trying to capture you, you've come to us." Bruce was as delighted as a devil could be. His long icy fingers surrounded me.

CHAPTER FIFTY-TWO:

In A Hot Mess

C hulie had been inside the Broussard's hot sauce plant for some time now and Chad and Maggie were getting antsy.

"I don't like this," Maggie said, her eyes shining through the dark interior of their car. "We need to do something."

"How long do you think it's been? What if we give it five …"

A piercing howl cut Chad off and he and Maggie locked wide eyes for a second before they jumped out of the car. That was unmistakably Chulie and neither of them could stand the thought of that little dog in pain, even if he was a bloodthirsty vampire dog.

They were still concealed at the edge of the parking lot, but it would surely not be long before Chulie's tormentors would wonder if he came with anyone else.

"I think we can make it to that clump of hedges near the restaurant. Maybe we can look in the windows?" Maggie suggested.

They hadn't planned on getting caught. With Chulie's skills that wasn't supposed to happen.

"I think we should call Strings for help."

Chad pulled out his cell phone. He had just typed SOS and their coordinates to Strings when a voice boomed from the building.

"Hey, who's out there?"

"Damn, they saw the glow of my phone screen," Chad whispered. He hit send and shoved the phone into his pocket. He and Maggie slipped away from the car as silently as humanly possible and ran into a thick grove of oak, sycamore and cottonwood trees with a smell so green, inhaling it could count for eating one's vegetables. It wasn't until they were behind a giant oak that they dared look back. There in the glow of the security light were two brutish men and one vampire Bruce holding Chulie. "Shit! I didn't anticipate facing off with a vampire," Chad said quietly.

The vampire pointed, and the men rushed toward their car. Chad was sure Bruce could hear their heartbeats. One felt the hood to see if it was still warm. They both scanned the grove where Chad and Maggie were hiding. At that perilous moment, Maggie did something brilliant. She picked up a rock and catapulted it far away from them. The thugs heard the noise and ran toward it as they hurried in the opposite direction.

This gave them the opening they needed to get out of there until Strings showed up. At least they thought it was, until Chad's boot caught on a root and he did a face plant in a bed of leaves. He tried to roll behind a tree and Maggie ducked behind another tree but their pursuers heard the commotion and quickly shifted focus in their direction.

"Trespassers!" one guy shouted. The two factory thugs caught up to them in mere moments.

"Not much of a vampdog posse. Just a couple of dorks." One guy laughed. Bruce was at their side in an instant, still holding Chulie.

The factory workers grabbed hold of Chad and Maggie as they tried unsuccessfully to wrestle free. One beefy dude had Chad in a chokehold and the other zip-tied his wrists. Meanwhile, Bruce had entranced Maggie. She stood perfectly still and stared at his face.

"Thanks for buying us dinner and sending us a clue," Maggie said in a robotic voice.

Bruce chuckled. "You were supposed to lead me to Lucy … or my son's killer."

Bruce directed his focus to the workers, "Take it easy on them, we just need to have a conversation." Then back to Maggie and Chad, "I have no ill intentions toward you. I am trying to solve the same mystery for different purposes."

They escorted Chad and Maggie into the building and shoved them into the employee break room.

"What do you think you're going to learn snooping around here?" Bruce demanded.

"Wouldn't you like to know!" Maggie spat out defiantly. The glamor had worn off. Chad didn't feel as bold as Maggie sounded. Maybe Bruce wasn't all that bad but he still terrified him. He'd still have Chad and Maggie for dinner if he had the urge. That was the way of The Darkness. He had dated Ms. Mimi back in the day. Small world. He tried to save a dog from the dog fight. The guy had many facets. Mostly he was a father who had lost a son, looking for justice. Maybe that was the angle to go for.

"You're looking for your son's killer, am I right? What if I told you Sister Eloise confessed to being involved." Chad offered. "It's true."

That really had Bruce's attention.

"Adam was a great person. He made me a better person and convinced me to have more compassion for humans. He didn't deserve the true death. I gave you that photo of Lucy's bloody dress at the restaurant. I've always thought she'd killed him because of that photo I found of her bloody debutante gown. I thought maybe she was mad about her dog."

"What was your business with Victor Broussard and the sauce hot?" Chad asked, his words getting a little jumbled. The stress made his blood sugar drop and he was feeling shaky. *When was the last time I ate?* he thought. He felt confused and clammy. He could pass out from hypoglycemia if his glucose level got too low. He needed his glucose tablets or some juice fast. This was bad timing.

Bruce looked at him and cocked his head to the side. Maggie noticed Chad's distress. "He's diabetic, he needs his medicine or some juice or you'll have a comatose captive on your hands!"

Bruce nodded at the two goons, and they came over to look at Chad. His vision blurred them together. *Oh god, please don't let me pass out!* Chad thought. What would become of Chulie and Maggie? His fuzzy brain wasn't taking into account that he could be in mortal danger here.

"Get some juice from that fridge and give him a sip!" Maggie insisted.

The two obliged. Chad soon felt sweet orange juice on his tongue and swallowed, while some ran down his chin. He took another gulp and started feeling a little better almost immediately. He'd have to get something to eat soon.

In the distraction caused by Chad's episode, no one was watching the entrance.

There was a loud crash. Strings, Mimi and Glory burst in like a hurricane.

"Remember me, Bruce? I've moved on," said Mimi. She wasn't full strength yet, being newly transitioned, but already exhibited the makings of a formidable vampire.

Chulie bit Bruce's hand and took a quick drink. But Bruce hardly reacted; when he saw the fury of Glory and Strings, he dropped Chulie. Glory held Bruce from running. Strings had the two factory workers pinned to a couple chairs. Mimi picked up Chulie who began furiously licking her hand.

"It's time we all had a good chat," Strings insisted.

"The dog and these two idiots were snooping around private property," said one of the factory workers.

"And what were you afraid we might find? What's going on here with Bruce?" Chad inquired with newfound bravado.

Chulie let out a bark from where he sat, now in Mimi's lap.

"And why are you all so bent on capturing the vampdog?" Maggie added.

"He's the key to everything, of course," Bruce said. "He was present at my son's murder."

"How does that relate to your business project with Victor Broussard?" Chad asked, trying to connect the dots.

Bruce sighed and raised his hands before he spoke. Glory had released him and the thugs had undone the restraints on Chad and Maggie. They all sat around the room, focused on Bruce.

"I might as well tell you now," Bruce started, "Ironically, my partnership with Victor Broussard was how Adam and Lucy met. We were guests in the Broussard home many times. Adam and Lucy were smitten at first sight. Victor and I chalked it up to typical teenage behavior that would run its course. But Fiona, she hated vampires with a passion. She was furious. I invested in a side project with Victor. We kept it hidden from Fiona and still do, even after his death. Together, Victor and I had developed a synthetic version of human blood for vampires and had bottled it up in hot sauce bottles. We called it Sanguine Sauce. Imagine the implications of having a way to feed without tapping into a human. Adam and Lucy knew about it and were all for it. They were progressive in their views about peace between humans and vampires."

No one interrupted Bruce's story.

"It sold like crazy on the black market and still does on the Dark Web. It gave Broussard Hot Sauce a surge in revenue. We were going to make it a mainstream product. But after Lucy disappeared and Adam was killed, Victor and I decided to keep it only a black market offering. We could never tell Fiona; her vampire hatred had reached a fever pitch when she lost her daughter. I still provide support anonymously in the background and it's still very profitable."

He saw the quizzical look on Chad's face and added, "Most people have it wrong about The Darkness. We aren't out to get humans. We just don't believe in denying a vampire's true nature. And sometimes that nature requires us to kill humans."

Strings got up and stepped in front of Chad and Maggie defensively.

Oh boy, thought Chad, *this could end up in a fiery debate amongst vampires.* But to his surprise, Strings changed the subject.

"This is all well and good, and I will be stocking up on Sanguine Sauce on my way out for troubling me to come out here. But how does this all connect to what happened to Lucy?"

The room went silent. But the factory workers Sam and Jake fidgeted uneasily.

"The two goons know something. They are hiding it," Mimi said. Bruce nodded.

"I can get the truth out," Strings said and began glamoring the lesser thug.

"Close your eyes, Jake! He's going to charm you like a snake!" warned Sam. But it was too late.

"Tell me what happened to Lucy."

"From what I've been told, she wanted to run off with Adam and her dog, to get away from her family. Fiona discovered their plan and had Adam staked. Lucy disappeared. Everyone wanted to find Lucy, but that could never happen …"

Chad could almost feel what Chulie must be thinking so he blurted it out, "Could never happen why? Did they kill Lucy, too?"

"It's almost certain. That's the rumor that circulated here at the factory."

Strings released him from the trance.

"Interesting," was all Bruce said. "Why have you never told me this before? Why did it take a vampire blogger to bring out the truth?" he boomed in the thug's face. The thug wet himself in terror. "We were afraid of what you'd do to Fiona and she still signs our paychecks."

"I will take care of you one night when you least expect it. Both of you, get out, you're fired!" Bruce yelled.

It didn't matter if he had the authority to fire them or not. Sam and Jake ran out the door and disappeared.

Chulie let out a long, plaintive howl. The sound held decades of longing and hurt. Chad and Maggie felt the pain of Lucy's death. It was the conclusion none of them wanted to believe. They all put their hands on Chulie.

"They'll probably call the cops," Chad said after a few moments.

"I don't think so, at least not for a while." Mimi held up their two cell phones. *Well played,* Chad thought. Being a vampire suited Mimi. It brought out her beauty in an ethereal kind of way, now and for eternity. No more worry about being an aging burlesque performer.

"So, all these dark secrets center on lust for profit and hatred for vampires? What folly," Strings said with disgust.

"I think it's time to visit Fiona Broussard. She needs to answer for what happened to Lucy." Maggie got up and rummaged through the office to find the address to the family estate. They had managed to avoid any digital trail and kept their residence unsearchable online. The things money can do. "Bingo!" Maggie said holding up an invoice addressed to Fiona and Victor Broussard.

Chulie let out another a long low howl that would melt even a vampire's heart.

CHAPTER FIFTY-THREE:

Fiona

I felt like someone had ripped my heart out. I just couldn't believe my Lucy had been killed by vampire haters and her own mother. It explained why she hadn't come looking for me—her death was the only explanation.

The idea that Lucy might be hiding seemed impossible now. If she was, though, she wouldn't have to worry about Bruce being after her now that they all knew the truth about Fiona and Sister Eloise. What if she'd been hiding at the Broussard's estate? That was probably my denial talking. I sank into the painful reality again. We'd all heard what the factory worker said. Rumor had it she was dead.

There were times, sometimes only in my dreams, that I had a sense of my Lucy, her energy. I felt like my entire body was paralyzed with the weight of it. Maggie stroked my back and tried to comfort me. But I could barely feel it. I guess in a small way I should be glad Lucy didn't give up on me or abandon me on purpose. Lucy loved me. I always kept a glimmer of hope that we would one day be together again. Without that, I wasn't sure how I'd go on. What would be the point of hunting and eating? I've heard vampires can starve to death and right now that sounded preferable to the way I was feeling.

Maggie and Chad had decided we'd go to Broussard manor straightaway. I hardly saw the point. I felt like my head was made of lead and could hardly lift it.

Strings, Mimi and Glory went on their way in Strings' red Mustang. We could hear the tires squeal in the distance. Chad and Maggie had me back in their Prius. No need for the tuba case yet, still several hours to dawn. I rode on Maggie's lap like a bag of bones, the life totally sucked out of me. I felt numb. We were pretty certain Bruce was following us.

"I'm worried about Chulie's frame of mind," Maggie whispered to Chad. *I can hear you, hello, I'm right here, I thought.* These two. Could I exist with them or without them? Or with my old nest mates in some semblance of a life? I wasn't sure what tomorrow would look like.

Chad and Maggie didn't have much trouble finding the remote Broussard estate with GPS after a few wrong turns. It was concealed from the road by thick trees and foliage, but a mile marker stood at the turn off. We pulled up the long drive lined with gracious oaks hung with curtains of moss. A wave of pain rippled through me at the thought of this family, now decades older… and my Lucy, never having the chance to be the middle-aged woman she should be at this point, but instead buried somewhere. We parked far away from the entrance and semi-circle drive. Before we got out of the car, Chad took out his blood test kit. He pricked his finger and put a drop on the test strip. "105," he proclaimed and Maggie nodded.

Then he pricked another finger and squeezed a big fat glob of blood and presented it to me.

"No biting please, Chulie."

I didn't really want anything to eat as the sadness had a grip on me. But I licked it up with my tongue and refrained from biting. It wasn't much but it did make me feel a little better.

It was the middle of the night and Chad and Maggie thought it best to proceed on foot. We had to park on the other side of an elaborate gate and tried to avoid the security cameras. We were able to slip through some hedges onto the main driveway. As we got closer, we saw the glow of a lamp and flicker of a fireplace in a first-floor room.

Maggie crept up to the window to peer in as Chad and I held back. She returned to tell us that there was just an old woman in the room dozing in a chair. I wondered if that could be Fiona. That would make sense.

"I think it's Fiona," Maggie whispered. *Well I called that one,* I thought. Chad and Maggie debated about the best way to gain entrance. We strolled around the perimeter and did not see anyone else. That's when I noticed a dog door. Chad and Maggie noticed it about thirty seconds after I did, but I was already there. I turned back to give them a quick nod before I plunged inside. I'm not sure what compelled me to do so. It's a dog door. I'm a dog. The burst of energy came from some instinctive place. As I gained entrance, I heard a mortal dog barking from some place in the back of the house. *They did get another dog,* I thought sadly. It had been so long, maybe they'd had a series of replacement dogs.

The foyer was dimly lit but still exuded splendor. A grand chandelier that looked like it may have come from Fischer-Gambino on Royal Street dripped with crystals shaped like fruit. I'd looked in the windows of that shop many times and listened to people coming and going. Even unlit this chandelier was opulent. A curving double staircase was the backdrop with red velvet pads on each step. A doorway on the left led to an ornate sitting room. The doorway on the right to a dining room with a grand table. Despite the grandeur, I noticed a few shabby things like a curl of wallpaper and scuffs on the baseboards, but it somehow added to the charm. Maybe it was a sign that everything wasn't sunshine and roses in the Broussard home.

I made my way to the left toward the room where the old woman sat. I stared at her sleeping in the chair and a flood of memories came back to me. She had a large silver cross hanging around her neck. I remembered how strict she was about Lucy going to church on Sundays. She didn't approve of certain types of music that Lucy would hide in her bedroom. One day, Fiona found them in her room and broke them to pieces after slapping Lucy hard across the face. The memory came flooding back vividly.

I nudged the old woman's hand with my nose to gently awaken her. She stirred and sat up, groggy. She gasped when she saw me.

"Where did you come from little one? You look exactly like our old pup, Chulie."

I barked softly to ingratiate myself. She smiled at me. She looked up and something gave her a fright. It was Chad and Maggie waving at the window. She jumped up and almost stepped on me. I ran toward the front door, wagging my tail to show I wasn't alarmed by these people, and she followed me. There was a soft knock on the door. The old woman opened it a crack.

Chad spoke first, "We're so sorry to intrude but it seems our dog let himself into your home."

"Oh, yes indeed. This dog looks like a pet we once had. Pekinese, poodle terrier mix, wonderful dogs. Although this one could use a grooming," she admonished. "Well come in." Maybe her eyesight was weak enough she didn't notice my red-rimmed eyes. I was glad she somehow didn't recognize Chad and Maggie, even though she had tried to warn them off the investigation. She didn't seem worried in the least to welcome strangers into her home.

Chad and Maggie entered respectfully and gave me some pets and head scratches. I didn't mind and understood the ruse.

"Oh, you rascal," Chad said to me.

She led us into the study and invited us all to sit. She confided that she welcomed the company since the whole household was off on a hunting trip. It occurred to me that's not something she should share with strangers. She must be referring to Lucy's brothers. I had forgotten them. The heirs to the hot sauce fortune.

"Dogs like this are a special breed, I'd love to hear about yours," Maggie probed.

"He belonged to my daughter." My heart leapt.

"Your daughter? Is she grown now with a family of her own?"

The old woman's face clouded over. She was silent for a while.

"No she is not," was all she said and she started to look distracted. Her reaction said it all, my worst fears. She went to a small table, opened a drawer and pulled out a small, laminated prayer card. She handed it to Maggie. Maggie gasped when she read the card.

"I'm so sorry," she said.

"We kept it quiet. My husband didn't acknowledge the funeral. He wanted to believe she was still alive. But you know all this, don't you," Fiona accused.

Oh no. Fiona was on to us. I had to distract her and get into her mind. I jumped up on her lap and stared into her face. Chad and Maggie knew exactly what I was doing, and soon I had Fiona entranced. Diving into her mind felt like going down a well, with decades and decades of information. Through her point-of-view, I saw my Lucy as a little girl being presented with a puppy. It was me as a baby! It was Christmas. Then I saw Lucy as an older girl, running with me in the yard. It was pure joy. Then the mood darkened as the father was sharing some bad news about my health with Fiona and Lucy. They both cried.

Her mind screen turned tumultuous as she was having a fierce argument with Victor. She was screaming, "You made a deal with the devil, and now what has become of our daughter?! Destroy them! She must be cured of this evil."

Fiona was indeed the instigator of the dark deeds that happened the night Lucy disappeared, or rather was killed.

The scene in Fiona's mind shifted to a gorgeous graveyard with lush trees and flowers and rows of white crypts topped with angels, crosses and other religious icons. *Oh god,* I thought. *My Lucy. My Lucy. What did they do to you?* I held firm to the mind meld. Time rolled forward on the scene until the white crypts glowed in the moonlight. Fiona's perspective was walking toward a crypt with the statue of a young woman angel on top, holding a dog. There were two of the scary Impaler priests in red and black cloaks guarding the entrance to the crypt. The woman handed one priest a transfusion bag of blood. They slid back a heavy stone just wide enough to slip the blood bag inside. A hand with long, slender fingers and long nails reached out to grab the bag. The priest immediately closed the stone door. He nodded at the person who brought the bag, presumably Fiona. Then the scene disappeared and all I saw was the prayer card Fiona handed to Maggie. It had a photo of my mistress Lucy as a teenager. It had a birth date and a death date.

My mind was reeling. Maybe they weren't guarding against something getting in, but rather something getting out. I broke the mind meld connection and the old woman was dozing off again. I thought about having a long slow drink of her but was bursting with what I just saw. We had to get out of here. We had to find that crypt. I bolted to the foyer and out the doggy door. Chad and Maggie hurried after me, not disturbing the sleeping old woman. She was Fiona, the matriarch of the Broussard household and vampire murderer. She was dangerous, but in sleep she looked like a sad old woman.

As Chad and Maggie stepped out of the front door, I heard a shout from the side yard.

"Hey! Who goes there? Stop you intruders!" A gunshot ripped through the night and Chad and Maggie were on the run toward the car. Oh no, for the second time today we were about to get caught in a place we weren't supposed to be. Not on my watch I decided. I lunged in the direction of the groundskeeper holding the rifle. He pointed the rifle in my direction.

"I'll take you out, you little varmint!"

Charming fellow. I zig zagged faster than his eye could see and his shots bounced off the ground.

"Chulie!" I heard Maggie scream. Her scream distracted the groundskeeper long enough for me to get my jaws around his ankle. He screamed and I took a long draw. I hadn't realized how ravished I was. As the big man passed out, I left him. I chanced a glanced back at the house, and there stood Fiona in the doorway.

"Chulie!" she shrieked, finally realizing I was indeed the one and only vampdog.

CHAPTER FIFTY-FOUR:

Crypt Search

Maggie and Chad made it back to the car and Chulie jumped in a moment later. They floored it to put some needed distance between themselves and the toxic Broussard estate. Chulie was vibrating in anticipation of sharing his latest mind meld images. Chad had a feeling the mind meld with Fiona would give them a major breakthrough in the mystery of Lucy's disappearance.

A look at the dashboard told Chad they needed to refuel and the rumble in his stomach told him he needed a refill too. He really should pay better attention to eating regularly after cutting it so close with his blood sugar levels in all the excitement. They pulled into a 24/7 gas station. While Chad refueled the Prius, Maggie ran in to get Vitamin water, almonds, cheese sticks, dried apricots and Swedish fish. Not the peak of nutrition but it would have to do. Chulie had his fill earlier with the groundskeeper at the Broussard estate.

They chose a parking space at the edge of the gas station lot. Chad felt more like himself after a few bites and was ready to engage. Maggie was still holding the funeral prayer card Fiona gave her for Lucy Broussard 1970 – 1987. She turned the card over and over in her hands. Fiona wanted people to know Lucy was dead, but her husband refused to believe it. But why? The back had a prayer that Maggie read aloud:

"Oh reaper great and dark and pure, I beg you to hear my plea, as all my life's work falls before me. Oh angel of death, so dark and clear, I pray to thee as my end draws near. A prayer for death, so black and cold, like all things lying upon this road, death is the release to life so cruel and so I pray that my soul be transferred safely to land of the dead, where dead is alive and alive is dead. Let me sit under my family tree, as I see my own branch crack and bear witness to my own destruction, let my soul be at peace here at the roots, as I find there is now nothing that I lack."

What a strange and dark prayer, they thought. Why would Fiona have had prayer cards made if the police were still treating it as a missing person's case? Did she know something the authorities didn't? Everything was pointing toward the likelihood that Lucy had been killed. How could Fiona deceive everyone this way? Was there a secret funeral? Something wasn't adding up.

Chad took Chulie on his lap and stared into the red-rimmed blackness of his eyes. He felt a sense of his animal innocence as well as the heavy burden of eternal wisdom. The images from Fiona flooded in. There was Chulie as a puppy with Lucy in a sunny yard, the screaming argument between Lucy's mother and father about making a deal with vampire Bruce, a torrent of religious imagery, and ultimately the crypts and statues in a cemetery, including the statue of a girl angel holding a puppy. But everything went sideways when Chad saw the crypt door guarded by two hulking Impalers.

What on Earth could they be guarding against? Then when Fiona appeared to drop off a bag of blood his mind reeled.

"Chulie, we need to find this cemetery." Chulie couldn't stay still. He bounced to Maggie's lap, paws on the window, his whole body wagging. Chad did his best to describe to Maggie what he saw.

They searched their phones and found dozens of cemeteries in Vermillion Parish where Abbeville was located, let alone hundreds in surrounding parishes. Chad closed his eyes and tried to pull up the images Chulie sent in his mind. But like many images we see in our subconscious, what's real is blended with what we imagine to fill in the empty spaces. He tried to focus on just what he saw. The priests in long cloaks. The surrounding crypts or trees. It was a lush cemetery. Given Fiona Broussard's zealous religious beliefs, he could rule out any that weren't Christian. More specifically it was likely Catholic given the Impaler priests standing guard, which narrowed it down to about five possibilities. In the distance from the crypt, he caught a glimpse of the back of a gothic looking chapel with pointy spires. He remembered touring a more obscure cemetery once with a gothic chapel. If memory served, it had something to do with a German priest in the 1800s and receiving divine protection against yellow fever. There was even a story of a ghost dog there. What was it called? He couldn't remember. It was coming to Chad in fragments.

He googled "cemetery gothic chapel." Voila! St. Roch's Catholic Cemetery came up right away. There were two in New Orleans and a third in Abbeville. No way to confirm it but worth a try. Unless Fiona let the cat out of the bag unintentionally.

"Let's have a closer look at that prayer card," Chad said.

Maggie handed the card to him and Chulie barked once to show his impatience.

"Down here in the copyright it says St. Roch Church Press. I think that could be the one." Chad shared with them the stories he knew about the cemetery and the ghost dog legend.

"St. Roch's," Maggie said, madly typing into her phone. "Yep, there is a New Catholic Cemetery and an Old Catholic Cemetery behind the church that's no longer in use."

"Sounds like a good place to start to me."

"Mapping directions now."

"We won't stop until we find the crypt with the girl and dog statue on top," Chad declared.

Maggie paused, looking at the sky outside the windshield. "Hate to be a buzzkill here, but we may need to wait until tomorrow night. The sky is lightening."

Chad let out an audible sigh. They were all anxious to find the crypt but he agreed.

"Back in the tuba case for you, Chulie. Let's get back to the motel to rest up until tomorrow night."

Chulie obliged.

CHAPTER FIFTY-FIVE:

Relocating

I was surprisingly comfortable in my tuba case and slept like a baby dog vampire. When we first arrived at the motel I could hear Chad and Maggie chatting with the desk attendant.

"Late night gig?" the guy inquired. It made me laugh a little to picture Chad as a tuba player, but that was a fair conclusion since he carried the case. Chad mumbled an affirmation and rushed us inside.

"Don't leave any instruments in your car," the guy warned. Good advice. I know from my time with the Plasma Casters that people steal instruments from cars regularly. Despicable. That of course would be deadly for me tonight.

After my deep sleep, nighttime had arrived once again and I lay awake staring at the inside of the tuba case until someone retrieved me. I pondered the possibilities of the new night. Once we found that crypt, and I had no doubt we would, what would we find inside? Was it vampire Adam who may have killed Lucy? Or dare I hope for a happier ending? Regardless, it had to be a vampire or why else would they deliver blood to the inhabitant. I heard voices outside the closet where I was stashed.

It wasn't long before Maggie's sweet face leaned over the open tuba case, cooing me awake like her child. She pulled me out and set me on the ground for my stretches and a good shake. I began running around in circles.

"There's someone here to visit us," Maggie said.

That's when I noticed good old Beanie, seated in one of our hotel chairs, looking well. I was so relieved and excited I almost forgot my urgency about our cemetery search. Almost. I jumped in Beanie's lap. He smiled and pet me. Chad sat in the other chair munching on fast food french fries. The smell was a bit nauseating.

"I told Strings where we were last night and gave him an update on what we'd learned," Chad informed me. "He sent Beanie to tell you something." I panted and wagged my tail at super speed to show my pleasure. It was truly so good to see this goof doing well.

"Hey there, Chulie boy," Beanie said as he gave a good scratch behind my ears. Heaven.

"The nest is moving once again. This time out of New Orleans. Just for a little while, until things calm down. That last fight with The Impalers took a toll, but I finally feel myself again. We'll be back. And Chad and Maggie have agreed to bring you to us any time you'd like to join up with the nest. We'll be there for you, Chulie boy."

I thought about my nestmates and I thought about Chad and Maggie. There were good things about staying with both.

"It's okay, Chulie," Maggie interjected, "We're ready for a change, too, and Chad and I can work from anywhere. We've been talking about it. We knew this was a possibility. We'll be here for you too, Chulie."

Even without my Lucy, I was starting to realize I still had my people, and my vampires. I could live with that. If being undead is anyone's idea of living. The Impalers were relentless, so we had to run away.

"Of course other cities don't have as liberal of vampire rights, but we can go low profile," Chad added. "Maybe we can return once the rampage against vampires simmers down. With Sister Eloise gone, maybe that'll happen. Plus Fiona won't be around forever."

I thought about Sister Eloise and whined a little. Beanie changed the conversation. He told us they were going to change the name of the band from Plasma Casters to Kin and would wear disguises with elaborate makeup and masks. They had always wanted to go Death Metal. They'd find legit gigs in their new city. Late night sets, naturally.

"This is just for now, Chulie. For your safety and ours. But we will see you again, you can count on it," Beanie reassured. "Glory said to give a belly rub from her." I flipped over and submitted to the pleasure of a belly rub.

"We will figure out our own next chapter, no worries on that Chulie," Maggie said. "We'll stick together."

"Of course we have a cemetery to visit and lots of planning to do first," Chad added.

I wasn't too worried. I'd survived many years without anyone. It was simpler. But I had grown accustomed to having other beings around. Chad and Maggie would do fine for now.

"Don't tell anyone this of course, but the next destination for the band is Memphis," Beanie informed us. "We board the City of New Orleans Amtrak tomorrow night and are hiding with different friends until then so no one follows us. Our coffins have already been loaded onto the cargo car."

It felt like the end of an era. But I've lived through eras before.

CHAPTER FIFTY-SIX:

Patron Saint of Dogs

C had, Maggie and Chulie took their places in the Prius after a long goodbye with Beanie. They tossed the tuba case in the back seat, ready for their next move. No one voiced it, but the heavy silence between them said they were all pondering the same thing—were they about to visit Lucy's final resting place? Maggie filled the dead air by suggesting that they discuss where they might want to go next. It was tough, because there was truly no place like New Orleans. They agreed Memphis, Key West and Miami were all fairly hospitable to vampires. The tourists and party culture in all three places would work, and they could get to all of them by car. They also talked about Jamaica or Cuba, but getting there would be more complicated. On the other end of the spectrum, St. Louis sounded like a place they could disappear to and the city hosted a big annual Mardi Gras parade. Chulie looked back and forth at their faces as they spoke, seeming to understand. The vampire stories Chad reported could come from anywhere these days, but nowhere as plentiful as New Orleans. Then, he thought about the rise of vampire hate in New Orleans, even at the highest levels. Bruce would avenge the murder of his vampire son Adam and The

Darkness would go on, hopefully a bit more enlightened. Humans would always be looking for ways to exploit the vampdog for their own gain. At least the dog fight ring had stopped. For now. The Light seemed committed to promoting peaceful co-existence. Maybe for a while The Light could win. Maybe the Broussard Sanguine Sauce could eventually go mainstream and lessen the need for human blood. Maybe that could help down the road. So many maybes. People and vampires had so much capacity for good and bad. But there was also the popularity of vampdog to contend with. Chad thought about how they could stay off the public radar and shake off the obsession with Chulie wherever they went. He had an idea that he kept to himself for now.

"Half mile ahead we'll take a right on 167, which will turn into Old Kaplan Highway. The church will be on the left with the old cemetery behind it. The new cemetery is further down the road," Maggie guided them with her GPS. They exited on Highway 167 and a landscape of empty fast food restaurants, muffler shops and strip malls melted into pitch black farmland. Chulie was trembling with anticipation in Maggie's lap. Or was it fear? Maggie stroked his back and scratched his ears. His body felt like other dogs she has known but a few degrees cooler.

"Almost there," Maggie said. "You ready for this?"

"Let's go over the plan," Chad said.

"We look for the crypt with the statue of the girl angel and her dog. I distract the guards and Chulie slips in to confirm who or what is inside. Then we get out undetected and call Strings for backup once we know what we are dealing with," Maggie said.

"Right. What could go wrong?" Chad joked. But neither of them laughed. Maggie started yoga breathing to psych herself up.

Maggie's Google search revealed that St. Roch Abbeville's oldest marked grave was Eufemie Broussard from 1852. The Broussard's had several plots in the cemetery. Victor Broussard was recently laid to rest in the newer cemetery down the road beside an empty plot for Fiona.

"Why would they have Lucy buried in the old cemetery and not the new one?" Maggie asked not expecting anyone to answer. She was trying on a wig from one of her disguises and checking herself in the side mirror, tucking in her strands of pink and combing through the gray curls with her dark, blue-polished fingernails. She'd left this one inside the trunk of the car after an audition for a staged version of Golden Girls. The disguise made her look very convincingly like an older woman. It was part of the plan to distract the guards. *Maggie never minded a chance to get into character*, Chad thought affectionately.

When they arrived at St. Roch, they cruised slowly by the gothic church, the wrought iron gate flanked by wingless angels and a sea of white stone crosses topping dozens of crumbling old crypts. As if to say enough of the sightseeing, Chulie started squirming and scratching on a window to be let out of the car.

They tucked their car by some trees at the edge of the lot and ventured out. The ground was spongy yellowish green grass, striped with white pebble walkways. The hum of insects had a cautionary tone and the night air was thick with humidity. If ever there was an atmosphere for supernatural activity, it was here at this cemetery.

Its rows of above-ground crypts stood like soldiers awaiting orders from the Beyond.

"This cemetery is named for St. Roch, the patron saint of dogs," Maggie informed them, as she read from her phone with an incongruent brightness in her voice.

"What about the ghost dog?" Chad asked in a hushed tone as if he might wake somebody up.

"The legendary ghost dog has been spotted many times by locals, a large black dog," Maggie said. Chad considered this. Ghost dog? Vampire dog? Perhaps anything is possible.

They had a lot of ground to cover. They decided Chulie and Chad would take the rows to the right of the chapel and Maggie would take the rows to the left. Maggie and Chad would text each other if either found the crypt.

"Chulie, what will you do if you find the statue of the girl angel and her dog?" Maggie asked.

Chulie responded with a convincing impersonation of an owl. That was the signal they had agreed upon. Turns out he was quite good at bird imitations. It was a skill that came in handy when looking for prey to feed upon.

Off they went. It hardly mattered that Chulie and Chad were paired up as Chulie bolted at his super speed and Chad was left behind to make sure he didn't miss anything. There were a lot of statues of girls, dogs, and girls with dogs as it turned out. But it wasn't more than twenty minutes before Chad's text alert sounded.

"Two big dudes in red and black robes standing guard at a crypt with a statue of a girl angel and her dog on top. Row 37E."

All she really needed to say was "found it," but Chad appreciated the detail. He whistled like a bird and the vampdog was back by his side in an instant. They crept as quietly as they could, Chad looking for the row numbers. Maggie motioned to them from behind a giant willow tree. They joined her to watch the priests undetected. The priests looked bored, stretching, smoking, chatting about the Saints—football players not the holy ones. She hunched over and shuffled toward the crypt while Chulie and Chad watched from behind the tree. She would distract them while Chulie rushed over to see if there was an opening in the crypt that he could squeeze through. Chad would keep watch. That was the plan, anyway.

"Can you please help me find the Stations of the Cross? I seem to have wandered off course," they heard Maggie say.

"What are you doing out here in the middle of the night, dearie?" one priest asked. "Cemeteries are not the safest of places."

They seemed to welcome the distraction from their boredom. They spoke to her and started pointing and hand gesturing directions. When one of the priests moved his arms, Chad could see he was armed. He guessed his gun was loaded with silver bullets like the one that almost finished Glory. Yikes. Maggie kept acting confused so they had to walk her a little way toward the Stations of the Cross. Chulie seized the opportunity and ran toward the crypt in a blur of fur. Chad watched him sniff at the crypt door and around the perimeter.

Then, Chulie crunched through some leaves and the sound cut through the night noises. The priests spun back toward the crypt and one whipped out a flashlight and the other a gun. They both abandoned Maggie despite her protests. The flashlight shown on Chulie, casting a giant, eerie, dog-shaped shadow on the side of the neighboring crypt.

"Ghost dog!" Maggie cried. The priests were startled and looked sufficiently rattled by the canine specter. Chulie came flying out of the shadows and lunged at the priest with the gun. The priest lost his balance and fell flat, while the gun skittered across the ground. Chad ran out to help and started wrestling the priest with the flashlight. Chad heard Maggie scream and turned for a second, giving his priest an open to punch him in the jaw. The priest was flailing hard and taking swings. Chad didn't know how long he could keep him down. Here they were, two gentle geeks, unskilled at fighting, taking on hired holy goons. Suddenly the priest stopped fighting and looked past Chad. Chad swiveled to see what caught his attention. There standing over them was Fiona with the gun.

"You! And that demon dog," she shrieked. "I should have killed the vampdog, too!" She pointed the gun at Maggie who had her hands up. Chulie saw it and ran over to protect Maggie. Fiona took a shot at Chulie and missed but started firing again and again. She pulled a silver-threaded net from her jacket pocket, the silver threads glimmering in the moonlight. She tossed the net onto Chulie and he immediately let out a heartbreaking, blood-curling howl. He had barely healed from the last silver net encounter. Smoke started streaming from his fur. Fiona took aim at Chulie again. Now it was plain to see Fiona was the Alpha of the Impalers hate group, despite her age. Perhaps, like Sister Eloise, she had indulged in some of the blood of the fallen vampires.

"You wretched bitch from hell!" Maggie screamed and dove into the old woman. Chad heard the sickening crack of a bullet as Maggie and the old woman tumbled to the ground. He scrambled toward Chulie to remove the awful net but one of the priests grabbed Chad around the waist while the other peeled Maggie off Fiona. Chad saw blood streaming down Maggie's shirt and almost passed out. Chulie continued to howl pitifully. Fiona was on her feet again.

"Chulie!" Chad yelled.

They heard a giant crack as loud as lightning hitting a tree and then a ferocious roar. The stone door to the crypt split and a pale young woman with honey-colored hair burst out. She was filled with decades of rage, grief and adrenaline of a lioness protecting her cub. She let out an ear-splitting, other-worldly screech. The sound of her beloved dog in pain gave her a newfound strength to break free. She was unstoppable now. A beast in a teenage girl's body.

"Stay back, Lucy," her mother commanded. But Lucy flew to Chulie's side and flung the cloak off of him even as it burned her own hand terribly. The little dog was limp but managed a yelp of joy.

Fiona was eerily calm when she spoke. "I have not come this far and killed so many of your kind to flinch from my duty now. My child has been lost to me for thirty-six years. I tried to protect you but I can't any longer now that the secret is out. Goodbye, Lucy. God have mercy on us both." She raised the gun and prepared to fire, eyes blank and staring above the barrel of the pistol.

Lucy shrieked again but didn't leave Chulie's side. Her agony was palpable.

Oh no you don't mother of the year, Chad thought. *Not after Chulie has waited so long.* With a bolt of energy, he wriggled away from the thug priest and threw himself at Fiona. With an "oof" she went down to the ground again. The old lady must be made of tough stuff but this time she was knocked for a loop. When the stunned priests decided they should be doing something they went for Lucy and Chulie. But Lucy hissed at them ferociously and they stepped back.

Not far away, Bruce was watching the scene unnoticed from behind a crypt. He had followed them again. Had it gone on another moment, he would have intervened. These people were no good to him dead. But it turned out he didn't need to.

Lucy bit her own wrist and let Chulie drink. The little dog started to heal enough to get back on his feet. His tail was wagging madly and Lucy held him while laugh-crying, bearing her fangs.

Fiona came at them again. In one swift move, Chulie leapt at Fiona and sunk his teeth into her ankle. The woman stayed down this time, yelping in pain. Lucy went after the priests and managed to sink her teeth into one of their necks while the other froze in terror. She left him weak but still breathing.

Chad caught a glimpse of Bruce behind a crypt. Bruce smiled nodded.

Chad was at Maggie's side assessing how badly she was injured. A bullet had grazed her shoulder and she was weak, but okay. They heard a siren in the distance.

"Someone heard the gunshots and called the cops I bet. We need to get you three out of here and someplace safe," Chad said with authority, gesturing they should go back to the car. He helped Maggie up and they made their way across the cemetery. As they walked, Chad couldn't help but notice that Lucy was nearly the image he had seen in the photos and in Chulie's mind, only thinner and paler. She was a little wobbly on her feet after being a prisoner in her crypt for so long. They took a quick look inside to see a comfy chair, a coffin, stacks of books, mostly religious, and empty blood bags.

"Yes, let's get out of here," Lucy agreed. "I haven't been out in a very long time. I have so much to catch up on."

While they started running to the car, Bruce swooped past them and gave them a nod. He rushed over to where Fiona and the priests were still standing. They heard him say, "Hello, Fiona. I believe you knew my son, Adam."

Chad knew in that moment Fiona would be finished. They didn't stay to watch, instead hurried into the car and zoomed away into the night.

CHAPTER FIFTY-SEVEN:

Reunited

What do you do when your greatest longing is fulfilled? When an impossible dream finally comes true? Savor it, don't question it, just take it in. Lucy and I were together again in our shared vampire state. Even after we endured great peril in order to escape, we made it. We sat in the back seat and she stroked my belly. One of her hands was still healing from the burn of the silver net, and my skin was still tender. But it was pure bliss nonetheless.

We listened while Chad and Maggie discussed what had led us to this moment. They were incredulous that Fiona could have held Lucy prisoner these past few decades, consumed by her hatred for vampire kind but morally conflicted when it came to her daughter. Of course she had the support of Sister Eloise and The Impalers. Fiona and Sister Eloise were responsible for the final death of numerous vampires including Adam.

Lucy filled them in on some details. Fiona had caught wind of Adam and Lucy's plan to go full vampire with Chulie and run away from their families when she intercepted a note from Lucy to Adam. Horrified, Fiona had shared it with Sister Eloise.

Chad and Maggie shared how they had been trying to find her, how many people had been, but Sister Eloise and Fiona had been doing everything they could to stop the investigation. Even recently with the shot at the rally, the warning on their door. The misdirection.

Sister Eloise worked within the covens as a familiar. Lucy explained it was part of her mother and Sister Eloise's plot to root out and destroy the worst of vampire-kind from the inside out. Lucy also explained the details of their plan the night of her debutante ball.

"Adam and I would save Chulie from his terminal disease by making him an immortal vampire. Once Adam turned him, he would wait until Chulie was stable and then turn me, too. I loved him," Lucy told them. "We'd live together forever away from my mother for good. My note confirmed the final details, including where we'd meet so Adam could turn me, the night of my debutante ball. But Mother's posse caught up with Adam after he had turned me. Sister Eloise staked him and cut his heart out, one of the only methods for final death aside from cutting off a vampire's head. They captured me but Mother would not let them kill me. She watched over my transition. I remember the sound of her desperate prayers. Chulie slipped out during the commotion and didn't even see that I was there. I felt like my heart was cut out too."

Victor had remained oblivious. He followed the news stories and police investigation of his missing daughter just like the rest of the world. If he knew anything, he buried it in denial. Fiona and Victor had been estranged for years, even though they remained legally married until his recent death of a heart attack. Victor grieved by burying himself in the growing hot sauce empire. Fiona did not approve of his vampire investors, but she justified it by using the family money and her allowance for her secret crusade to eliminate vampires. Lucy's brothers were now running the business and were mostly kept in the dark about their mother's escapades and had no clue about Lucy.

We decided not to return to Chad and Maggie's apartment. Not ever again. Who knew how many Impalers might still be out there seeking revenge. Our new life would need to start sooner than expected. Maggie contacted a discreet realtor and the signs went up later that week. It would all remain untraceable, the proceeds of the sale handled by a trust. They couldn't be too careful.

Maggie found us a vampire-friendly Airbnb in Lafayette. They had a coffin in a large crawl space and I could sleep in there with Lucy. It was the most peaceful sleep I have ever had in my vampire state, despite our injuries and trauma.

Maggie and Chad stopped at a drug store for essentials and we settled in for a few days. It was a single house set on a rural road backing up to a wooded area, perfect for hunting. Lucy and I had so much to catch up on. We frolicked in the backyard in the moonlight and rekindled our happy times. She wasn't much of a hunter, so I showed her how and even caught enough for both of us. Squirrels, possums and even a nasty human who was abusing a cat.

We only dared stay in the house for a few nights while Chad and Maggie made plans for our new life. We decided to make our way to a place Chad and Maggie called Key West. I had never known any other place than New Orleans, so this was a leap. But I could adjust to anything now that Lucy and I were back together. Home to me is wherever she is. Chad and Maggie told us there were beaches with late night parties and we would be there in time for peak tourist season and to see the red ruby slipper drop on New Year's Eve, whatever that means, but it had something to do with a mortal dog named Toto so it was fine by me.

Chad and Maggie got hitched at one of those drive-in chapels in Key West and legally changed their names to Brad and Janet Weiss, after the characters in Rocky Horror Picture Show. It suited them. But Chad would keep his real name on his blog only for his followers.

We heard from Strings, Mimi, Glory and Beanie on occasion when they would send a note through an encrypted message on What's App. They were loving life (if that's what a vampire can call it) in Memphis although they said the local blood had a hint of barbecue and whiskey flavor that took some getting used to. Their new masked band called Kin had a late night residency at Paula & Raiford's Disco and were quite a sensation. Mimi had gotten in on the act as their dancer. We made plans for them to meet my Lucy in the near future. Chad also kept in touch with his copy buddy Frank on What's App, after a slightly painful attempt to teach him how to use it he caught on. For safety, we did not share that we found Lucy or where we were but did share what Fiona was up to with The Impalers.

One day we spotted an Impaler priest in Key West. He didn't see us. And fortunately Chad (now Brad) had a plan to throw them off my trail for good.

CHAPTER FIFTY-EIGHT:

Alligator Tears

*B*loodlust, a Blog for Vampire Enthusiasts – January 30, 2024 By Chad Russo

Hello Dear Readers, both vampire and mortal,

Thanks as always for your blood loyalty and for sending in all of your comments and stories. This connection with New Orleans means more than you know, and now your stories are flooding in from all over the world. This blog is officially expanding beyond New Orleans which is the good news.

But today I have terrible news to share.

It is with great sadness that I must inform you of the passing of a beloved vampire dog, the one and only of its kind that we know of. I have it on good authority that while roaming the bayou, Chulie the vampdog was swallowed by an alligator who then dove deep into the swamp where Chulie met his fate.

The Krewe du Vampdog has been informed and they are hosting a massive second line parade on Saturday, February 3rd at 3:00 pm starting at Buffa's on Esplanade and Burgundy. Humans, vampires

and canines with benevolent intentions are all welcome. Rest in peace, Chulie the legendary vampdog. This reporter has been privileged with more than one encounter and I can say, the world is minus one spectacular creature.

The disappearance of his Lucy may forever remain an unsolved mystery. But I've heard it on good authority, they've opened the investigation again and have a solid lead.

In related news, new management has taken over the Broussard hot sauce company along with Lucy's brothers who may retire soon. They are looking for humans and vampires to work the night shift. It could be a great opportunity. The matriarch Fiona is no longer with us.

Until my next post, be well, be safe and stay oh positive.

For all the latest vampire news, please like, follow and share. @ Chadrusso #bloodlust

#

Chad closed his laptop. Maggie and Lucy were playing records in the next room and giggling. Chad stroked the little vampire dog who sat in his lap and felt the vampdog sigh. He was like a little black mop. The pit bull from the dog fight ring lay next to them on the couch. They sent for him and a volunteer drove him out to them from the shelter where Bruce had left him. They named him Gumbo.

This last blog post was the least Chad felt he could do since his Bloodlust series was partially to blame for bringing so much attention to Chulie. He got the idea from the way Fiona made vampire Lucy "disappear." They thought it best to let the Lucy mystery persist although the trail would inevitably lead back to

Sister Eloise and Fiona. They hoped the news of Chulie's fake death would spread quickly especially after the second line parade. That should buy them some time off the grid. At least for now, until another vampdog sighting might be reported. The Krewe du Vampdog had already started to shift their focus to all supernatural animals instead of this one infamous pup.

Maggie came in to join him with two glasses of beer.

"Hey husband."

"Hey wife."

She raised her glass and simply said, "to Pete." She knew him so well, knew that he'd had his brother Pete on his mind a lot these days. He would have loved hearing how this story played out and Chad would have loved telling him about it.

"To Pete," Chad replied as they clinked glasses. *Maybe he is watching this all play out after all,* Chad thought and felt a profound sense of closure having solved the disappearance of Lucy.

Chulie, still in Chad's lap, turned his face up toward Chad and fixed him with his black, red-rimmed eyes. That was all the thanks Chad needed.

THE END

www.ingramcontent.com/pod-product-compliance
Lightning Source LLC
Chambersburg PA
CBHW022148170626
46807CB00005B/2124